I Let Him In

JILL CHILDS

D1211221

Published by Bookouture in 2021

An imprint of Storyfire Ltd.
Carmelite House
50 Victoria Embankment
London EC4Y 0DZ

www.bookouture.com

ISBN: 978-1-80019-024-5
eBook ISBN: 978-1-80019-023-8

For Alice

I Let
Him In

BOOKS BY JILL CHILDS

CHAPTER ONE

LOUISE

I pour myself into pedalling. *Pump, pump. Left, right.* Body and mind raging into the beat.

I'm under attack from the wind, the steadily growing rain. I lower my head for the grinding climb, sinking into myself, slowly pulling up through Blackheath village, away from the glistening pavements, the lights spilling from bars and restaurants, the knots of people intruding here and there on the road as they step off the kerb to skirt the crowd.

I leave them behind and enter the emptiness of the open heath, heading higher, over the top towards Greenwich.

As the landscape opens, the wind blows up in a moment, snatching my breath and almost knocking me sideways off the road. I steady myself and battle on, piston knees, hands knuckle-white on the handlebars.

A car appears from nowhere, driving too fast in the wet darkness. Its headlights surge and ebb as it rises and falls with the dips in the road. Suddenly, it's on me, passing me on the other side of the road in a flash of light.

For a moment, it illuminates the falling sheets of rain, thicker than I'd realised. I stay steady and focus on the road, fighting the dazzle, and blink away the spangled darkness in its wake.

The night folds in again. Still and silent. All I hear is the lashing rain and my own breathing, blood pumping hard in my ears, beating time with my legs. I press myself forward from one solitary pool of streetlight to the next, cutting across the heath. I'm exposed now, at the mercy of the wind and rain. Sharp pellets pepper my nose, strike my cheeks. My skin is almost numb.

I still see Toby's face, tight with hurt. *You don't mean it.*

Water streams from the curves of my helmet, flying into droplets as the wind whips it away. My legs ache. I want to crest the heath and start my descent towards the docks, down into Greenwich.

I want to be home, packing, getting ready to fly away from all this. From him.

You'll regret it.

The noise explodes from behind me. From nowhere. One moment, I'm alone on the open expanse of heath, inside the wind and driving rain and the rhythm of my own hard breathing; the next moment, an engine roars in my ears. It's right there in the darkness, at my shoulder, too fast, too close. I try to swerve away, into the ditch. Too late.

I'm flying, soaring through open air, tossed, arms flailing. I fall through emptiness, blinded. Time stops. Everything hangs. Silent. Suspended.

Then the bubble bursts and I crash. My body, limp, pounds into cold metal, skids sideways, hits the ground with such force I can't breathe. I imagine my body smashed into a thousand fragments.

Bright lights pulse in my head. Pain explodes everywhere, a firework burst, shooting white sparks through black. Then nothing.

CHAPTER TWO

Burly men with deep voices pin my limbs and lift me, swinging my weight. I smell stale cigarette smoke.

I try to move, to struggle, to scream for help but the sound sticks in my throat.

A face looms. A distorted mask of grotesque features and devilish eyes.

Then, those accusations from long ago, inside my head. Always with me, even now.

You killed her! You wicked, wicked girl.

I toss from side to side, trying to shake myself free but it's impossible.

The skin on my arm feels a sudden chill, then, my arm tightly held, the sharpness of a needle.

I sink back and again disappear.

Something wet and cold on my lips. Parched tongue. It's a supreme effort to prise open my eyes.

The light is hard and bright and hurts. I blink.

The feathery pressure lifts from my lips.

'Lou?' A rustle of clothes. Josephine, my sister, looms and fills my vision. 'Lou? It's me. Jo. Can you hear me?'

I try to nod. My head is the weight of a cannonball. The slightest movement sends shoots of white pain through my neck and shoulders. I sink back and blink up at her. Her eyes are full of worry.

'You had an accident. Can you remember? Someone knocked you off your bike.'

I frown. *Darkness on the heath and rain.* I look past her at the dappled cream panels of the ceiling. I don't know where I am. Not at home.

A pink foam square appears and she runs it along my lips. Ice cold and wet, trickling water into my mouth. That's good. I breathe deeply and pain sears across my chest.

Jo looks panicked and twists away from me, looking round. 'Don't move,' she says. 'I'll get a nurse.'

I let my eyes fall closed and keep very still. I'm frightened of moving and stirring pain. There are noises. An occasional rhythmic whirr and click, the low, steady hum of a machine. I smell disinfectant and another, kinder scent. A distant whiff of coffee. Hospital?

Am I dying? Paralysed? Panic flares and my breathing quickens. I concentrate on trying to check my body. My hands lie heavy at my sides, palms upward, fingers lightly curled. I twitch my fingertips, stealthily. They seem to respond. I steady myself. I'll try my toes next, far away down the bed.

The mouse squeak of hurrying soft shoes on a polished floor.

A loud, clear voice. 'How are you feeling, Louise?'

I open my eyes. A nurse leans over me, her hair pinned back severely. She peers for a moment into my face.

I want to ask what happened, what state my body is in, but I barely croak. Already, she's turned away, fiddling, checking something with busy fingers.

Elsewhere, down my body, slim, warm fingers stroke my hand. Jo's touch. 'It's all right.' Jo's voice. Softer now. 'Try to get some rest.'

Tears spill from the corners of my eyes, surprising me. They slide down my temples and pool in my hair. *Am I OK?*

The nurse says something but softly and not to me. I can't keep hold of the words; they shimmer and slip through my senses.

I fall backwards again into nothingness. The only sound is the *boom, boom, boom* of blood banging around my skull.

CHAPTER THREE

'Louise? Can you hear me? If you can hear me, can you open your eyes?'

A man's voice. It's artificially loud and blasts at me. It's the tone some men use to speak to children or the elderly.

I want to tell him not to be condescending. *I'm not a fool. I'm strong. I'm a professional. I'm a...* I have to concentrate hard and chase the words around my head before I winkle them out: *I'm a travel writer. A journalist. Yes.*

'That's it, Louise. Now, can you open your eyes for me?'

I prise open my eyelashes and light floods in, blinding me. Slowly, as I blink, shapes form. Blurred at first, then gradually sharpening.

A man stands over me. My age, maybe, late thirties. His chin is dark with stubble and his skin is furrowed with tiredness. But his eyes are very clear. Blue-green.

'I'm Doctor Kennedy. How are you feeling?'

I manage to croak through dry lips: 'Not great.'

He smiles. 'You've had an accident. Do you remember?'

I frown. My mind is still clouded by the memory of the strange, misshapen face looming over me. By the accusations. *Where were you? How could you?*

Not him. Not his voice. As I focus, frowning, the dream face recedes.

'You've fractured your tibia.'

Jo, further away, puts in: 'You've broken your leg, lovely.'

'And you had quite a bang on the head.'

Jo again, her mothering tone: 'Thank god you were wearing your helmet, Lou. You might've been killed.'

The doctor holds up his fingers and tells me to focus. He's looks pleased when I count them and whisper the number three. I hope I've got it right. He moves them this way and that and peers at me as I make my eyes follow them. Strong fingers. A sensible gold wedding ring.

More questions. I strain to do my best but the sheer effort of listening, of trying to do as he asks, is exhausting. I don't know what day it is. I can't hang around here. I've got a flight to catch.

I think about Jo, spending all this time here, with me. Mike won't like it. There'll be an argument. He'll moan about looking after Mia. *Mia*. I don't want her to see me like this; she'll be frightened.

Pain washes over me in a hot, violent wave: *leg, chest, head*. I grimace. Moments later, I dip under again, my mind a mess of swirling shapes and colours, starbursts and whirlpools, drawing me in.

CHAPTER FOUR

'I can't remember.'

The nurse has elevated the head section of the bed. I don't like it, but she insists. I need to get used to sitting up again, apparently. So far, even like this, flat on the pillows, against the mattress but with my head and shoulders inclined so I can see around the small bay, I feel dizzy and that makes me feel sick.

There are two police officers. The young woman has drawn up a chair by my bedside. She's the one asking the questions. Her colleague, an even younger man, stands at the end of my bed, keeping watch. He's removed his cap and tucked it under his arm and his hair sticks out in clumps around his temples. He takes notes as we talk.

The area proscribed by the curtains, drawn now around the bed in a nod towards privacy, is so small that there's barely room for all three of us, as well as the bed, the bedside locker and all the medical apparatus. My arm lies limply on the sheet, palm up, a clear liquid surging into the vein through a tube. My bedding is distorted by the cage protecting my leg, reset now and encased in plaster.

The young policewoman tries again. 'So, you left your boyfriend's house—'

I say: '*Ex*-boyfriend.'

She continues, unruffled: 'You left your ex-boyfriend's house at about ten past ten at night.'

I nod. 'We'd had an argument.'

She considers. 'How would you describe your state of mind at the time of the accident?'

I remember my gritted teeth, the rain and buffeting wind. 'Determined. I wanted to get home.'

'You say you and your ex-boyfriend had just had an argument. Is it fair to say you were upset?'

'A bit.' I shrug, wondering how much to tell her. 'I broke up with him a week ago. He was the one who was upset. He wanted to talk. That's why I went over. I thought I was being…' I hesitate, trying to find the right word. Why had I gone over? Because I felt guilty. Because he refused to believe it. Because he wouldn't let go. 'I was trying to be kind. I'm going away soon, for work. I didn't want to leave it like that.' I remember his face, tight with anger. 'I think I made it worse.'

'Had you consumed any substances? Anything which might have impaired your senses?'

'Substances?' I blink. 'Pizza. A glass of wine.' I hesitate. 'Is that what you mean?'

The other police officer's pen pauses and I sense him look up.

She says: 'How much wine, would you say?'

I frown. 'One glass. I'm not a big drinker.'

'Drugs?'

'No.'

'Were you taking any medication?'

'No.'

She keeps her gaze on the edge of the bed as we talk but if I look away, I sense her eyes jumping to my face. I don't like that. I sense that she doesn't trust me; she doesn't believe me.

She tells the bed: 'So you remember cycling through Blackheath village and up onto the heath. It was windy and it started to rain. You didn't see the vehicle until shortly before the collision.' She leans a fraction further forward. 'Can you tell me anything about the vehicle? Anything you saw before the impact? A colour, perhaps, or outline? Whether it was a car or a van, small or large?'

I strain. All I can remember is the terrifying sensation of being hit, flying through the air, then crashing into the ground. 'I don't know. I'm sorry. It was dark.'

She seems disappointed. She and the other officer exchange a glance. It's a signal but I can't read it. He closes his notebook and stows away his pen, settles his cap back on his head. She gets to her feet and nods down at me. 'I can assure you, we'll do everything we can to identify the person who hit you,' she says. 'It's a serious offence. Not just the accident, but fleeing the scene and failing to report. That's a crime.'

I watch her eyes. Her words suggest she's on my side, but I'm not sure I trust her.

She says: 'We'll leave you to get some rest. I'll keep you informed.' She draws a batch of brightly coloured leaflets from her case and sets them on the locker. 'Are you happy for me to pass your details to Victim Support?' She pauses. 'Have you heard of them? They might be able to give you practical advice. You may be eligible for compensation, for example. It's a confidential service.'

I manage to nod. I don't want to look suspicious by telling her that of course I know Victim Support, I've had dealings with them before.

Finally, she withdraws a card – Detective Sara Blakely – and indicates the case number written neatly in pen across the back. 'If anything comes back to you in the meantime, anything about the vehicle or what happened, just give me a call.'

The male officer holds open the curtain for her as if they're both leaving a stage. She's about to pass through when she hesitates and turns back. 'One other thing. The paramedics said you were very distressed at the scene.'

I swallow. 'Was I?'

'You kept struggling. Saying something about going to jail.'
For the first time, she looks me straight in the eye. 'Any idea why?'

I fix my eyes on the heaped sheet over the bed-cage. I feel
suddenly very hot.

She waits, but I don't answer. Finally, she says: 'Anyway, thanks
for your time. We'll be in touch.'

The curtain swishes shut behind them and their boots thump
away down the ward.

CHAPTER FIVE

'Told you not to leave. See? You should've listened.'

Toby looks pleased with himself. He tips the bouquet of flowers towards me so I can see the flash of red roses inside the cone of paper, then sets them down on the locker by the plastic jug of water and box of tissues.

He pulls up a chair and plonks himself down. 'Does it hurt?'

'The leg?' I sigh. 'Yes. I can't sleep at night.' I hesitate. 'My head aches.'

He pulls a packet of mints out of his pocket and half-heartedly offers me one, then takes one himself and sucks noisily. 'Just what you needed, a good bang on the head.' He laughs. 'Don't look so shocked. I'm only joking.'

I manage to say: 'Thanks for the flowers.'

'That's all right.' He reaches for my hand and holds it firmly. It's the arm with the drip and I can't easily pull it away from him. 'I told my mate at the *Gazette*. They might do a story on it. Apparently, there've been a few accidents around there. None as bad as yours, though.'

I sigh. 'You might have asked me first. I don't want to talk to the *Gazette*.'

'You don't have to. I did. Anyway, it might help them find out who did it. Someone must have seen something.'

I turn away my head, trying to hint that I'm tired, that I want him to go.

'What?' He laughs and starts to crack the half-sucked mint between his teeth. 'Just looking out for you, that's all.'

'I don't need you to do that, Toby. I'm looking out for myself now. Remember?'

He snorts. 'Yeah, clearly that's going well.'

We sit in silence for a few moments.

'Anyway, sorry about your trip.' He manages to sound sheepish. It must be an effort. 'I didn't want you to go, you know that. But even so.'

'I'm still going.' I try to sound more determined than I feel right now. 'I just might have to delay a bit, that's all.'

'Right.' He shakes his head, disbelieving. 'Sure you are.'

I can't bring myself to look at him. A stout, middle-aged man is crouching by the neighbouring bed, unloading cartons of drinks and packets of biscuits from a carrier bag and stocking his wife's locker.

Toby reaches closer. 'Don't let's fight, Lou.' He lowers his voice. 'You don't mean it, not really. Look, I know I said some... you know, some unpleasant things the other night. I'm sorry. I really am. I was upset.'

I turn back to him and open my mouth, but he lifts his hand and carries on.

'No, hear me out. I've been thinking a lot about it. Maybe I am rushing you. It's a big deal, having a kid. I get that. I know you love your freedom. Jumping on and off planes all the time and all that.' He hesitates, looking everywhere but at my face. 'It's just, I don't know, going to see Dave and Claire's baby the other day, it just got me thinking – why not us? Why won't you ever even talk about it? You'd be such a great mum, Lou, you—'

'Maybe this isn't—' I say, weakly.

He ploughs on, regardless. 'But then I thought: you've got to feel ready too. I know that. And if you need more time, well, maybe I just have to live with that. I'll try. I really will. But if you could at least think about it.'

'Toby...'

'Hang on, I'm not done yet.' He squeezes my hand harder. 'This accident. It feels like a wake-up call. I worry about all these daredevil trips you do. I don't want to lose you. I love you, Lou. I do. I know you don't want me getting all soppy but I just want to be with you, see? So, here's what we do: we put all this behind us for now and take it one day at a time and see how we go. Right?' He looks down at the bulge of the bed-cage over my broken leg.

I take a deep breath. My head throbs. I haven't got the energy for this, not right now. 'Toby, I'm sorry. But—'

He cuts in and talks over me, as he so often does. 'Another thing. I've been looking on Dr Google and it might be a long haul. Have they said that? You'll have that cast on for weeks. I know you don't want to hear it but you're grounded for a bit. That's just the way it is.'

'People can still—'

He ignores me. 'So, here's what I think. Makes more sense for you to be at my place, just till you're back on your feet. Or foot.' He grins, affable. 'I'll look after you. And I've got more room, that's another thing.'

I twist sideways and finally manage to extricate my hand from his. 'No, Toby. No!'

'Keep your voice down!' He nods across to the middle-aged man who's turned to have a look. Toby gives him a 'you know what they're like' roll of the eyes and grins.

I take a deep breath. 'Toby. I meant what I said. We're through. The accident doesn't change anything.'

Something shifts in his face. The bravado is gone and he looks suddenly tight-jawed and wounded.

He says: 'I just thought—'

'No. I'm sorry.' My tone is more brutal than I meant. I swallow. I need to be firm. Otherwise, he won't understand.

Toby leans over me. For a moment, I think he's going to kiss me but he doesn't. He says, too loudly: 'You haven't listened to a word I've said, have you? Rachel warned me about you. And you know what? I always stuck up for you. More fool me.'

I blink. 'Rachel?' He knows exactly what I think of his colleague – always hanging around him, batting her eyelashes. Finding a reason to ask him over every time I'm away. And that's not all. Toby makes light of the rumours about her, the gossip about her bullying junior staff and the whispers about her stabbing rivals in the back. Toby has always seemed oblivious when we're out with his work crowd, but I've seen the way the younger ones look at Rachel when her back is turned, their lips pursed.

I take a deep breath. 'What does she know, anyway? She has no right—'

Toby carries on, regardless. 'I give up, I really do. Two years I've put up with this. Kicking my heels while you go on endless holidays. Yes, they are holidays, Lou! It's not real work, writing about crossing the Rockies or swimming with bloody dolphins or whatever it is. All this time I've been waiting. And you know why?' He prods a finger in my face. 'I've been waiting for you to want to be with me, to love me back. Frightened of telling you every time another mate gets married or has a kid, worried how you'll take it.' His face contorts. His body's shaking. 'I'm forty-two, Lou. I love you. And I also want to be a dad. Is that so terrible?'

He grabs back his bunch of roses from the locker, picks up his jacket and sweeps off without another word.

Beside me, the middle-aged man's shoulders stiffen and he sits very still, embarrassed for me, trying to pretend he hasn't heard.

CHAPTER SIX

On Saturday, Jo and Mia come to take me home.

I sit, waiting for them, in the chair beside my hospital bed. My holdall sits at my feet, packed to bursting with the overnight things Jo brought in for me, and my new medication.

My broken leg sticks out in front of me, rigid with plaster. The doctors are pleased with the X-rays. It should heal well. But Toby's right: it will take weeks before they get the cast off. I sigh. Just getting dressed, hobbling to and from the toilet and packing my stuff has left me feeling exhausted. I'm not a patient person. I hate being dependent on anyone. Most of all, I hate sitting still.

First thing on Monday, I'll get on the phone to the travel company. Maybe I could fly out late and find a way of catching up with the rest of the journalists going on the trip? If I still make the main days, I might convince my editor.

Mia's voice drifts down the ward before she comes into sight. 'This one, Mummy? This one?' She skips around the corner, screams when she catches sight of me and dashes towards me for a hug.

Behind her, Jo, worried, calls: 'Careful, Mia!'

'Are these yours?' Already, Mia has seized the crutches and is trying them out, hopping up and down at the end of my bed like Long John Silver. Her stubby plaits bounce on her back.

I smile. 'You figure out how to do it, would you? Then you can teach me.'

'Easy peasy.' Mia shines with all the confidence of a seven-year-old. She drops the crutches and peers into my unzipped bag. 'Did you pack my card?'

'Of course!' I show her. 'It's a fabulous card. My favourite. Love the colours. Will you find a good place for it, as soon as we get home?'

When we set off, she bounds ahead, running back to us and off again, like a puppy. Jo and I make slow progress. The crutches are bruising the soft flesh under my arms and I struggle to get the rhythm right. Jo hovers beside me, my bag on her shoulder. Her arms are tense as if she might suddenly need to catch me.

By the time I stagger into my flat, I'm out of breath and sweating hard. I make it to the lounge and drop into a chair with relief.

'At least the lift's working.' Jo goes through to the kitchen and I follow her movements by sound. Running tap, filling kettle, cupboard doors opening for mugs.

Mia brings a stool over to me, places a cushion on it and watches with a frown as I heave my leg onto it. 'Is it tricky?'

'Pretty tricky.'

She looks disappointed. 'We won't be able to play Tag for ages.'

'Sorry.' I try to be brave and smile. 'Not for a while. But it's cold and wet out, anyway. We can do other things when you come over. Play Ludo. Draw. Paint.'

She cheers up at once. 'Great idea, Auntie Lou!' She pulls my get-well cards out of my holdall and arranges them on the mantelpiece, her own taking pride of place. She then turns to look at me again. 'I can do this. Watch!' She does a ragged forward roll on the rug and jumps up. 'Ta-dah!'

'Very good.'

'And a handstand. Well, nearly.' She finds a patch of empty wall and tries to kick up her legs.

I want to jump up and demonstrate and then catch her legs and guide them into position as she tries again. That's what I would have done a week ago. Now I can't. I feel exhausted again. My heart races and the throbbing in my head worsens. I've never had such intense headaches.

Jo, carrying in a tray of tea and biscuits, seems to read my expression. 'What?'

'Just tired, that's all.'

She sets a mug down at my side. 'Something hurting?'

I nod. 'Head.'

She sits down across from me with her tea. She looks tired and worried, ever the big sister. She's made a point of looking out for me since we lost Mum, nearly ten years ago now. I can barely remember Dad. He and Mum split up when I was tiny and, the last we heard, he'd disappeared to Australia and settled there. 'They said it was normal with concussion, didn't they? Headaches. Dizziness.'

'Apparently. All part of the package.'

'Do you want a painkiller?' She looks over at Mia, who's still struggling to kick up her legs and falling to the floor each time with a colossal thud. 'Mia, come and sit down for a minute. Have a biscuit.'

I force myself to smile. 'She's all right.'

I sip my tea and look around the room. It's a traveller's mish-mash, crowded with souvenirs from years of trips. The painted wooden screen, with lattice insets, from Rajasthan, straddling a corner; the black and white pottery vase from Cyprus; Chinese silk cushion covers in emerald and a rich, blood red.

A set of framed art deco travel posters, a present from Jo years ago, hangs around the walls. Istanbul. Cairo. Amsterdam. New York. All places I've been.

I grimace, thinking again about the big trip to Chile. It was going to be epic. A perfect way to escape the start of cold, grey

December here in London. Bungee jumping out of a helicopter over an active volcano. The pictures online look amazing.

'Maybe I could go anyway, on a later flight?'

'Where?'

'Villarrica – Chile. I'm in the heli for most of it. Maybe they'd still let me jump. It's not impossible.'

'With a broken leg?' Jo snorts. 'Actually, yes, it is.'

I carry on, regardless. 'It's not like parachuting or sky-diving. You don't have to land by yourself. With a bungee jump, you just have to fall out and then it tows you along. I'd make it part of the story, doing it with a cast. It might inspire people.' I pause, thinking. 'I might even get the cover.'

'You might even get killed.' Jo shakes her head. 'Look, I'm sorry, Lou. Really. I know how much you were looking forward to it. But it's not happening. Not right now, anyway.'

She drinks her tea, trying not to notice that I'm glaring at her. We sit in silence for a moment, watching Mia, who is panting now, practise her moves.

A few handstands later, Jo softens and passes me a biscuit. 'I know you're disappointed. Can't you just postpone it? Go in the spring?'

'I wish.' I sigh, thinking about all the planning that's gone into this. 'I'm not the only one going. The travel company has invited a group of journalists, not just me. Anyway, I can't pitch the same story, months after everyone else's done it.'

She doesn't have an answer to that. 'You're always travelling, Lou. Maybe you should try to enjoy being at home for a bit.'

'I know.' My shoulders droop. 'It just sounded amazing. They're taking them white-water rafting as well.'

Jo looks around the room. 'You've been saying for ages you want to repaint the flat. You have the time now – you could get someone in. Shouldn't cost much. It's only small.'

'Maybe.' I don't usually 'get someone in'. I do everything myself.

'No, really. You should.' She straightens up, energised. 'Bit of company while you're stuck at home. And you'll be here to keep an eye on them. It's perfect. And if they're any good, let me know, would you? I need to get the café redone over Christmas. Before it gets any shabbier.'

Within a few minutes, she's surreptitiously checking her watch, then drinking down a final mouthful of tea and marshalling Mia to stop poking about on my desk and get ready to go home. I wonder what Mike's doing today and if he's really so busy planning lessons or catching up with marking that he can't look after Mia for a few hours, but I don't ask. I know better by now.

She stands by the front door, poised to go, and considers me: 'Do you need help going to the loo?'

Mia squeals: 'Mummy! She's a grown-up!'

'I know. But she's also got a broken leg, sweetheart. That's what I mean.'

'I'll be fine. Honestly.' I feel a surge of love for them both. I don't want them to leave. I normally love my own company but, suddenly, I don't want to be left on my own. I feel something I haven't let myself feel for years: vulnerable.

Jo, sensing my mood, hovers. 'Is Toby coming over later?'

I just shrug and let her make what she wants of that. I haven't got the strength for an argument about Toby, not right now. I know what she'll say.

Jo looks guilty. 'I'd stay a bit longer but I've left Angie in charge.'

'Oh, no.' Mia rolls her eyes at me. 'You know what happened last time. She nearly set the café on fire.'

Jo tweaks Mia's plaits. 'It was just a tray of lasagne, actually. Got a bit charred.'

I say: 'Off you go.'

'We'll pop back tomorrow.' Jo opens the flat door and Mia rushes out. She's growing up fast, but she still likes pressing the button to summon the lift. Jo turns back to me. 'Just text, won't you, if you need anything? There's fresh milk in the fridge. And bread. And a few other bits and pieces to keep you going.'

'I'll be fine.'

'Call Toby, OK? Tell him to get over here and look after you.'

After the door finally closes and the lift carries them away, the flat feels very still. I sit in the silence, looking down the barrel of my huge, white leg, too tired to move. My head aches.

When I close my eyes and start to melt into sleep, I fall backwards. I feel as if I'm flying down a dark tunnel, arms outstretched, hair flying, mouth open, struggling to scream.

Toby's voice comes again. *You'll regret it.*

Then that other voice which always lives inside my head. *How could you?*

CHAPTER SEVEN

I hadn't realised how hard this would be. Trapped. Alone. A prisoner inside my own home.

It takes a long visit from Jo and Mia to help me get through Sunday. Jo cooks a casserole in my kitchen, fussing about the state of the oven and the broken grill. I've never cooked very much. I'm more an eat out and takeaway sort of woman. Or at least, I was.

Then Jo rushes off for a couple of hours, probably to do more cooking and cleaning, while I help Mia with her weekend homework, drawing and colouring a Viking village and then making a longboat out of stiff card.

That's my job in the family. Arts and crafts. Making things out of old loo rolls and tissue paper. Painting. That's the way it's always been. Jo, the big sister, is the practical one, the care-giver. I'm the arty one. The rolling stone. The oddball. Jo's husband Mike probably has worse words for it – he's never been a fan – but I try not to think about that.

On Sunday night, my head and leg both ache. I struggle to sleep. I'm practising in my head all night what to say to the travel company, how to persuade them to let me go. I can't get comfortable, flat on my back. I swallow down painkillers and doze, on and off, but can't sleep deeply.

At five, I give up and start the day, already feeling ragged and anxious about the morning to come. Routine tasks which would normally take me a matter of moments are suddenly major events.

The process of washing, getting dressed and making breakfast is prolonged and exhausting.

Monday is a cold, damp November day. The trees across the road are heavy with mist. I look at the pile of bright summer clothes I'd put out for the trip. In Chile, spring is slowly turning into summer. Even in the mountains, it'll be pleasant. Now, instead of getting on a plane in a few days to go halfway around the world, I can barely get from the bedroom to the lounge.

As soon as it hits nine o'clock, I call the travel company to see if we can salvage something from the trip. Anything.

They're sympathetic but practical.

No, I can't bungee jump out of a helicopter with a broken leg. Even if I wanted to take the risk, the local partner would never agree and neither would their insurers.

No, I can't go along for the ride to watch the others. It's jumpers and instructors only inside the helicopter. If I can't jump, they need the place for someone who can.

I do my best, but it's clear they won't budge. It's not a cheap trip, I know that. They need to be sure they'll get value for money in terms of coverage.

I give up arguing in the end and force myself to write the email I've been trying to avoid, to the section editor who was taking the story. *Maybe there's still time for one of the other freelancers to step in*, I write. I send all the details across. My bad luck is someone else's lucky day.

I bite my lip. *After all that lobbying. After all that planning.*

I make myself another coffee and sit, staring at the travel posters, wondering how I'm going to get through the next few weeks.

Even that little screen time has set off another headache, so I'm just reaching for more painkillers when the door buzzer sounds. I hesitate. It's rarely for me: it'll be a parcel delivery for another flat in the block or someone selling door to door. I almost decide not to bother but the buzzer sounds again, insistent, and I sigh, organise my crutches and hop to the flat door.

I peer at the blurry image on the security camera. A woman. Probably.

'Hello?' She doesn't look like anyone I know. I'm poised to see her off.

She looms as she presses her face closer to speak into the microphone. Her voice cuts through the static, anxious but determined. 'Hello! Is that Louise Taylor? It's Tanya from Victim Support. Did you get my email?'

I hesitate. I've had so many follow-up emails since the accident. I think there was one from Victim Support, I just didn't really read it, not properly. I try to think what to say, embarrassed about wasting her time, but before I can answer, her voice pipes up again: 'Is this a bad time?'

I shake my head, weary but resigned, and press the door release. 'Come on up. Second floor, on the left.'

I unlock the front door and leave it open an inch, then propel myself through to the kitchen, set out mugs, tea bags and milk on a tray and put the kettle on.

'Hello?'

Her voice, already in the hallway, makes me jump. That was fast.

Before I can answer, she appears in the kitchen doorway. She's around forty with a mess of blonde hair, pushed behind her ears. She's wearing a baggy jacket which looks as if it's seen better days and a pair of black trousers.

'Tanya.' She puts out a hand, her expression uncertain, and repeats: 'Victim Support.'

We have tea in the lounge. She perches on the edge of an armchair, head to one side like a bird, and listens solemnly while I tell her the story of the accident. She doesn't interrupt, just gives little nods and occasional grimaces to show how keenly she's paying attention. She mouths 'ooh!' and 'oh, dear!' now and then. Once she's finished her tea, she opens up her voluminous bag and hands me several leaflets. Some look familiar – the same colourful pamphlets about road traffic accidents that the police gave me in hospital. She adds a couple about Victim Support and the help it can give. 'And how are you feeling now?'

I consider. 'My leg's not too bad. It's just awkward. But I'm still getting headaches.'

She makes a note, very earnest. 'And is anything coming back about the accident?' She flicks to a different page. 'The police report suggests you can't remember much about the vehicle?'

'Nothing. I've had a few flashbacks.' In the night, I'd felt myself flying again, falling, heard the voices in my head. 'But it was so dark. They hit me from behind.'

She tuts sympathetically. 'It's hard to imagine, isn't it? How anyone could just drive away like that. Not knowing if you were dead or alive.' She nods to herself. 'Look, the mind often blanks out a traumatic incident like yours. It's very common. Don't worry about it. But in the future, if you do think of anything that might help them catch whoever did this, just call the police. Or me, if you'd rather. None of us wants this happening to anyone else, do we?'

She winkles out a new leaflet, about compensation. 'Even if they don't catch them – and I'm not saying they won't – you may still be able to get compensation.'

I shrug. 'It's not really about money.'

'Of course. But even so. It might help.' She counts off the points on her fingers as she makes them. 'Injury compensation. Trauma. Loss of earnings. And also damage to property. The cost of a new bike, for example? A new cycling helmet?' She looks embarrassed and lowers her voice a little, as if she's awkward talking about money. 'There's a central fund that pays out for hit and runs. See?' A neat index figure points me to the right paragraph. 'The MIB. Motor Insurers' Bureau. I can get you all the forms and help you fill them in.'

She rummages again in her file, then bites down on her lip. The light catches a small diamond ring on her wedding finger, pressed against a wedding ring.

'Oh. I'll have to bring that form next time. Sorry. I was sure I put one in.' She shakes her head as if she's disappointed in herself. 'How about shopping? Have you been out yet?'

She moves on to practicalities, establishing that yes, I plan to stay here on my own but with a sister on hand to help out, that I'm a freelance journalist but with enough put by to see me through.

'Do you need help making any changes to the flat?' She looks around the lounge. 'Any equipment you need or anything to make you more comfortable here? I'm guessing you're going to be at home a while.'

I try to imagine the flat through her eyes and remember what Jo said. 'I wondered about getting it repainted, actually. Seeing as I'll be stuck here for a bit.'

Her face falls. 'I'm not sure that would qualify—'

I smile. 'I wasn't looking for money. Sorry, I was just thinking out loud. My sister thought it might cheer me up. A way of doing something positive, since I'm here anyway.'

She nods, relieved. 'Well, have you got someone in mind? Because we've got a database of approved contractors. Locksmiths, handymen. I'm sure there are painters and decorators in there too. If I can find them, shall I email them over? Say you heard about them through Victim Support. Some of them give a discount.' She makes a note in her file, then stops for a moment, hesitates and leans forward. 'Look, I'm only supposed to give you companies in the database. But do you mind if I go off script for a moment?'

I nod, amused by how careful she's being.

'I probably shouldn't do this but you're, you know, living on your own and you'll be spending a lot of time with whoever comes and, well, I'm guessing you need someone you're sure you can trust. And someone you can stomach, right? Not someone who plays loud music all day when you're trying to rest or wants to tell you their life story.'

I laugh. 'Definitely.'

'Well, it's not really for me to recommend people. That's not my job.' She pauses, her eyes on mine. 'But I know a lovely local guy. I use him myself. I totally trust him to do a great job and… well, I totally trust him, full stop. He gets booked up, but you never know, he might have a gap.' She writes out a name and number on her notepad and tears it off. 'Ed. Ex-army. Tell him you know me, if you do call. He'll give you a good rate.' She pauses and looks worried. 'But it's up to you. Obviously. I can email you the official list as soon as I'm back in the office.'

As Tanya packs up her bag, she asks if she can drop by again with the compensation forms and see how I'm doing. She hands me a Victim Support business card with her name, email and phone number. 'Any questions, just give me a call, OK? Happy to help.'

Once she's gone, I sit and stare for a while at the scrap of paper she gave me. *Ed Spencer.*

I look thoughtfully around the flat. Maybe Jo's right. Maybe it is a good time to give the place a facelift. I listen to the stillness. I'm not used to being on my own all day. Jo will do her best, I know that, but she's busy, running the café and looking after Mia. I can't count on her coming often.

It might be fun to have someone in for a few days, and the flat does need doing.

Before I can change my mind, I reach for my phone and dial the number.

CHAPTER EIGHT

I'm slowly adjusting to life on crutches but it's physically harder than I'd imagined. I'm using different muscles in my arms and back and by the end of the day, I ache in strange places. I'm growing some impressive bruises under my arms too, where the crutches press when they take my weight.

All day Tuesday, I do my best not to think about Chile. I try to stay positive by working on chasing down some other trips for early next year. All being well, I'm hoping to get the cast off by February.

I spend a while day-dreaming about where to try and making a short list. Cape Town's worth a shot. At least it'll be warm. Maybe Naples? I check the dates of the Venetian Carnival and start doing some quick internet research, then send out some exploratory emails in the hope one of the travel companies might bite. When I first went freelance, in my twenties, the travel sections still had budgets for trips and most of my time was spent having lunch with commissioning editors. Now that's all gone and we have to scout around for freebies from tour operators and hotels in return for a favourable write-up.

After dinner, I take another painkiller and get ready for bed. Jo's right. It's been a long time since I just slowed down. Maybe it will do me good. I go across to the small bookcase of travel books in the lounge and run my eyes down the spines. I've got a couple on Venice. I pick one off the shelf. I could start mugging up. It might give me some fresh ideas for pitches.

I sit up in bed and start to read about the history of Venice. Sounds drift in. Music plays somewhere in the block, the low distant rumble of bass. Now and then, footsteps trot along the pavement, a man's heavy tread and a woman's clipping heels. A steady procession of cars splashes through the wet.

I think about the smooth ceiling panels at the hospital, always so brightly lit day and night; the constant soft tread of nurses, back and forth; the rattle of trolleys; the moans and cries in the night from neighbouring beds, and feel grateful to be home.

I soon find my eyes closing and the book slips from my hands as I slide backwards into sleep.

The roar of the wind on the heath surrounds me again. The pumping of blood in my ears, the hard breathing. Then, from nowhere, the car, tossing me into the air like a puppet. The dizzy, terrifying flight through the air, through nothingness.

I snap my eyes open, propping myself up on my elbows and fumbling for the bedside light. I must have slept. It's twenty past two. I half sit, half lie, blinking, trying to force myself awake, anxious, staring into the empty room, my face sweating. Something woke me. Was it my own voice, pulling me out of my nightmare? Did I cry out? I don't know. The room is still and silent. I strain to hear. I'm sure there was something...

I lift my plastered leg and swing it to the floor, then grope for the crutches and head slowly out into the darkened lounge. I stand against the wall, biting my lip, and listen. From the kitchen, the fridge hums and whirls. The heating system clicks.

Then another sound comes, just outside the flat. A mechanical noise. It takes me a moment to place it: it sounds louder than usual in the stillness of the night.

The grind of the lift, rising from the ground floor. It passes the first floor, then reaches mine, the second. Then it stops. I hold my breath. The doors open with a whoosh of air. Silence.

They close again. Has someone stepped out? Is someone there, on the tiny landing, right outside my door? My breath quickens.

An elderly lady lives alone in the other second floor flat, across the landing. She barely goes out nowadays. I can't imagine her having visitors in the middle of the night. I hobble to the front door, my crutches noisy in the silence, and put my eye to the peephole.

The fisheye image swims, blurry. It's dark with shadow. I can't see anyone. But the fisheye doesn't cover everywhere. What if someone's against the wall, to one side? Or low and close, against my door?

I sense someone there. My skin creeps and hairs bristle on my neck. I can feel them. I lift a hand to the safety chain, wondering for a moment about sliding it quietly off, easing back the bolt and pulling the door open to see for myself. I hesitate. If someone is there, they must be listening too. Maybe they can hear my fast breathing. Maybe that's what they want. They want me to open the door.

My leg aches with standing. I try to change position, to shuffle around and shift my weight. One of the crutches slips from my hand and falls to the floor with a clatter. I curse under my breath and it takes me a while to steady myself; then, one hand clutching the door handle and the other stretching down, I ease low enough to grab it.

As I right myself again, the lift doors close and, a few seconds later, the mechanical whirr sounds again as it slides steadily down the shaft to the ground floor. Whoever was there – if anyone was – has already gone.

CHAPTER NINE

The next morning, I wake with a jolt.

My neck is stiff. I'm not in bed. There are no sheets, just a blanket which has slipped to one side, trailing to the floor. I blink, looking around. I'm lying sprawled on the sofa, my leg sticking out over the arm. My cheek is hot and uncomfortable where it's been pressed sideways against the rough fabric. My mouth, slightly open, is dry.

I'm agitated, remembering what happened in the night. Someone was there, weren't they? Someone was in the building, was on the landing by my door? My heart races.

I try to shake myself out of it. This is ridiculous. I'm in suburban London, not Baghdad or Beirut. Maybe I am just tired. I've also been taking a lot of painkillers – maybe they're making me jumpy. *Come on, Louise. There was no one there.*

But even as I reassure myself, I don't buy it. I'm not the nervous sort. Every time I've ever been in a hotel room in a strange city and sensed something wasn't as it should be, I was always right. I've got good survival instincts. A broken leg doesn't change that.

I wash, dress and sit over a strong coffee, looking out at the street. The road surface glistens with rain. The trees along the far side are leafless scribbles against a dull sky. I frown, thinking about what happened overnight and wondering why anyone would come creeping to my door in the small hours.

I think about Jo and check my watch. It's just after eight. Mike'll be gone by now, on the train to school. She'll be getting

Mia ready, then rushing her out to school. I picture the two of them, hand in hand, hurrying down the road, Mia's backpack bouncing on her back.

Below the window, the door to the building block clicks shut and a middle-aged woman, smartly dressed, appears on the path, clipping over the stones to turn into the road, heading towards the high street. She walks with short, poking steps, impeded by her heels. A leather bag dangles from her shoulder and she cradles a re-useable coffee cup. Her face has the tight look of an efficient, urban professional, someone who's on a schedule and doesn't wish to be interrupted. A younger man, twenties maybe, approaches our block from further down the road and lollops past her with ease, swinging a battered bag in his hand.

I have a sudden yearning to be outside again, back in the real world. I'd like to be heading to an airport but if I can't do that, I could at least try leaving the flat. I can't stay cooped up inside all the time, crutches or not.

I smile at myself. I've travelled the world but I'm suddenly excited about hopping down my own street to the café on the corner. I could get a decent coffee, maybe have a croissant and bring something back to have later, for lunch.

It takes me a while to make my way around the flat, finding a coat and balancing while I put it on, gathering my keys and wallet. I head onto the landing with a sense of achievement, leaning my crutches against the jamb as I lock up.

Outside, the air is crisp and chilled. Wet leaves form a slippery mulch underfoot and I progress carefully, taking care not to fall, swinging my way down the path and out onto the pavement. The flow of commuters heading towards the high street is thickening and they make a point of overtaking me, skirting me, sometimes stepping off the kerb to give me a wide berth.

It's a good workout. I pause after a while and stand, leaning on my crutches, catching my breath. A woman, right behind me, makes an exaggerated arc round me, making the point wordlessly that I'm in the way.

I watch her stride off. It's usually a few minutes' brisk walk to the end of the street but I'm struggling already and I'm only halfway there. I brace myself, imagine I'm in the sunshine in St Mark's Square in Venice, smelling the salt water of the lagoon and hearing the gaggle of tour groups, then reposition my crutches and head off again.

Inside the café, I'm triumphant. I find myself grinning inanely as I wait along the side of the counter, looking over the pastries and cakes, the macaroons and biscuits, as if I've never seen them before. The air is rich with the smell of fresh coffee and steamed milk. Normally, I'm in as much of a rush as the rest of the people here, grabbing a coffee, swiping a card and dashing out again to jump on a train or bus, but today I take time to smile at the harried young baristas and ask if one of them could kindly carry my tray to a table so I can eat in.

I sit in the window, nibbling a sweet, warm almond croissant and sipping a strong coffee, looking out at the bustle and stir. My fear last night seems distant now. I was right. I just needed to get out of the flat. I imagine telling Jo about popping down here for breakfast, as if it were nothing at all, and smile at myself.

Afterwards, as I head back, I start to tire. I'm still in training on crutches and fresh aches are setting in. I think about my elderly neighbour and wonder for the first time if she too feels it's an achievement to make it to the end of the road. Maybe, when I'm back on my feet, I should make more effort to befriend her and see if she wants me to do her shopping.

The leaf mulch is treacherous and I pick my way with care, unsteady now. I'm a few steps from the block and about to turn off the pavement onto the path when I'm distracted by two young boys, racing on scooters, heading right for me.

I stumble to get out of their way and totter awkwardly, thrown off balance. My crutches tangle for a second, one knocking the other from under me. I stab at the ground with one, trying to stay upright, but the crutch skids on the leaves and suddenly I'm falling backwards, crutches clattering in all directions, grasping at air.

I'm right by the kerb and a car speeds past, too fast, too close, a blur of dark metal. I cry out. For a second, I'm back in the darkness, feeling myself flying off the bike, arms wide, crashing against a bonnet, then thrown off onto the ground.

I land with a bang, first my back, then my head hitting stone. I lie still, winded, blinking away spangles of light.

For a moment, I can't move. I just stay there, looking up at the sharp edge of the block of flats and the grey autumn sky above it. It's not darkness. Not the heath. I struggle to make sense of it, trying to remember where I really am.

It starts to come back. It's morning. I'm outside the flat. The car didn't hit me. Somewhere nearby, dropped on the ground, there's a sandwich. It's almost as if I'm looking down on someone else, wondering how much damage I've done this time.

'Don't move. Just for a moment.' A man's voice, deep and confident. 'You're all right.'

A paramedic? How did they get here so soon? I didn't pass out, did I? Whoever it is, I'm grateful for their help.

A man in a leather jacket is stooping over me, checking over the plaster cast and organising my limbs back into a less awkward position. He reaches my head. He has a mess of dark hair flopping over his forehead as he looks down at me. He's a little older than me, maybe early forties. A tanned, lived-in face with creases around the corners of the eyes. 'Don't try to move yet. Just tell me: any sharp pain?'

I consider this. 'Not really.' What's a sharp pain? A break, maybe. Crashing off the bike – that was sharp pain, for sure. 'I think I banged my head. My back. But I'm fine.'

He nods as if that's a good answer, then gathers together the crutches and leans them against the low boundary wall of the garden around the flats. 'Have you got much further to go?'

I point to the path. 'I live right there.'

He comes behind my head and crouches down, puts his hands under my shoulders and raises them a fraction. 'That hurt?'

'Not really.'

'Good. Here's what we're going to do: I'm going to count to three and on three, I'll lift you up onto your feet. Try to take your weight on your good leg if you can. I'll support you while you get your balance. Right?'

I'm about to say I'm not sure about this. There's part of me that would rather stay where I am a bit longer, lying right there on the damp pavement, than try to get upright again straightaway. But it turns out that he isn't asking my opinion, he's informing me and already, he's counting down: 'One. Two. THREE.' He presses his knee between my shoulder blades and lifts me, his hands now firmly under my arms.

I brace myself, jaw set. He hauls me upwards and I scramble to right myself, leaning heavily on him. It's only a dozen steps to the front door, but it seems a mile. He holds me up with one arm, a solid ledge of muscle, while he reaches for the crutches with the other and hands them to me.

I stutter: 'I'm sorry, you must—'

He cuts me off. 'You're fine. Focus now. Get your balance.'

I feel such a fool, held up by his arm. I want to say: *This isn't me. You don't know me. I've travelled across deserts, up mountains, jumped out of aeroplanes. I never accept help, especially not from strangers.*

He walks me, step by step, up the path, into the lobby, into the lift.

I lean back against the side of the lift, shattered. 'Second floor,' I manage to say.

'I know.' The lift shudders into movement. He's already hit the button. 'Flat B.'

I stare at him, suddenly tense. I think of last night and the lift doors stealthily opening.

'You said nine-thirty. I've been sitting in the van for ten minutes. Just as well, as it turns out.' He holds out a hand. It's warm and strong in mine. Capable. One of the hands that just picked me up off the pavement and half carried me inside.

'Louise Taylor, right? There can't be many one-legged women in the block.' He smiles. 'I'm Ed. Come about the painting and decorating. Remember?'

CHAPTER TEN

I hand Ed my keys to open the front door and ask him to help me to the sofa, then put another chair in front of me so I can rest the plaster cast on it.

'You want to watch it.' He's cheerful. 'You know what they say – one broken leg is a misfortune, two looks like carelessness.'

I have to think about that. 'Is that Oscar Wilde?'

He just grins to himself. 'What do you want me to do with this?' He takes a long bundle out of his pocket. It takes me a moment to realise he's recovered my sandwich from the ground, battered but still edible.

'Fridge, please.' I point him towards the kitchen. A moment later, I hear the soft suck of the fridge door. I blink. I'm hit by a sudden, intense memory, one I can't place.

He calls through: 'Shall I make you a cup of tea? How do you take it?'

'Sure. Strong, please. Milk, no sugar. Have one yourself. Mugs are in th—'

'Yup, got them.'

Running water, then a click as the kettle goes on. Cupboard doors open and bang closed. The kettle murmurs and starts to boil. I stare at my plastered leg, still disorientated. I can't work out why this scene suddenly feels familiar, as if it's something that's happened before.

He calls through: 'Got any biscuits?' Then: 'No worries, found them.'

He carries in two mugs of tea, a packet of biscuits under his arm, and sets it all on the table. He shucks off his leather jacket and folds it with care, then sits opposite me. He's wearing a plain black T-shirt underneath, biceps spilling out of the short sleeves. His broad thighs are encased in workman's jeans. He rests his elbows on them as he sips, as if they were shelves.

I sip my tea and grimace at the sweetness. 'Is this yours? I think it's got sugar in it.'

'That's for shock.'

'Really?' I raise my eyebrows. 'Isn't that an old wives' tale?'

'Never underestimate an old wife.'

I gesture to him to help himself to the biscuits, then sip the sweet tea. My hands tremble on the mug. My heart rate's slowly settling back to normal again, but I still feel peculiar. I sense a memory of this man, just out of reach. A shadow I can't yet grasp.

'Ed?'

He nods, dunking a biscuit.

'Have we met somewhere before?'

He shakes his head while he eats his biscuit, then swallows the crumbs and says: 'Not that I'm aware.'

I frown. *Something. It'll come to me.*

He considers me. 'Are you OK?'

I nod, still thoughtful.

'You cried out,' he says. 'When you fell over. Was it the car?'

'I suppose so.'

'It wasn't that close.' He looks at me. His eyes are very clear, intelligent and intense. 'Was that what happened?' He nods at my broken leg. 'A car?'

'Knocked me off my bike.'

'Ouch.' He pulls a sympathetic face. 'I'm guessing not long ago, either.'

'What makes you say that?' I give him a sharp look. *How does he know that? From Tanya?*

'Just the state of the cast.' He shrugs. 'Hardly a mark on it, apart from just now. You're not long out of hospital, are you?'

'Three days.'

'That's hard. Suddenly being on crutches. Does it hurt?'

I shrug. 'Not too much. But you're right, not being mobile is a pain.'

'I bet.' He pauses.

'Let's just say, I could have done without it,' I say. 'I'm not used to being stuck indoors all day. That's not me.'

He nods. 'I get that. It wouldn't be me, either.'

I put down the over-sweet tea with an unintended bang, sloshing it over the rim. 'Tanya said you were in the army.'

'Yep.' A long silence. I expect him to say something else, but he doesn't. Just sits there and slurps his tea.

I hesitate. I'm not sure how much I can ask about it without sounding nosey.

Finally, I say: 'So, are you painting and decorating full-time?'

'Correct.' Again, he doesn't elaborate. A man of few words, then, when it comes to talking about himself. Suits me. I think about what Tanya said about being stuck with someone who wants to tell you their life story. Not much chance of that here.

I try to sound businesslike. 'You said on the phone that you might be able to fit me in straightaway. What do you think, now you've seen it?'

'I've got a week, basically. My next job's been put back.' He gets to his feet and strolls around the room, his fingers reaching out now and then to touch a lump in the paintwork, his eyes checking out the chipped skirting. 'If I start now, I could get the lounge done. Probably the hall, too. As long as I don't run into problems.'

I wait, watching him. 'Kitchen?'

'Not in a week. I can come back to you, but it might be January.' He sits down again. 'Look, I do things properly. Strip right back, replaster if needed, then two coats, at least. Maybe three.' He nods to himself. 'It's not fast. But you'll see the difference. And it'll last.' He pauses, looking around again, thoughtful. 'Have you thought about colours?'

'Not really. Nothing over-powering that might clash with the pictures. Something fresh.'

'Well, we can figure that out. I'll bring you a paint chart.' He hesitates, considering the room. 'Green's popular. Not a strong green, just a hint. That might look good with the frames. Or maybe one of the Willows? Or a Wattle. I'd stick with off-white woodwork, myself. Keep it light and airy. It's quite a small room.'

I just nod. I'm not a big fan of green but he's right, I need to see a chart and have a think about it.

He gets to his feet. 'I'll get started then, shall I? Just need to get my stuff off the van.'

I hesitate. *Did I even hire him?* 'You haven't told me what you charge.'

He picks up his mug and calls over his shoulder as he takes it into the kitchen, his voice rising in volume as he turns on the tap and washes it up. 'A hundred and fifty a day. Plus materials. Cash in hand, if that's OK – no rush. I like an early start to beat the traffic. Say eight o'clock? And leave about four, four-thirty. Light's starting to go by then.'

He's back in the lounge, still drying his hands on my kitchen towel. He's so solidly built, he seems to fill the place. I wonder for a moment what it'll be like, the two of us together all day in this tiny place. I remember what Tanya said: *I totally trust him, full stop.*

'OK, then.'

He nods. 'OK, then.'

CHAPTER ELEVEN

His work is methodical, almost mesmerising.

I'm trying to write pitches for trips next year, but the cast makes it hard to sit comfortably for long. I perch on the sofa, laptop on knee, trying to ignore the dull ache at the back of my skull. *What about Estonia? That's somewhere I've never been.* I do an internet search and note down who's written what from there in the last few years.

I make slow progress, struggling to concentrate. It isn't only the cast.

I keep finding my eyes lifting to watch Ed work. He feels the walls with his fingers, sanding off bumps and filling crevices, stripping off old paint where it's been thickened by several coats. He seems unhurried, moving at the same steady pace, hour by hour, working his way around the lounge, then into the hall, re-laying his dustsheets as he goes, cleaning up behind him with a hand-held vacuum cleaner.

Muscles knot and twist down his back as he stretches and bends. His T-shirt sticks across his shoulders in a dark line of sweat. He wears earbuds, the wire running down to the smartphone in his pocket. Now and then, when he moves, a hint of sound leaks out, a rumble of bass. Not enough to tell me what sort of music he's chosen.

His presence bothers me, and I can't figure out why. It's more than the fact he's a stranger, suddenly working a few feet away from me in a small room; I can't shake the feeling that we know each other from somewhere. I just can't work out where. It's unsettling.

Also, maybe I'm imagining it, but it feels as if he's oddly attuned to me. If I make the slightest move to get up, he seems instantly aware of it. I might be wrong. After all, he doesn't say anything. He doesn't even look round. He just seems to slow his movements, as if he's waiting to see if I need help.

It's as though, if I faltered, he'd be there at once, wiping off his hands on the splattered rag tucked into his belt and quietly striding over to help, holding me upright until I got my balance again.

At lunchtime, he stops work and disappears into the kitchen with his brushes and tray for a quick clean-up. 'Are you having this?' He appears in the doorway, hands clean now, and brandishes the battered sandwich.

When I nod, he says: 'Cup of tea?'

'Only if it's sugar-free.'

He grins, and goes back into the kitchen. The kettle goes on.

He comes out again carrying an old tray from the back of the kitchen counter. It belonged to Mum years ago, one of the possessions I salvaged from the house after her death. 'Lunch is served!' He sets it down on the coffee table with a flourish. He's unwrapped the sandwich, cut it in half and put it on a plate, alongside a mug of tea.

I smile. 'You can always get a job as a waiter if the decorating doesn't work out.'

'Never say never.'

I point at the tea. 'Did you make yourself one?'

'I'm fine, thanks.' He heads out of the room, calling over his shoulder: 'See you later.'

As soon as the front door closes, the flat feels lifeless.

I reach for the tray and start on the sandwich.

Already, the room's changed dramatically. Ed's folded the wooden screen and stowed it away in the hall. The framed posters, now neatly stacked against the wall outside my bedroom, have left a succession of dirt rectangles. Several smaller items – the occasional table with the black and white lamp; a pair of large, china elephants from Hong Kong; the outlying rugs, rolled now – are huddling together, away from the walls.

I shake my head, trying to work out what's the matter with me. I've felt weird all morning. Unsettled. Spooked. I still can't shake the sense I know this guy. My head aches so much, it's a strain to think. Maybe he just reminds me of someone.

I take the chance to check my phone. I've been keeping it switched off or on silent since I came home from hospital, partly because I keep drifting off to sleep during the day but mostly because of the deluge of messages from Toby. Looking now, I power through a series of voicemails from him and delete the lot.

He just rants. Sometimes he says how much he loves me, that he wants me back. At other times he's bitter, listing everything he's ever done for me, all the times he's waited at home while I was swanning off on foreign trips. 'Holidays', as he calls them. I'd no idea he'd resented it so much, all this time.

I've heard enough already. Since this morning, he's sent half-a-dozen texts, telling me with mounting anger to call him back, then two chatty emails. It's like dealing with several different people rolled into one. I delete these too and switch my phone off again. I really haven't got the energy for all this.

When I've eaten as much as I can face, I pull myself up and take the plate and cup back to the kitchen. I pause by the window and peer out. Ed's down there, sitting in the front of his van.

He's parked just past the block and he's eating his lunch, lolling, relaxed, in his seat, gazing forward through the windscreen at the empty road. Homemade sandwiches, from the look of it. The sight of him makes me smile. I'll tell him, I decide, that he doesn't have to eat in the van. It's cold. He can bring his lunch in here if he wants.

As I watch, he suddenly heaves himself into a more upright position, quickly sets down his half-eaten sandwich and fumbles in his pocket, then pulls out his phone and answers it. I can't tell what he's saying but his body language changes in a moment. He hunches forward, his free hand tracing the curve of the steering wheel. Whatever's being said, he looks tense.

I turn away. I shouldn't be watching: it's intrusive and none of my business, anyway.

By the time he comes back, I'm on the sofa again, trying to pretend I haven't spied.

The steady rhythm of scraping and filling resumes. I power my laptop up again and open a document, but I barely look at it. My eyes are on him, watching him work, trying to figure him out.

At about three, I hobble into the kitchen and make us both a drink.

'Quick break?'

He sizes up the coffee. 'Lovely. Just there, please.'

I set the mug down on the nearest table, go back to fetch my own mug and perch nearby him, companionable.

He was right. He's good at his job. Deft. Thorough.

When he finally reaches down to take his coffee, he glances at me. He must take in the way my hands, cupped around my own mug, are trembling.

'You still a bit shaky?'

I nod. 'I have been since the accident. Shock, I suppose.'

'Must have been quite something.'

I shrug. 'It's not just the leg. I had concussion.'

He looks concerned. 'Headaches?'

'Yep. Dizziness. And flashbacks. All that stuff.'

He sets his mug down again and turns back to the wall and, for a moment, I think the conversation's over. I feel a stab of disappointment, then embarrassment as I wonder what he makes of me. Needy woman desperate for company? That's not me at all.

After a few moments, he stops scraping again and says: 'You might have a bit of PTSD. You know what that is? Post-traumatic stress.'

Do I know what PTSD is? I tighten my lips. *You have no idea, mister.*

He seems to mistake my silence for scepticism. 'I'm just saying. That car frightened the hell out of you, earlier. I saw. It's a perfectly normal reaction. But you need to keep telling yourself you're actually safe. Just because it happened once, it doesn't mean it'll happen again.'

'But it might.' The words come out before I can stop them.

He pauses. 'What do you mean?'

'It was a hit and run. Whoever it was, they're still out there.'

He turns and fixes me with a long, steady look. 'Are you saying it might not have been an accident? Someone might've hit you on purpose?'

'Who knows?' I shrug. 'I'm just going to be careful, that's all. It's unfinished business.' I see his frown. 'Look, forget it.'

I take some painkillers and go through to my bedroom to lie down.

By the time I wake up, it's dark and, when I hobble through to the lounge to look for Ed, he's already gone.

CHAPTER TWELVE

'What's he like?'

Jo's cooking Mia's evening meal – sausages, by the sound of it: popping fat and the metallic scrape of the grill-pan drift down the phone as we chat. She usually feeds Mia at about half past five, then cooks again later so she and Mike can eat together in peace. Couple time, once Mia's in bed. I picture their kitchen as she strides round it, setting the table, opening a tin of baked beans and spooning them into a dish. Peas from the freezer.

'He's… you know, fine.' I hesitate, thinking about the last two days. How do I describe Ed? His calmness, his strength, his silence. 'He was in the army. You know the type – focused and no-nonsense. Gets the job done.'

'Muscle man?' She chortles to herself, rustling something. 'He sounds quite a find.'

'Don't be silly.' I frown. 'It's not like that.'

She's already heard about the way he scraped me up off the pavement and half carried me home. She's made me promise not to try going out on my own again, at least not for a few more days, until I'm steadier on my feet.

'Is it weird, being stuck in the flat with him all day?'

'Not really. Not yet, anyway. He doesn't talk much.'

'Can we come round and check him out soon? Mia's dying to see you. She wants you to paint the walls rainbow. I keep warning her that mightn't be the look you're going for.'

I smile to myself. Of course she does. Everything has to be rainbow at the moment.

'I've been looking at Willow.'

'Beg your pardon?' The beep of the microwave. Dinner must be nearly done.

I tell her what I've just been checking online. 'It's a sort of pale browny-green.' I put on a TV advert voice. *Understated and yet subtle. Modern and yet of all time.*

'Blimey.' Her voice comes and goes. She's probably got the handset jammed between her shoulder and her cheek while she uses her hands to cook. 'Is that the painter's idea? He sounds in touch with his feminine side.' She moves the phone away and hollers: 'Mia! Dinner!' Then comes back to me: 'Sorry, Lou. Look, I'll have to go in a minute. But while you're on—' The kitchen clatter suddenly recedes as if she's moved somewhere else, into the echoing downstairs bathroom, maybe, where Mia won't hear. 'Can you hear me?' Her voice falls to a whisper.

'What?'

'Toby called me today.' A pause while she lets that sink in. 'In a real state.'

Silence. I clench my jaw. He has no right to pester Jo. He knows how much I hate being talked about behind my back.

She carries on. 'What's going on? He said you've walked out on him.'

I tut. 'Not quite the right turn of phrase, just at the moment.'

'All right, chucked him. Broken it off. What do you want me to call it? Have you?'

I hesitate. She sounds annoyed. What right has she got to make me feel guilty for not telling her? It's nothing to do with her. And, anyway, so much else has been happening.

'I have, as it happens.'

'As it happens? You didn't think you might just mention it? Or were you just going to let me go on assuming you were still together?'

I shrug to the empty flat.

'Why've you done it? Did you have a fight?'

I squirm. 'I just don't think we're right together.'

'That's a bit vague.' She sounds cool. 'Any particular reason?'

'He's never supported my job. You know that. He's always moaned about the fact I travel a lot, even though he knew from the start what I did.' I hesitate. 'He was dead set against the Chile trip. Kept lecturing me about how dangerous it was.'

'I was worried about it, too. You do push it, Lou.'

'Well, there you are, then. You'll be pleased I'm not going.' I huff, annoyed with them both. 'And it's not just that. He's suddenly got all serious on me. He thinks I ought to move in with him and think about having kids.'

'What's so awful about that?'

'Oh, come on.'

'What? I'm just saying. You've been going out for – how long – three years?'

'Two and a half.'

'Well, then.'

She always does this. I say, 'Could you just not take his side, please? For once.'

'That's not fair.' She sighs, then there's a creak as the bathroom door opens. 'Coming, Mia. Just hang on a sec. I'm on the phone.' She closes the door again and comes back on the line. 'He adores you, you know that, don't you? He's a really nice guy.'

I think about the barrage of wheedling, injured messages. 'You sure about that?'

'Stop being silly.' Her big sister voice, straining to stay sensible. 'Do you think it's just nerves? Maybe you should move in with him for a trial period. Just give it a go. You're not getting any younger, Lou.'

'I can't believe you just said that.'

'Well, it's true. You love him, don't you?'

I hesitate. Do I love him? *Not enough. Not the way Jo loves Mike.*

'Lou. I think there was someone with him when he called.' Jo's voice sounds careful, as if she's weighing her words. 'I heard a voice. In the background.' She pauses. 'A woman.'

My stomach folds. *Rachel. I bet it was bloody Rachel, rushing round to offer her bony shoulder to cry on.* I can just imagine. Bad-mouthing me again too, no doubt. Sticking the knife in. What did he say when I was in hospital? *Rachel warned me about you.*

I take a slow, deep breath and force myself to say: 'Well, why shouldn't he?' My heart races. *It's not my business. If he wants to hang out with her, that's up to him.* 'Good for him. Really.' I don't like the woman. I don't trust her. But he's not mine any more.

'Lou! You're the one he wants. You know that.' Jo can read me like a book. Always could. 'And maybe he's right, in a way. Thirty-six, Lou. Come on. If you want kids, you need to get on with it.'

'Well, I don't. OK?' I'm on the verge of ending the call. Then Mia starts singing in the background and I soften a fraction. Her young voice is confident, however high-pitched and off-key.

'I just wonder, sometimes, why you're so desperate to be on the road all the time. I could understand it when you were younger. Seeing the world and all that. But when's it going to end?'

I'm stung. 'Why does it have to?'

'I just don't want you to miss out on a family,' Jo says. 'And it keeps happening, Lou. Doesn't it? Rob. Lovely guy. Super keen on you. Then Simon. Perfectly nice bloke. Wanted to marry you. And now Toby. It's like you can only go so far with these guys and then you run away.'

I don't answer. What can I say to that?

'It's as if you're still punishing yourself,' she says, softly. 'As if you think you don't deserve to be happy. Is that what's going on?'

'Jo?' Mike's voice booms in the background. Just home, probably.

I shake my head. 'You'd better go.'

That's enough unwanted advice for one day. We say goodbye, and hang up.

CHAPTER THIRTEEN

That night, I dream about the past for the first time in years.

I thought I was over it. I thought I'd finally learned to block it out.

But I'm right back there, all over again, inside the house.

It's horribly vivid, as clear as if it were yesterday.

The room's dark, the corners black with shadow.

Then, the scream.

I wake and sit up abruptly in bed, eyes wide and staring, feeling the dream slip away, leaving me shaking and damp with sweat.

An hour or so later, Ed's van draws up outside. I expect him to head straight up the path but my phone pings with a text.

Going for coffee. Want one?

I text back.

Black Americano, pls. NO SUGAR!

Something in me eases when I open the door and see him standing there, a shy grin on his face, takeaway coffees in hand.

I think about it as I sip my Americano, pretending to start work but actually watching him bustle about, setting up for the day. The flat seems safer with him here, this man I've only just met but somehow already feel I know. Finally, the menace of the dream, which has hung around me since I woke, evaporates.

It rains on and off throughout the morning. The sunlight across the bare walls is watery.

At lunchtime, I go to make myself a sandwich. I rummage in the back of the fridge and turn up some stale cheese.

When Ed stops work and comes through to wash, I say, trying to sound casual: 'You're welcome to eat lunch here, if you like.'

He doesn't answer. I can't see his face. It's lowered over the sink as he concentrates on scrubbing flakes of dried paint off his fingers.

I stutter on. 'I mean… just, it's cold outside.'

He glances sideways at the breadboard where I'm making my sandwich. 'Did that cheese crawl out by itself?'

'Pretty much.'

We don't talk as we eat. It isn't awkward, we just don't need to. Again, I have that strange sense that we've spent time together before.

As he's getting up, ready to go back to work, he notices one of my rugs on the far side of the room. It's a faded Tree of Life in muted shades of brown and orange.

He points. 'Where's that from?'

'A market in Islamabad, years ago. They said it was Afghan and pretty old.' I shrug. 'Who knows, though, maybe they made it round the back.'

'I don't think so. Looks authentic to me.' He pauses for a moment, considering it. 'Nice piece.'

At the end of the day, when he's packing up to leave, I try to press a few pounds on him for the coffee. He folds my fingers around the coins and pushes my hand away.

'All included,' he says, his eyes amused.

'I'd have asked for a large if I'd known that.'

He just raises an eyebrow to acknowledge the joke, then he's gone.

*

In the evening, after Ed's left and I've eaten a tasteless microwave dinner, I lie quietly on the sofa and watch the daylight fade to dusk. I look at the pale, scraped walls. Here and there, patches of filler glisten where he's smoothed out a crack. The wooden skirting is back to its natural brown, lightly mottled with stubborn flecks of white paint. The flat smells of turpentine, underpinned, just faintly, with his smells: fresh sweat, soap, his leather jacket.

When I close the lounge curtains and switch on the lights, motes of plaster dust shine in the brightness. I wonder what Ed would say if I told him I wanted to keep it like this. *Don't bother with fresh paint, I'll stick with the fleshless skeleton look, please.* Why do I feel so at home like this? Because there's something honest about seeing the bones of the place exposed. Something brutal.

I switch on my phone for the first time since lunchtime and it rings almost at once. It's Toby. Either it's a fluke or he's been trying all day. I take and end the call in the same movement, without speaking. The handset vibrates and starts to ping as a flurry of messages and voicemails, no doubt mostly from him, rush in.

I check through the messages. As I expected, a torrent of texts and emails from Toby. He's persistent. Some are pleading. Others confused. Some angry.

> *You can't treat me like this. You think you're so special, don't you? Take a look at yourself.*

This is the man I'm supposed to start a family with? Is he really the same one who was saying, a few texts earlier, that he adored me, that he couldn't live without me? I shake my head. I'm sorry. I really am. I never meant to hurt him. I should never have let it go on so long.

The problem is that Toby thinks he knows me, but he doesn't. He doesn't know the half of it.

I check through the missed calls and voice messages in case there are any I do want to hear.

Jo, checking in on me, followed at once by Mia, her voice high and excited, asking if she can come and see me on Saturday, telling me about her homework. We're on to 'What did the Vikings eat?' apparently. I smile to myself.

A few messages from friends, asking if I'm in London at the moment, wondering if I fancy meeting up for dinner or seeing a film at the weekend. I'm not in the mood to call back, not yet.

Then, amid more ranting calls from Toby, a voice message from the police. That female detective who interviewed me in hospital, Sara Blakely, asking me how I am, if I have anything more to tell them.

I press the phone to my ear, my pulse quickening, concentrating on her words.

The CCTV checks haven't brought any new leads so far, she says. They've appealed for witnesses. The mangled frame of my bike is with forensics. They're backed up, but she hopes to hear from them soon.

She's just signing off in her curt tone when the front door buzzer sounds, long and urgent. I jump. It's dark outside and getting late.

A moment later, a new message pings on my phone. Toby.

It's me. Let me in.

I delete it. The buzzer sounds again. My heart races. I just want him to go away.

A new message in angry capitals: *I KNOW YOU'RE THERE. LET ME IN*

I type back, angry: *Go away or I'll call the police.*

I switch off my phone, heave myself to the door and fasten the safety chain. If he hangs around down there for long enough, someone else will let him into the building. They always do in this block, assuming someone's just forgotten their key or that it's a courier, delivering fast food.

I switch off the lights and hobble through to my bedroom. I lean back against the edge of the window frame in the dark and peer out, trying not to be seen. Below, the road is quiet, the blackness broken here and there by pools of lamp light. I stare out, waiting, my palms sweaty.

The buzzer sounds again. I don't move.

After a while, Toby appears below, stomping down the path, stopping every now and then to twist and look up at the windows. His face is hard with anger. He's in his best coat, the one I helped him choose last winter. I imagine him picking it out to wear this evening, as he gathered his courage and decided to come over. I wonder if Rachel knows he's here. What she'll have to say about it if she finds out.

I expect him to stride off towards the high street and disappear from view. He doesn't. He hesitates, then crosses the road and stands on the far pavement, deep in the shadows, under the trees. I blink. He's barely visible, his dark coat merging into the night.

I stand for as long as I can bear, waiting for him to leave. He doesn't move.

I creep into bed, leaving the curtains undrawn, and try to get to sleep, knowing that he's still there, angry but determined, his eyes on my window, watching me from the darkness.

CHAPTER FOURTEEN

Ed arrives promptly just after eight o'clock on Friday morning. Already we're falling into a relaxed routine.

I make sure I'm washed and dressed and waiting by the security camera when he buzzes, smiling at the blurry image of his floppy black hair, broad shoulders, leather jacket.

He bounds up the stairs and arrives with his work bag slung over his shoulder and two takeaway coffees, his latte and my black americano. I've stopped trying to insist he takes money for mine.

Today, he spends the morning on finishing touches, sanding and smoothing. At about twelve, he takes out his earbuds and turns to face. 'It's make-your-mind-up time. Are we ready?'

He's already given me colour charts. This is my last call before he buys the paint.

He chooses a tester wall, close to the window but not in direct sunlight, and brings some mini tester pots out of his bag. 'So, madam. Here' – he gives a theatrical flourish – 'we have "Willow One".' He daubs a broad streak on the wall. 'And here: "Willow Two".' Another.

I sit, leg propped on a chair, and try to tell one from the next, laughing at the crazy names as he tries the rest of the testers: 'Mole's Breath', 'Mouse's Back', 'Smoked Trout'…

'What's that one, again?'

'One of the Willows. Hang on.' He bends down to the pots to check. 'Willow Green, I think?'

'You know what? Surprise me,' I say at last. 'Any of those willowy ones. They all look good. From here, they're practically the same.'

He looks at me with those intense, see-it-all eyes.

I laugh. 'Was that the wrong answer?'

'I'm shocked.' He gives me a mock frown. 'Are you really suggesting there might be more important things in life than the difference between these four shades of willow?'

'I'm afraid I am.'

He breaks into a smile. His face lights, younger suddenly. His eyes crinkle at the corners.

'In that case, I'm going to make an executive decision. I'm going for Willow Two. This one.' He points it out on the wall. 'OK?'

'Perfect.'

He puts down his brush, cleans off his hands and shrugs on his jacket. 'I think I'll head out now and pick up the paint, so I can start first thing on Monday. OK if I store it here over the weekend?'

'Of course.'

He strides to the door, then stops and turns back. 'By the way, I've noticed you're getting low on fresh food. Do you want me to pick something up on my way back? Milk? Ham? Loaf of bread?'

'Are you sure?' I hesitate. 'Well, I would be grateful. As long as you let me pay for it.'

I write a quick list and hand it to him with a ten-pound note.

He heads out. I imagine him bounding down the stairs, his hair flopping across his forehead, then bursting out of the front door onto the path. His engine revs into life in the street below before his van moves off.

I look at the walls, calculating how long he'll need to paint them. I'm not fooling myself – I know why. I don't want him to finish and move on, not just yet.

CHAPTER FIFTEEN

He arrives back with the paint and a carrier bag bulging with food.

'That must've cost more than a tenner.'

'I added a few things for myself, that's all,' he says. 'Besides, I couldn't stand by and watch you eat another mouldy cheese sandwich. That's a violation of human rights.'

He sets out plates on the coffee table and starts to unpack. First, the items I asked for: sliced ham, a wedge of Cheddar, a fresh loaf of bread and a bag of apples. Then he sets another set of parcels on his side of the table: bread rolls, a thick piece of Stilton, salami and plastic pots of taramasalata and olives.

'We can always share,' he says, quietly. 'If you like?'

'That doesn't seem quite fair.' I smile. His stuff looks far more expensive. 'But if you're sure, thank you. Great idea.'

I watch as he slices the salami. He does it the way he seems to do everything: with care and precision, as if it matters.

'Is that your army training?'

'Cutting stuff?' He doesn't look up, his eyes on the meat. 'Yep, that's basically what I did. Lunch specialist.'

I hesitate. 'You're joking, right?'

He doesn't answer, just finishes up, then rips the top off the olives and pushes the pot towards me. 'Dig in.'

He sits across from me as he eats, perched on the edge of the armchair, using his broad thighs as a personal table.

'What music do you listen to? When you're working.'

He pauses and looks across at me, amused. 'Guess.'

I think about London's radio stations, the ones that play almost non-stop pop. 'Capital? Magic?'

'Wrong.'

'Am I close?'

'Nope.'

I frown, cutting myself some Stilton and helping myself to olives. I think of the leather jacket. 'Heavy metal? Punk?'

He raises his eyebrows.

'OK. I give in.'

He takes out his phone and detaches the earphones, then presses play. The music that comes through the phone's tinny speakers is the last sound I expected: the kind of old-fashioned song my grandparents liked. A deep, mellow female voice croons about a lost love.

'Ella, today.' His eyes are on my face, enjoying my surprise. 'I like to mix it up. Bit of Frank. Bit of Bing.'

I laugh. 'Bet that went down well on the battlefield.'

He smiles back. 'Why not? No harm being—'

He's interrupted by a bang on the flat door. The wood shudders. It comes again, the repeated crashing of a fist.

'Open the door!' The voice is muffled and shouting: 'Lou!'

Ed's on his feet and going to answer it, even as I call: 'No! Don't!'

He doesn't seem to hear me, my voice drowned out by the fresh hammering and I can't get to my feet to stop him.

After that, it all happens in a blur.

Ed clicks the lock and, as he starts to open the door, it bursts right open, knocking him back. Toby forces his way in, his face flushed with rage. 'You bastard!'

He jumps Ed, one hand clawing at his T-shirt, the other pulled back, ready to punch him in the face.

I try to shout out again, but I can't breathe, let alone yell. I'm in shock. I've never seen Toby like this, so pumped up and aggressive.

His fist swings towards Ed's face.

CHAPTER SIXTEEN

They're completely different builds.

Toby is shorter than Ed and thick-set, but more flesh than muscle. Ed is lean and strong and clearly quicker on his feet. Toby lumbers forward, his fist slamming towards Ed's head.

I struggle to get up quickly and find myself toppling sideways. My plaster cast catches on the seat of the chair where it was resting and anchors me, so I swivel and end up in a twisted heap on the carpet, my broken leg off at an angle and my body contorted. I scream as I hit the ground.

When I manage to strain round and look at what's happening over by the door, the two men are in different positions entirely. Ed, far from lying, felled, on the floor, is standing, holding Toby tightly across his front. Toby's facing out, away from him, his arm pulled behind his back in an arm-lock. His face is puce.

As I watch, Toby tries to attack in the only way he can and kicks wildly backwards, hoping to catch Ed's shins. Ed sidesteps as if he knew exactly what was coming. Toby grimaces as his bent arm jars.

Ed's phone, still playing, runs seamlessly into the next mellow, breathy love song, oblivious to the unfolding drama.

Ed turns to me. His tone is unruffled. 'This a friend of yours?'

I glare at Toby. 'What the hell? How did you get into the building?'

Ed says calmly: 'Look, mate, if I let go, are we done?'

Toby looks over the flat, taking in the exposed walls and dustsheets, then the food spread out on the table. The romantic music. The two plates.

'I knew it.' He glares at me. 'It's him, isn't it? You lying cow.'

'Don't be stupid.' I'm trying to get myself up from the carpet, but my plastered leg is still caught. I wince as something pulls. 'You're being an idiot.'

Ed says again, quietly: 'You've got it all wrong, mate. I'm just a painter doing a job, that's all. Ask her yourself.'

Toby nods at the remains of our lunch. 'Right. Looks like it.'

'So,' Ed carries on, calmly, saying again: 'Are we done here?'

He slowly lets go of Toby's arm and takes a step back from him, watching him closely. Toby makes a show of massaging his shoulder and checking his wrist. His lips are pressed so tightly together, they're white.

'Stop spying on me, Toby!' I'm shouting now, close to tears. 'Enough! Just go. Leave me alone.'

'You don't love anyone, do you? Not really. Apart from yourself.' Toby pokes a finger at me. 'Do you even know what the word means?'

Ed lifts a hand in warning. 'I think she asked you to go, mate.'

'I'm not your mate.' Toby squares up to him again, all bravado. 'What's it got to do with you, anyway?'

Ed just stands his ground and looks at him. It's the disappointed look a parent gives a naughty child.

Toby hesitates, then shakes his head at me in disgust, turns on his heel and storms off, trying to salvage what little dignity he thinks he still has.

CHAPTER SEVENTEEN

I can't stop apologising. I'm mortified.

'No need. Really.' Ed reaches down and switches off the music on his phone. It seemed suddenly very loud, very out of place. 'None of my business.'

The door's safely shut again. Ed has helped me off the ground and back into my chair and now stands by the window, looking out. I consider some more painkillers to take the edge off the ache in the newly strained muscles.

'I broke up with him just before the accident. That's why I was cycling home late, in the rain. He hasn't taken it too well. OK, understatement of the year. He just keeps saying I don't mean it.'

Ed comes back to the chairs and sits down again, picks up his food. He goes back to eating lunch, chewing methodically, his eyes on his plate. He doesn't need to say anything. I sense, just from the tilt of his head, from his quietness, that he's listening to me.

'I know he looked like a total dick just now. But he isn't. He's a nice guy. I've done this to him. I've really hurt him.' I take a deep breath, tears pricking my eyes. 'I think he's right. I'm not sure I'm capable of loving anyone. Not deeply. Not the way he means.'

I push a bit of food round my plate. Whatever appetite I had before, I've lost it now.

I glance over at him. His expression is calm and neutral, his eyes focused down, on his food. Something about him makes me want to confess, just a little.

It's so strange, but whatever the reason, I realise I want something from him that I haven't wanted from a man since I can remember. I want to feel heard and, if not absolved, at least a little understood.

I say very quietly, 'I did something terrible, you see. Years ago. Something unforgivable. No one knows. I never talk about it. Toby doesn't have a clue. But I carry it round with me every single day. The guilt.'

He's stopped eating but he doesn't raise his eyes or give me any other sign of what he thinks. Maybe I'm embarrassing him. This crazy woman, stuck in her flat, baring her soul to him. Maybe he's keeping his eyes low because he doesn't know where to look.

But I've gone too far now, I can't stop. My voice falls further, almost to a whisper.

'So that's it. It's not his fault. He's right. It's not that I don't want to have a proper relationship. It's that I can't. I can't ever get that close to someone else. I don't deserve to.'

For a moment, there's silence. I feel myself flush. This is where he gathers his stuff together and heads for the door, goes all fake-cheery with me: *Well, I'm done. Have a great weekend!* And, if he ever comes back, we both spend next week painfully pretending none of this happened.

He slowly lifts his gaze and it fixes on mine. 'Believe me, I get it.'

I frown.

He blows out his cheeks. There's a weary look on his face that I've never seen before, and it suddenly convinces me he's for real. 'I'm in pretty much the same boat,' he says, quietly. 'Except I'm laying bets that what I did – and no, trust me, you don't ever want to know what it was – is far worse than anything you're capable of doing.'

I open my mouth to speak, and he lifts his hand.

'Don't.' He talks rapidly. 'I don't talk about it, either. And I won't again. But I can tell you this: I've no hope for my own life, not now. The only thing I pray for, every single day, is the chance to go back and do it differently. Put it right.' His jaw clenches. 'What I'd give for that.'

I just nod. He's right. *What I'd give for exactly the same chance...*

His phone rings and he jumps abruptly to his feet to answer it. 'Hi. Yes, I am.' He sounds tense. 'I can but, just hang on a minute, will you?' He nods to me that he needs to take the call, then heads into the hall. His voice drifts through. 'Calm down. OK? Take a breath.'

The front door opens and closes. I start to gather up the packets and pots of food and pile them onto the plates to carry to the kitchen. My cheeks feel hot. My heart's thumping. What was I thinking, talking to him like that? I probably embarrassed him. I hardly know the guy.

That's probably his wife or girlfriend on the phone, part of his real life. I know so little about him, about where he goes when he leaves here, what he does.

I pause and remember the way he slowly raised his eyes to meet mine and the look on his face that convinced me he was telling the truth. Maybe that's why I sense we're somehow two of a kind. Maybe we're both paying the price for mistakes we made a long time ago.

CHAPTER EIGHTEEN

EDWARD

2007

When I was overseas with the army, I was one of the only officers who didn't have a girl back home.

But there were days I kidded myself about Kath.

I'd met her at university. She was one of the few girls who hung around with the rowing team, starting off as a rower herself with the women's squad but being small and slight, never quite made the cut. She coxed for us, now and then, mostly in training. She wasn't an obvious looker but funny, more than holding her own if the guys tried to mess with her. And kind.

I always sensed there might be something between us, just from the way she looked at me sometimes. She seemed curious, as if she couldn't quite figure out why I was so much quieter than the other lads, why I kept myself to myself. She made an effort to be friendly with me, which was more than most girls did.

In our third year, she stopped coming. One of the other women rowers said she'd dropped out to concentrate on final exams and that, I thought, was that.

Except I missed her. I had no right to: I'd hardly known her. I didn't even have her number.

I bumped into her at a post-exam party. We were all well-oiled and party-hopping from one student house to the next. I'd just pitched up at my third, standing for a moment in the doorway, beer in hand, surveying the tangle of sweaty, leaping bodies on the makeshift dance floor.

It was after midnight and inhibitions were being stripped away into a final mania, a medieval painting of hell with all its hinted debauchery: girls draped around guys; dancers stumbling into furniture as they gyrated to the beat, arms flailing, heads banging; down in a corner, a girl with streaming mascara crying to herself. Another hour and the neighbours would have the police round, telling us to keep it down.

Kath came out of nowhere and threw herself at me, bodily. 'Come on!' She took the beer from my hand and set it down on a table, then grabbed my hands. 'Let's dance!'

She swung her arms, her movements uncoordinated. It was hard to keep a grip on her hands, they were so slick with sweat. Her hair was pasted against her forehead, her cheeks shining. She struggled to focus on my face. I'd never seen her so wild and I'm sure, if she'd seen herself, she'd have been horrified. But to me, she was gorgeous. Alive and free and euphoric.

When the tempo slowed, I opened my arms to her and she pressed herself into them. She smelt wonderful, her hair, her skin, even her sweat was intoxicating.

'It's over,' she kept saying. 'I can't believe it. Can you?'

I touched my lips to her damp hair and kept my arms around her, steadying her on her feet. Around us, the crowd was thinning at last. People were stumbling out into the street, their voices raucous in the quiet night, or curling up in corners on cushions and grabbing some sleep.

'Shall I take you home?'

Kathy nodded and tilted her face to mine. I kissed her, but gently. She barely knew what she was doing.

The air outside was cool, even in June, and I took off my jacket and slipped it around her shoulders, then managed to wave down a cab. By the time I settled her in the back, she was fading, slumped in my arms. I took her back to my room, forced her, mumbling, to drink a glass of water, then eased off her shoes and tucked her into bed.

I spent the rest of the night on the floor, my head on a cushion, keeping an eye on her.

The next day, she slept until lunchtime. The best thing for her. When she surfaced, groggy and shamefaced, I fed her aspirin and a mug of weak tea and, once she was up for it, took her round the corner to my favourite greasy-spoon café for a fry-up.

She wore one of my baggy jumpers over her strappy dress. Her hair was matted and her pale face splotchy with stale make-up. She looked beautiful to me. I reached across the table as we ate and took her hands, kissed them.

'I wish we'd done this earlier,' she said. 'Why didn't we?'

I smiled, thinking: *Because I'm shy. Because if you hadn't been drunk and hurled yourself at me, we wouldn't be doing this, even now.* 'That's a good question.'

She dunked bread in her fried egg, breaking the yolk. 'I'm supposed to be packing. I'm off tomorrow.'

I tried not to look dismayed, to say: *But you can't, I've only just found you.* 'What comes next?'

'Teacher training in York. I'll save money living at home for the year.' She raised a hand, staving off criticism. 'I know, back with Mum and Dad at my age. But you know what? I can't wait.' She tucked into the bacon and sausage, finding her appetite. 'How about you?'

'I've joined the army.'

'You never have!' Her jaw dropped. 'You!'

I shrugged, trying not to look offended. 'I'm off to have adventures. See the world.'

'But the army?' She reined herself in, struggling to be more polite. 'Well, each to their own.'

Later, as we said goodbye, she said: 'Did anything happen last night? I mean, is there anything I need to know?'

I kissed the tip of her nose. 'Not a thing.'

She gave me an odd look. 'Have you got an address in the army? I can write to you.'

So she did.

CHAPTER NINETEEN

EDWARD

2007

From then on, all through basic training and beyond, Kath wrote me entertaining letters about teaching and mishaps and unruly pupils, about life at home with her mum and dad.

I wrote back. I thought long and hard about what to write, searching sometimes, when we were lolling around on base or out on patrol, for choice phrases to bring it all to life. I had plenty of time. That's the bit about warfare they never tell you: how boring it can be, most of the time.

I wrote to Kath about my first glimpse of Afghanistan, when we flew in at dawn after an endless night freezing our balls off on military transport. It looked like the moon. Stark, rocky mountains, jagged and stripped of life. No trees. No grass. No houses. Barren as hell.

The plane dipped down over the mud sprawl of tiny, low-storey houses and narrow streets as it headed up the valley to the base.

We climbed out of the plane, bristling with kit, lugging our stuff onto the base. It was basic, but not bad. Decent food in the cookhouse, most of it fresh. Lukewarm water in the showers, if you got there early, standing in line in the dust in flip-flops and shorts, the roar of transport planes shaking your ears, your washbag and towel in hand.

It was all right. When I think back to that bit, I remember banked-up excitement. *Finally. After all the training, all the briefings, here we are. Ready for action.*

Then we were off again, heading south to Camp Bastion. The eerie green light on the aircraft turned us all into ghouls as we sat crammed around the shell, clipped into harnesses, facing a few tons of crates and boxes in the centre, all trussed up with netting and straps. Troop class, never comfy. Deafening, even with earplugs. Tremors from the engine right through your bones.

Half the boys dozed, heads hanging forward, resting cheeks or chins along the top ridge of their body armour, on their kit. A few plugged their ears into music. Heaven knows how much they could hear. Me, I just stared into space, thinking, gearing myself up.

They seemed a good bunch of lads. One or two had been out before, done a six-month tour with some other unit before joining ours. They didn't brag about it, but it was clear they'd seen a few things, they'd had contact. It showed in their attitude. They really listened, as if their lives depended on getting it right. Maybe, soon enough, it would.

They knew I was green, they all did. They smelt it on me. They showed respect to my face – they had to, as I was their officer – but they were wary, sizing me up.

I was older than most of the privates, even though I'd seen less service. I'd done my degree, then a year of officer training, then another six months of special training. Then six months wasted, in my view, kicking around on bases, organising kit stores and wondering if I'd ever get deployed. I'd ended up a lieutenant faster than I expected, as much on promise as performance.

Some of this lot were barely old enough to buy a beer in a bar. Never left England before. They were tough nuts, though. I saw it in the way they handled themselves, the latent aggression in their eyes. Dragged up on sink estates, no book learning to speak of but up for a fight.

I hung around with Adam Johnson, mostly – another newbie lieutenant. We were both just promoted and ready to cut our teeth on our first overseas tour, hoping for some action. He was street smart, rougher than me. He liked to take the mick about my college education. *Professor,* he called me sometimes. Or in the middle of the bloody desert, he'd pipe up: *I say, Professor, fancy starting a book club?* Stupid stuff like that. He liked a laugh but, more important than that, I sensed he had what it takes. All the training in the world doesn't tell you how someone's going to react when he's under fire for the first time. You hope you'll keep your head and man up but until it happens for real, you wonder. About yourself, for sure, but about your mates, too.

As for Camp Bastion itself, I struggled to explain it to Kath. That massive container city, stuck in the middle of absolutely bloody nowhere, a barbed wire fortress surrounded by endless scrubby desert; a wild west troop city of swirling dust and giant satellite dishes, water towers, trailers and tents. The world's biggest, grimiest airport terminal. *Mad Max, eat your heart out.*

We watched terrible films in hangers, jogged around the running track, sweating our guts out in throbbing heat, weapon always to hand. It was filled with guys either killing time, waiting to get on and see some action, or killing time and waiting to get a ride home.

It was eeriest after dark. I kept away from the perimeter fence. The guards, in night vision goggles, did their best to penetrate the blank blackness of the desert. Overhead, the sky was as clear and as bright with stars as a planetarium. Now and then, a dog barked or, more chilling, wolves howled. I sensed the vast strangeness out there and the unknown enemies slinking across the scrub.

And, in case you could forget why we were there, there was a bloody great hospital. We watched the helis ferry in the wounded. All day, surgeons stitched them back together, patching up some boys and sending them out into the field again; putting others in boxes and sending them home, covered with a flag.

The day before I was properly deployed, out into the field, a letter arrived for me from Kath.

Guess what? She'd met someone. James. A fellow teacher. She was so happy, she said. He was amazing – witty, clever, kind. She couldn't believe he liked her back. She really thought he might be The One.

I was happy for her, I really was.

Kath had sent me her photo and I kept it just the same and carried it around Afghanistan, tucked inside a plastic pouch with my papers. Sergeant's wisdom: always wrap your sweetheart in plastic. You never know when you might bleed.

I wasn't in love with her. That was James's prerogative. She was just a very nice girl who wrote me letters once in a while. Sometimes, in the middle of a war, that's all you need.

CHAPTER TWENTY

LOUISE

That night, after Toby's crazy assault on Ed, I fasten the bolts on the front door, put on the security chain and wedge a chair under the handle, just to be sure.

Alone in my bedroom, I dose myself with painkillers and crawl under the covers. I lie on my back. My cast protrudes at the side and shines eerily in the darkness. My toes are cold and itchy.

Outside, a wind's getting up. The dying leaves on the trees sigh and rustle. Cars whoosh past. Now and then, brisk footsteps sound, swell, then fade.

I close my eyes but my heart thumps. I'm frightened of going to sleep, scared of having the dream again.

I lie quietly, trying to stay calm. Jumbled memories rise in my head.

I see Toby, his face contorted with anger, barging into the flat, braced to take a swing at Ed. If I hadn't seen it myself, I wouldn't have believed it possible. It's not like Toby. I shake my head, thinking about the way he's been behaving. The abusive messages. The bitterness. The rage, tipping over so easily into violence. Maybe I never really knew him, all this time.

My thoughts move on to Ed. The anguish in his eyes as he spoke haltingly about something terrible in his past. I had no idea. He seemed so straightforward, so strong.

What had he said?

I have no hope for my own life. The only thing I long for is the chance to go back and put it right.

I blink hard. My chest tightens until I can barely breathe. I thought I was the only one living like this. Weighed down. Alone. Maybe there are two of us, after all.

I'm finally slipping into sleep when another memory comes for me.

I'm pedalling hard, lungs bursting. Blood pounds in my ears. The road is rising, drawing me out of the village, up onto the open heath. The wind quickens and throws rain into my face, numbing my nose, my cheeks.

A first car comes towards me, dazzling me with the sudden glare of its lights. My vision spangles with shards of colour as I settle back to the darkness.

Then, almost at once, a car's approaching fast behind me, the roar of the engine is so sudden, so close, it's deafening and already, even as I realise, it's too late, it's sending me flying into the air.

I open my eyes with a cry and scramble to sit up. The bedroom is quiet and still. My heart pounds.

All this time, something about the crash has gnawed at me. My mind couldn't quite reach it, but I knew something wasn't right.

Now, finally, it's come to me. Now I know.

CHAPTER TWENTY-ONE

'This is so weird! Auntie Lou!' Mia dances around the flat on Saturday morning, loving the strangeness of it: the bare walls, the exposed fittings, the displaced light switches dangling on wires like gouged eyeballs. She stops in front of the tester stripes of colour that Ed daubed on one wall. 'Wicked! Can I do some? Pleeeease?' She pauses and throws herself into a ragged handstand, kicking her shoes against the plaster.

Jo opens up the carrier bag of shopping she's brought over, showing what she's chosen. When she goes into the kitchen to stow it away in cupboards and in the fridge, she calls through: 'Have you been out?'

'Not since falling over on Wednesday.'

'Where's all this stuff from, then? This cheese is pongy. What is it, Danish blue?'

'Stilton.'

She appears on the threshold with the pot of olives in her hand. 'You hate olives!'

'No, I don't.' I feel myself flush. 'Anyway, Ed bought them.'

'Ed bought them?' Jo stares. 'What's that about?'

'It's not about anything. He got some shopping in, that's all. I paid him for it. And he bought a few things for himself.'

'So, why's it sitting in your fridge?'

I shrug. 'Maybe he wants it for lunch on Monday.'

Mia, still upside down, pants: 'Is he your new boyfriend?'

'Don't be silly.'

Jo narrows her eyes. 'Well, I hope Toby doesn't find out.' She must see something in my face because her mouth widens. 'What? Something's happened, hasn't it? Are you back together?'

'No.' I take a deep breath. 'Toby made a fool of himself, actually. He came round yesterday and found Ed here and went mad.'

'Really?' Mia stands up, interested. 'Was he super jealous? Did they have a duel, Auntie Lou?' She clasps her hands together. 'That's so cool.'

Jo looks annoyed. 'Fighting is never cool, Mia. What do we do when we feel angry with someone?'

Mia sighs. 'Use our words.'

'Exactly.' Jo turns back to me. 'So, what did happen?'

I hesitate. 'In fairness, it wasn't Ed. He stayed totally calm. But Toby took a swing at him.'

Jo turns away.

'Don't give me that look.' I know what she's thinking without her saying a word. 'You're not listening. Toby was out of order. Don't you get it? How do you think he knew Ed was here? He's been spying on me.' I snort, thinking of the angry messages, the insults. 'You don't know what he's been like.'

Jo shrugs. 'I just think—'

'How would you feel if Mike suddenly stormed into the house and punched some completely innocent workman?'

'That's totally diff—'

'Well, anyway. Let's not talk about it.' *Time to change the subject.* 'Mia, come and show me your homework. What've we got to do?'

She drags out her school books and we set to work, planning a Viking meal and drawing a picture of it. As we work, Jo runs a cloth over the kitchen: it's 'covered' in plaster dust, apparently. I can't say I'd noticed.

Once we've finished, I let Mia set herself up with her drawing pad and crayons at the desk and she concentrates on a picture while Jo and I talk over tea and biscuits.

I tell her about the investigation and the latest news from the police about progress, that nothing yet has come from CCTV footage nor from the appeal for witnesses.

Jo nods. 'Can't say I'm too surprised, given where you had the accident. You were right up on the heath.'

I lean in closer and lower my voice. 'I think I've remembered something, though. Just last night.'

She looks up. 'What?'

'You know I kept saying I couldn't remember the vehicle? Nothing. Not even what size it was – a family car or a van or whatever.'

'And you have?'

'Not exactly.' I frown. 'The accident's come back to me once or twice. Flashbacks. And all I see is darkness.'

'Oh.'

'But don't you see?' I lean in closer. 'Darkness. Why? Why wasn't I dazzled?'

She frowns. 'Because it came from behind you. It wouldn't be right in your eyes.'

'I know. But I'd be right in its headlights. Lit up. I'd see something, wouldn't I? The glare. I should have got a sense of it reaching me, just before it hit me. Unless…' I pause, expecting her to jump in and finish the thought.

'Unless what?'

'It didn't have its lights on.'

'Is that what you've remembered? That it was too dark to see anything?' She looks confused. 'How does that help?'

I glare. I want her to be excited about this too. 'Surely that tells us something about the driver? Who'd drive across the heath, in pitch dark and rain, without their headlights on?'

Jo shrugs. 'I don't know. Someone very stupid.'

'Or someone who doesn't want to be seen. A criminal. A burglar? A people trafficker? The police need to make a big deal out of this.'

'A people trafficker?' She snorts. 'Don't you think—'

I ignore her and carry on. 'No wonder they hit me. How could they see me, with no lights? And no wonder they didn't stop. Too frightened of getting caught for the other thing too.'

Jo gives me an odd look, then reaches forwards to gather up the mugs. 'Tell the police, by all means. Why not? But don't get too obsessed about this, will you, Lou?'

'Obsessed?'

'I'm just saying.' She heads towards the kitchen to wash up. 'Maybe you need to move on. We should think about getting you out of the house this week. You can't stay cooped up indoors all the time.'

I think about the lift doors opening and closing in the night. How can I feel safe until I know who hit me and why? How can I know, until they're caught, that it won't happen again?

Mia slips down from her chair and runs over to me, her eyes half on the kitchen door, making sure her mother can't see her. She points at the last biscuit, waits until I nod, then takes it.

'I'll help, Auntie Lou,' she whispers through the crumbs. 'I'll use my detective kit. I can do fingerprinting and secret codes and everything. I'll investigate for you.'

'Thank you, sweetheart.'

I open my arms and she pushes into them for a hug. She smells of outdoors, of mud and late autumn leaves. I hold her tight.

'Can you come to the park yet?'

I pull away and point to my plaster cast. 'I'm sorry, Mia. I can't. Not yet.'

She frowns. 'How about tomorrow?'

Jo, appearing, reaches for Mia's coat. 'Maybe. Let's see what Daddy wants to do. We'll definitely see Auntie Lou again soon. Come on, now, Mia. Time to go.'

CHAPTER TWENTY-TWO

I'd be in Chile now, heading for the mountains.

I try hard not to think about it but I find myself traipsing around the flat after Jo and Mia have left, and it seeps in. I really wanted this one. It sounds like the trip of a lifetime and not one I'm ever likely to be able to afford myself. I shake my head and try to push away the thought.

I spend the afternoon lying on the sofa, drinking tea and watching an old black and white film on TV. I think about Toby. He hasn't tried to contact me since he left yesterday. No texts. No emails. No missed calls. I keep checking my phone. His silence is almost worse.

I imagine him pottering inside his tiny house, all white walls, state of the art stereo speakers and massive framed photographs of space. I think of all the weekends I've spent there. It's odd to imagine never seeing it again. Never seeing him again. I don't regret it, but it's going to take time to adjust.

I wonder if Rachel's there, getting her feet under the table. I shake my head. I shouldn't care. It's all history now. I just don't like her. The way she's simpered and fawned over him for the last year, sending him late night texts when she knew full well he was in a relationship with me. He just laughed if I said anything, pleased to think I might be jealous. For a man in his forties, he can be very naïve about women.

Stop it. I bite my lip. *It's his problem, now. He's free to see anyone he likes, even her.*

After a while, I get a grip on myself and switch off the TV. I push small pieces of furniture to the sides until I've got a clear circuit around the lounge, setting up my own indoor training course. If I want to get out and about, I've got to build up more muscle and get faster on my feet. I shout to the smart speaker to set a timer and head off, trying to set a new world record for round the lounge on crutches.

I'm on my third lap when the door buzzer sounds.

I stop and wait. It might be Toby. I don't want to see him. He's got to stop this. He's got to back off and leave me alone. I hop to the camera to see if it's him.

The picture's grainy. I squint. Not Toby. Definitely not. A woman.

I press the speaker.

'That Louise? Hello again! It's Tanya. Victim Support.' She sounds hesitant. 'Is this a good time?'

I buzz her in and try to set the lounge straight before she arrives.

Tanya's wearing the same baggy jacket and trousers as before. Her blonde hair, scraped back today, looks as if it needs a good wash.

'I hope you don't mind me popping round at the weekend. I should have called first, I know. Don't tell the office!' She stops, taking in the messy, half-finished decorating and the stray pieces of displaced furniture, still pushed back here and there to make room for my training circuit. 'I've been meaning to come by with those forms for you. I'm sorry. It's been non-stop.'

I find myself smiling. She seems so apologetic.

'May I?' She settles herself down on the edge of an armchair and starts rummaging in her bag. 'I definitely put them in, I know I did. Ah, here you go.'

She starts to gabble as I look over the compensation forms.

'I thought I'd pop in because I was just nearby. You don't mind, do you?'

I'm only half listening. The forms look pretty straightforward. Tanya's already filled in some of the details for me: my name and address, the police reference number and so on.

She points a finger down the page. 'You need to say how much it'll cost to get a new bike. Did you buy it new? Good. That's easier. Look it up online if you can't find the receipt.' She pauses, eyes on my face. 'How've you been? How are you managing? Been out at all?'

'I'm doing fine, thanks.' I nod. 'I'm not sleeping properly yet, but the headaches aren't as bad and my leg's stopped aching.' I hesitate, wondering how much she knows about progress on my case, if she gets any access to the file. 'I've been thinking a lot about what happened,' I go on. 'I'm really trying to remember. I keep thinking: what if there's some small detail I can come up with that could help? I really want them to catch whoever did this to me.'

She puts her head slightly to one side, doing her active listening. 'And how's that going?'

'There is something. I don't think the car had its lights on. That's why I didn't see it coming. Do you think that's worth telling the police?'

She frowns slightly. 'Well, no harm.'

I hesitate. She seems as unimpressed as Jo was.

'But don't you think it's significant? I mean, it's so suspicious. Who'd drive over the heath at night without lights on?'

She takes a slow, deep breath and clasps her hands together. 'Why not give the officer a call on Monday and mention it? You never know. But…' She looks down at her hands.

'But what?'

'Can I be frank?' Her eyes come back to my face. 'I'm not sure it's such a good idea to be dwelling on the accident. It's awful, what happened. Any traffic accident is awful, especially a hit and run. But it sounds to me as if you're really searching for something you may not get. Closure.' She hesitates. 'It's one of the toughest parts of victim support. Honestly. And you're not alone – it's only natural for anyone who's been a victim of crime to want justice. I would!' She leans in closer, sharing a confidence. 'I had another case this week. An elderly lady. In her eighties. Lives alone. Burgled while she was asleep in bed. Kids, probably. They didn't take much, but you can imagine what a shock it's been for her. I've helped her get new locks, fix the window they forced, everything. But she's still scared. She doesn't feel safe in her own house any more. She says she won't be able to sleep until those lads are caught and punished. Locked up. And I'd love that too, believe me!' She sighs.

I nod, thinking how shaken the elderly woman must feel.

She continues: 'But the truth is, most of the time, they're not caught. It's all wrong, I know. The police do their best. It's not their fault. They haven't got the resources, the manpower.'

I bite my lip.

Tanya says softly: 'I know it sounds brutal, but I'm going to say the same to you as I said to that lady on Thursday. Sometimes things happen for a reason and that helps us make sense of them. But sometimes they don't. They just happen. It's hard to accept but, the fact is, you'll probably never know who was driving that car and why they didn't stop. You have to find a way to put it behind you and move on. Look forward. Get on with your life.'

I think about Jo, telling me not to get obsessed. 'That's pretty much what my sister said too.'

She nods, thoughtfully. 'Well, she wants what's best for you, surely?'

'I know.' I sigh. 'I do find it hard to accept, though.'

She straightens up and points to the bare walls. 'I see you've got cracking on the decorating. That's great.'

'That's Ed's handiwork.' I smile, thinking about him. The leather jacket and black T-shirts. The Ella Fitzgerald. 'Thanks for putting me in touch. I was lucky. He'd just hit a gap.'

'Perfect. You're in safe hands with Ed.' She closes her bag and seems about to leave.

I realise I want to keep her talking, partly because I want to know more about Ed. 'How did you find him?'

'Through my husband. Long time ago now.' She shucks her bag onto her shoulder, smiles and gets to her feet. 'Don't get up. I'll see myself out.' She heads for the door, then pauses with her hand on the handle and turns back. 'Look, give me a call if you have any questions about the forms, won't you? And keep me posted if the police do get any leads. I'll keep everything crossed.' She looks rueful. 'I'd love to be proved wrong.'

CHAPTER TWENTY-THREE

EDWARD

HELMAND, AFGHANISTAN, 2007

Our deployment came through. They found us a heli out of Bastion, swerving and swooping as it followed the twists of the Helmand River down below. The water sparkled like cut diamonds in the hard sunlight. Tempting to dismiss it as a mirage. Along the floodplain, the land grew lush and fertile and towns and villages clustered, drawn from the dusty, barren wasteland beyond.

We thought ourselves lucky to be posted to the biggest military base in Helmand, in the provincial capital, Lashkar Gah. Other units were heading further north to the sharp end, off to man some dodgy Forward Operating Base, surrounded by enemy. The Taliban had control of the vast Helmand hinterland – and its wheat and poppies.

Officially, these FOBs were called 'ink spots'. That sounded to me like something indelible that might slowly spread. A classic example of positive thinking in government. They were actually more like lily pads across a treacherous pond. You hopped from one to the next, surrounded by deep, dangerous waters, just about keeping your feet dry. But the further out you got, the flimsier they became and the greater the chance you'd drown.

All we had to do was patrol the streets of Lashkar Gah which, by day at least, was pretty secure. We made the local population feel safer as they stood at their market stalls or cycled the narrow streets or shepherded their kids to and from school. We guarded dental and medical clinics, which were run by army personnel and meant to win over hearts and minds. It was our job to check for trouble: a shifty-looking guy who might have a suicide vest under baggy clothes, a few kids on nearby rooftops with grenades to hurl or AK-47s to shoot.

We saw pick-up trucks swing through the market as we patrolled, the backs filled with cocky young men sporting Afghan headgear, eyeing us up with unconcealed hostility; ancient motorbikes with a teenager or two perched on the back, suddenly appearing from around a corner, checking us out, then disappearing in clouds of filthy exhaust, gone as quickly as they came.

'Dickers,' the sergeant muttered. Taliban spies. Passing on info. Keeping watch. Planning, perhaps.

It had its own dangers, being off base. You could never relax, not even for a moment. You were always on guard. But it wasn't fighting. It wasn't action. It wasn't a daredevil story to tell your mates back home in the pub.

The younger lads grumbled. We felt it, more than heard it.

I understood. We were all relieved – and ashamed of being relieved. We liked being alive. We liked surviving. But we also wanted to fight, to creep through waist-high wheat fields, as we'd been trained to do, to use silent hand gestures to motion each other forward like commandos, to cock our weapons and tighten our fingers around the pin of a grenade.

Our commanding officer, Captain Miles, gave us pep talks: 'Keep morale high, lieutenants. This is good work. Hearts and minds win wars, that's the real battle. Never mind shoot-outs.'

Johnson especially didn't believe a word of it. He put on a good show for his men, but he was short-tempered. In Camp Bastion, he'd been so pumped up, pulsing with energy, anticipation. If his time was up, he liked to say, he wanted to die a hero. He wanted to make his folks proud. Now, with each routine mission, each uneventful patrol, his spirits sank a little further. After he'd called home, he slouched back to barracks, looking deflated.

'They were frantic,' he told me one evening. 'Some poor sod copped it on Tuesday, up north. No names yet. How can I tell them back home how cushy we've got it here? They'd be ashamed.' He kicked out at his kit, sending a tin mug crashing against the pre-fab wall. 'I'm such a wuss.'

And then I met Abdul, and everything changed.

CHAPTER TWENTY-FOUR

EDWARD

AFGHANISTAN, 2007

Johnson started it. He had a way with young lads. They hung around him as if he were the Pied Piper.

'Hey, mister! What your name? What country?' Dirty-haired kids in hand-me-down clothes that had been pummelled so often in wash-tubs and bleached dry so many times by the sun that they were threadbare and colourless. Only the seams held the memory of the shade they'd once been.

They kept their distance as we patrolled, their eyes all over our uniforms which bristled with interesting kit. We were just the latest batch, as green and wary as the last guys had been six months ago at the start of their tour. They just needed to break us in, to tame us.

'Hey, mister, pencil? Candy?' Their hands out, begging, cheeky-grinned.

Johnson was relaxed with them, handing out the odd treat from his pockets. He had presence. They knew without asking that he was the guy in charge. They knew not to mess with him. His men watched his back, staying at a distance, weapons ready, keeping formation, their eyes turned to the outside, watching the street for movement, for danger.

It could be oddly normal in the centre of town: old women in *burqa*s shuffling to and from the market with baskets; older kids lugging armfuls of flat, warm Afghan bread; hawkers everywhere sitting cross-legged along the road, side by side, keeping an eye on identical pyramids of potatoes or tomatoes, apples or lemons, misshapen and lightly coated with dust but always fresh from the field.

After a few weeks, Johnson got the go-ahead from Captain Miles to take a few men down late in the afternoon, when the worst of the day's heat was fading, and kick a football around the nearby dried-mud pitch for half an hour or so. Never too long. Never the same day, the same time – too predictable. He'd just show up, weapon always in hand, and start messing about with the ball; within a few minutes, young lads appeared, grinning and cheering, dodging and tackling, delighted to have something new to do.

Johnson was careful. He was no fool. While he and a few of his men played, others, including me and some of my platoon, stood around the edge of the pitch, facing outwards, scanning the narrow streets, the marketplace, the doorways and windows of the concrete and mud-brick boxy shops and their rooftops, checking for trouble.

A journo came out once, a young lass from one of the nationals, and did a story about Johnson and the lads. The kids had started calling him Beckham by then and the journo lapped it up. She sent him the piece by email. Big photo of Johnson in action, bulky with kit, SA-80 in his hand, dribbling the ball, surrounded by a ragged gang of laughing kids. It's what people back home wanted to read, I suppose. They were sick of mangled bodies and bombs over breakfast, and I don't blame them.

I was standing guard one of those evenings when a lad came up to me. He was a scrawny kid, all bone, and short, barely up to my waist. He had a look about him. Different from the rest. Quieter, more thoughtful. Or maybe just shy. I could relate to that. I was a scrawny kid myself, back in the day. Even after I'd bulked out, I still kept myself to myself more than most.

He looked me over and gave me a nod. 'Hello, mister.'

'Hello.' I barely gave him eye contact. I didn't want to be distracted. I nodded at the knot of kids racing to and fro around Johnson and the others. 'Not playing?'

He said: 'My name is Abdul. What your good name?'

'Spencer.' I kept my focus on my job, keeping watch.

'Spencer.' He pulled a face. 'What does it mean?'

'It's a name. It doesn't mean anything.' I shrugged, considering. 'Well, I suppose it did, once.'

He looked confused. 'Once?'

'It's just a surname. You know what a surname is?'

He frowned and shook his head.

'It's the name everyone in the same family has. Your last name. My first name's Edward.'

'Edward?' He brightened. 'What does that mean?'

'That doesn't mean anything, either.' This kid was getting tedious. 'It's just a name.'

He looked concerned for me. 'My real name is Abdullah. It is meaning "servant of God".'

'Well done.'

I thought he'd take the hint and push off, but he didn't. He lowered himself to his haunches in the dirt near my feet as if he were settling in.

'I want to go to England.'

'Do you? It's very cold.'

He considered that. 'My country is very poor. My family, also. My mother and I live alone. Now I am learning English, learning, learning, so I can get scholarship and study good in England. Then I will help my mother.'

I glanced down at him. 'How old are you, Abdul?'

He looked up, his face grave, as if it were a matter of some importance. 'I'm not knowing. My mother forgets. Now I am studying in class nine. So maybe I am fourteen. Maybe older, maybe younger. Only Allah is truly knowing.'

He struck me as tiny and under-developed for fourteen, but maybe that's what lads looked like here, with poor diet and not much healthcare. On the pitch, Johnson was high-fiving the lads and handing out chocolate. The sun was a red ball in the cloudless, dusty sky, turning the light amber. Time to go.

'Well, good luck, Abdul.' I nodded goodbye. 'Keep working hard.'

He beamed. 'I will. You will help me.'

I shook my head. 'Not me, mate. Sorry. Gotta go.'

I started to walk steadily across the end of the pitch, eyes scanning, gesturing to the men, making sure they were moving into position, ready to head back to the Snatch Land Rovers we'd driven down in.

'Not now, Mister Edward.' He was still smiling, full of confidence. 'Next time. Now, I am thinking, you and me, we are good friends.'

'You and I,' I corrected automatically.

He clapped his hands, gleeful. 'Yes, Mr Edward. Yes, thank you. You and *I*, we are good friends.'

CHAPTER TWENTY-FIVE

LOUISE

I get dressed late on Sunday.

I didn't sleep much last night and at ten, I'm still groggy and under-caffeinated. I'm just hanging out in sweatpants, trying to decide whether I dare try to make it to the corner café again for a decent coffee, when my phone rings. I snatch it up. Toby. I sit for a moment, heart racing, feeling it vibrate in my hand as it rings. It feels mean not to answer, callous.

I imagine him in his lived-in jeans and an over-sized sweatshirt, slumped on the sofa at home, thinking about me. Reaching out. I blink. All the Sunday mornings we've shared there, just being together. It's so vivid, I can almost smell it. The fresh coffee and burnt toast, his skin, warm and stale with sleep.

The ringing stops as it clicks to voicemail. I shake myself. *He's not the one. I'm right to break it off. It's time.* I swallow hard.

A moment later, a text from him comes through.

Don't ghost me. We need to talk.

I'm looking at my phone, trying to decide what to do, when another text comes through.

Can you talk?

This one's from Ed. Toby can wait.

I hit the call button before I can stop myself.

'Sorry to bother. Is this a bad time?' His voice sounds echoey, as if he's in a hall or bathroom.

My heart thuds. 'No, not at all. Something up?'

There's a moment's silence. I clamp the phone to my ear.

Finally, he says: 'Look, it's probably a bad idea—'

'What?'

Another pause. When he speaks, his breathing sounds shallow. 'I just wondered how you were feeling about the colour? The paint. I know I've bought it, but it's not too late to swap, if you wanted to. I'm sure they'd be OK.'

I blink, trying to catch up. 'That's thoughtful. But no, I haven't changed my mind. Honestly, I—'

'I could pop around with another sample, if you like? I'm pretty close to your place. It's no trouble. Just to put your mind at rest.' He sounds so unlike himself, so nervous.

I pause. 'What, do you mean now?'

'Well, not if you're busy. I just thought—'

'Fine.'

'Sorry?'

'I said fine. Come round, if you like. I'm here.'

For an awkward moment, he doesn't say anything and I wonder if I've misunderstood. Then he says in a rush: 'Right, then. See you soon,' and ends the call.

I call Jo.

She's in the supermarket, almost drowned out by tinny background music and the din of noisy shoppers. I imagine her pushing her trolley down the aisle as we talk, checking prices and picking her fresh fruit and veg with care.

'He said what?'

I go through it again. 'He sounded weird. Nervous.'

Jo sounds distracted. I can tell she's only half listening. 'If you don't feel comfortable, call him back. Tell him to wait til Monday.'

I hesitate. I don't want to do that. 'Maybe he's lonely.'

Jo tuts. 'If he is, that's not your problem. He's just there to paint the walls, Lou, remember?' Something crackles near her handset as if she's opening a paper bag. 'Don't get involved.'

I think about that. The trouble is, I already feel involved. I've felt involved since the moment he picked me up off the path. That's what's so hard to understand.

Jo says: 'You still there?'

'I'd better go.'

'Call me later, will you? Tell me what happened. Mike's working, so I can always pop round with Mia to check on you. She'd love to see you.'

I hang up and sit quietly in the flat, thinking. I know why he's coming round. It's not about the paint. It's because he wants to see me.

I know, because I want to see him too.

*

He seems different.

Ed's wearing jeans, not exactly smart but paint-free, a denim shirt and the usual leather jacket. But it isn't the clothes, it's his manner. He's usually so confident, so efficient in his movements, so sure. Now, as he hands me the new paint sample, then heads inside to sit across from me in the lounge, he's oddly jittery.

We sit and make small talk for a while, hardly looking each other in the eye. We talk about paint and the pros and cons of different colour schemes in this room. About London and how different it feels each season. About what we like most about Christmas.

Finally, the conversation lulls.

I take a deep breath. 'Is everything OK? I mean—'

He says, at the same time: 'Would you like a coffee?'

We both stop, then there's an embarrassed: 'Sorry.' 'You first!' 'No, after you.'

He swallows. 'I just thought, well, have you been out of the flat since Wednesday, since you had that fall?'

I shake my head.

'Maybe you should try. Just for an hour or so. We could grab a coffee. There's that place on the corner.'

'Hmm.' I hesitate. 'Well, I don't really—'

He drops his eyes and stares fixedly at his hands. 'No, of course, I shouldn't have…' He starts to stand.

I push on. 'No, it's just – I'm still really slow. And wobbly. Even getting to the corner, you know? I'm not sure I won't fall again.'

He nods, still not quite looking me in the eye. 'I don't know if…' He looks worried. 'This might make you angry…'

'Try me.'

'Well, I figured you might be anxious. So… I've got a wheel-chair in the van.'

'A *wheelchair?*'

He grins, looking more himself at last. 'Don't worry, it's not mine. I just borrowed it from a mate. He used to take his gran out in it.'

I roll my eyes. 'Great.'

His smile broadens. 'You don't have to use it. But it takes the pressure off. You need to get out of the flat for a bit, don't you? Get your confidence back. So, how about it?'

I smile back, thinking how much effort he's put into this. 'OK.'

'I'll go and fetch it.' He stops at the door and turns back. 'It's pretty sunny. I could push you round the park afterwards, if you like?'

I consider this, thinking about my conversation with Jo earlier. 'I might ask my sister, Jo, to come along, if that's OK? Her daughter, Mia – well, she loves the park.'

He shrugs. 'Why not?'

As soon as he's gone, I text Jo.

You and Mia free later? Mr Muscle here. Maybe meet in the park?

She shoots back.

In the park???

I try to explain:

He got a wheelchair.

She takes time to reply. I can't tell if she's just busy with shopping or deciding how to reply. Finally, her message pops through:

Be careful.

I'm not sure if that's a warning about the wheelchair or about Ed.

I'm taken aback by how vulnerable I feel to be out, how fast and loud the world seems.

Ed wheels me along the pavement to the corner café and parks me at a table. He shrugs off his backpack too, then folds his jacket and drapes it across the chair beside mine, saving his place, then goes to buy coffees.

He's nearly at the front when his phone, in his jacket pocket, starts to ring. I rummage for it, pull it out and wave it at him, thinking it might be a call he needs to take, but he's speaking to a barista now and doesn't see me.

I glance at the screen. It's someone in his contacts: *Ellie.* As I look, she hangs up and a moment later, the screen darkens again. I push his phone back into his jacket pocket.

'You had a call.' I nod to the jacket when he comes back. 'Sorry. I didn't know whether to take a message or not.'

He has a look at the screen, then frowns slightly. 'I won't be a minute. That OK?'

I watch through the windows as he paces outside, shoulders hunched, listening more than talking. When he comes back, he doesn't explain and I don't ask.

We drink our coffees almost in silence. He seems thoughtful. Other women check him out now and then as they pass, and I see him through their eyes. He is good-looking. The floppy hair. Those eyes. He's certainly well-built. But he seems oblivious to them, in a world of his own.

I remember his slow, methodical movements as he works, unhurried, his music in his ears. Now, in all this bustle and noise, the screaming toddlers and harried baristas, he still seems separate, his eyes steady, his mouth soft, as if he's visiting from another time, another place, and knows none of this daily scurry really matters.

Afterwards, he clears away for us both.

'Time for the park?'

I text Jo to come and meet us at the children's playground in about twenty minutes, then settle into the wheelchair. Ed puts his jacket and backpack back on, then steers me outside and starts to push me up the hill.

Something loosens in me as we head in through the gigantic iron gates, nose our way through the stream of people coming and going: locals walking dogs; parents with children; tourists in gaggles, clutching guidebooks, calling to each other in the music of foreign speech. High above us, on the hill, the statue of General Wolfe gazes down, black and solid, the rim of his cloak eternally flowing. I turn back to Ed. 'That's the best view in London, from up there.'

'Is that right?' He looks down at me, then up the steep path to the brow of the hill, thoughtful. 'Have we got time?'

He sets off, trotting, barely out of breath despite the incline and the weight of the chair. People part to get out of our way. Others, panting, stopping to get their breath back, follow us with tired eyes as we pass.

The air is crisp, heavy with the smell of leaf mulch and churned mud. As we near the top, the winter breeze, swirling round the summit, bites my cheeks.

When we reach the statue, Ed parks the wheelchair by a bench on the flat, grassy area just below it and sits beside me. I gaze down across the grand sweep of Greenwich Park and sigh. 'Amazing, isn't it?'

He just nods. I have no idea what he's thinking, but it doesn't matter. I'm glad he's here, just the same.

I switch for a moment into travel-writer mode and point out the landmarks. 'You know what I love about this view? It's not just the fact it's dramatic. Though it is. It's the sense of all the layers of London history, concertinaed.' I turn to check if he's listening. His eyes are facing front and it's hard to tell. 'So, here, the cafés and restaurants and gift shops. Victorian, mostly. Then, right there, the National Maritime Museum and the Old Royal Naval College.' I point to the Georgian façades and grand courtyards at the foot of the park. Beyond them, the silvery loop of the Thames slides silently towards the sea. 'And then, right at the back, on the other side of the river, Canary Wharf.' Skyscrapers crowd together in the distance, their multi-storey windows gleaming and winking in the low winter sun. 'Modern London.'

He says: 'Don't give up the day job.'

I smile. 'This is the day job.' I didn't expect to impress him. After all, he lives here too. I'm just happy to see it all again, spread out before me, a time map. 'Well, sort of. I'm a travel writer.'

He just nods, as if he isn't surprised.

'And mustn't forget the tourist magnet behind us.' I struggle to get round far enough to see. 'The Royal Observatory. Jewel in the crown.'

He raises his eyebrows. '*Jewel in the crown?* Really?'

'OK. Maybe not the best line. But it's still amazing. Aren't you proud?' I point to the slowly rising stream of people working their way up the hill towards us. 'People come halfway round the world to visit the Observatory. Take a photo on the meridian line. Straddle two hemispheres. It's time travel, you know that? A human obsession. Jump that line and you can say you've travelled, just for a fraction of a second, through time.'

He looks thoughtful for a moment, then spoils it by checking his watch. 'When are we meeting your sister?'

We head back down the slope towards the playground.

'Jo's a workaholic,' I say. 'She runs her own café. The Canny Kettle – do you know it? Over there, off Stockwell Street.' I point vaguely in that direction. 'I often bring Mia here on Sundays so Jo can get on with baking and making soup and everything.' I point to my leg. 'Well, I used to.'

He nods. 'Is Mia the one who did the homemade card?' He doesn't miss a thing.

'She's seven. I'm in her bad books at the moment. She seems to think having a broken leg is a bit boring. She thinks I ought to be running around again by now.'

He just says: 'I've got something with me she might like. Let's see.'

*

Mia breaks away from Jo and comes pelting across the grass as soon as she sees us trundling along the path near the playground. I wonder what Mia will make of Ed. She never really warmed to Toby, I don't know why.

Mia reaches us and considers Ed. 'Are you Auntie Lou's painter?'

'Edward Spencer.' He holds out a hand and they shake. 'You can call me Ed, if you like. Are you her niece?'

She nods, grave. 'I'm Amelia Hilary Watson. But you can call me Mia.' She turns to introduce Jo as she catches up. 'This is my mum, Josephine. Everyone calls her Jo. Those two are sisters. I'm an only child, did you know?'

Ed takes it all in his stride, shaking hands with Jo with an easy smile. I'm the only one who knows Jo well enough to read the tension in her face as she greets him. She gives me a quick kiss on the cheek, then heads for a nearby bench and takes out her phone, leaving us to it. Ed beckons Mia forward and shrugs off his backpack. 'You want to see what I've got in here?'

I twist to watch too. He draws out a bulky fabric bag.

'What is it?' Mia stands, frowning with concentration, her hands obviously itching to touch.

Ed's carefully opening out a thin bamboo frame, covered with panels of multi-coloured plastic. He unwinds a tail, made up of thin plastic strips, tied together into bows.

'Is it a kite?'

He nods.

'Are they plastic bags?'

'They were old ones, worn out.' His voice is thoughtful. 'Better than throwing them away, you see?'

'Much.' Mia nods, sagely. School lessons have made her self-righteous about the environment. 'Plastic clogs up the ocean,' she says. 'Fish swallow it. And birds.'

He leans in, pointing with his long, gentle fingers to show her how he looped the plastic sheets over the bamboo and secured it. I lean in too. He's so close, I feel the heat rising from his body and smell his scent of soap, fresh sweat and coffee.

'Where did you learn that?' Mia is wide-eyed. 'Online?'

'A young lad taught me,' he says. 'You're seven, aren't you? Well, he said he was fourteen but he wasn't much bigger than you. He probably didn't know his real age.'

She stares. 'He didn't know how old he was?'

'Not everyone keeps count. He lived on the other side of the world.'

Mia pulls a face. 'So how did they know how many candles to put on his cake?'

He laughs. 'He didn't have candles. Or a cake. Or even a birthday, I don't think.'

'Everyone has a birthday.' She scoffs, dismissing him now. 'That's stupid.'

He looks at her, thoughtfully. 'Not stupid. Just different. After all, he knew how to make a kite out of rubbish, didn't he?' He considers her. 'You know what else he taught me?'

She narrows her eyes, not sure now whether to believe him.

'If you coat your kite string with homemade glue, then rub it in broken glass, it cuts through another kite's string like butter.'

She blinks. 'Why would you want to do that?'

'That's how you win. Where he lives, they don't fly kites just for fun, like us. They make them fight. They take it very seriously. It's a sport. Dangerous, too.'

'Dangerous? Flying kites?'

'Sometimes.' His eyes flick to mine as if to reassure me that he knows not to tell her too much.

He holds the kite high enough for it to feel the breeze. It flaps and stirs in his hands.

'So, Mia, do you want to fly it with me?'

She can't speak, just jumps up and down and windmills her arms.

He parks my chair beside Jo's bench, out of harm's way, then goes back to show Mia what to do.

Jo waits until he's out of earshot, then says in a low voice: 'What's going on?'

I turn to look at her. 'Nothing. He's just being kind, that's all. Getting me out of the flat, for a change.'

'Right.' She stares across at them. 'Just being kind.'

I sigh. 'What's the big deal?'

'What about Toby? Have you stopped to think how he'd feel, if he saw you right now?'

I bristle. 'So what if he did? It's over. I've told you.'

Ed gets Mia to hold the kite as high as she can while he walks backwards, unrolling the string, then lifting it until it's taut. As she throws it up into the air, he runs. The kite rises at once, in a frantic flutter of plastic, taken by the autumn wind.

Jo, still stony-faced, says: 'You need to be on your own for a while. You always do this. You jump right into the next wrong relationship as soon as you end the last one.'

'I am not jumping into anything. He's just painting the bloody flat, that's all. It was your idea, if you remember.'

'Yes, to get someone in. Not to get involved with them.' She twists to look at me, her cheeks flaming. 'I saw the way you looked at him. I'm not blind.'

'For heaven's sake. That's the most ridiculous—'

'Whatever.' She lifts a hand to interrupt me. 'Just be careful. That's all.'

I shake my head and we sit rigidly side by side, watching the kite.

Once the kite's flying well, Ed positions Mia in front of him, encircles her with the cage of his arms, and guides her hands on the rim of its plastic handle, showing her by his own movements how to tease it and help it ride the currents of air.

Her eyes, riveted to the sky, shine. The tip of her tongue protrudes from the corner of her mouth. Gradually, he hands over control.

'I'm doing it! Look, Mummy!'

I glance at Jo. She just manages to crack a smile and mime clapping her hands.

I shout: 'Well done, Mia! Go, girl!'

I let my head fall back and watch the kite, rising and falling against the moving clouds.

Jo says quietly: 'What do you really know about him, anyway?'

I don't even reply. *I know enough*, I think. I know we're two of a kind, both messed up in a way Jo could never understand. I think of the way he quietly listened to me, of the look on his face when he told me that he too was haunted by something so terrible he too doesn't feel he deserves to be happy. I imagine what it would be like if we really could go back in time and put right our mistakes. What a relief that would be.

Finally, even those thoughts dissolve into nothingness and I focus my eyes on the kite as it twists and dances, hypnotic, graceful and free.

CHAPTER TWENTY-SIX

EDWARD

AFGHANISTAN, 2007

Once he'd met me, my young Afghan friend Abdul glued himself to my side.

Every time I headed down into town, either on patrol or to back up one of Johnson's impromptu kick-abouts, he appeared, a skinny figure emerging from the shadows, his dusty sandals flapping, a puppyish smile on his face.

His devotion to me wasn't lost on the men. 'Sir's shadow' was one of the kinder nicknames I heard, and there was plenty of sniggering.

Johnson made a joke out of it, of course, as soon as we were back in barracks, out of the men's earshot. 'He had you down as a college man, Spencer. You sniff each other out, you book-learners. Birds of a feather.'

Abdul's main goal was to practise making conversation. He was desperate to improve his English, which was already pretty good, for a maybe-fourteen-year-old. If I taught him a new word, he frowned and muttered it over and over to himself as he memorised it, then made the effort to slip it back into our chat another day, to show he hadn't forgotten. You've got to admire a kid who tries that hard.

For my part, I was careful, never losing concentration, ignoring him if I needed eyes on something unusual. But he also taught me a lot about his life, about his country, without even realising. That had to be useful.

His dad had been a policeman, he said. Blown up in a roadside bomb a few years ago. That was one of the reasons he kept himself apart from the other boys. His family was seen as tainted now, having taken the government's shilling and paid the price. You never knew who bore a grudge, he said, wiser at his age than he had any right to be. Besides, he had his eyes firmly set on England and the scholarship he planned to win to study there.

I didn't ask too much. I didn't want to get involved. Next it might be: 'Mister Edward, where you live? Can I visit you in England?'

I might have been green, but I knew where to draw the line.

His mother rented a sewing machine and made clothes. She rarely left the house, according to him. He was the one who ran to and from the market, who haggled for cloth at the tailor's and took round the paper parcels of finished clothes. Mostly, he went to school in the morning and sewed buttons in the afternoons. He didn't like it, he said. Their small mud-brick house was always in darkness and stitching made his eyes hurt.

Clearly, judging by the state of him, the lack of meat on his bones, he and his mother struggled. I started buying him a chocolate bar at the NAAFI store on base now and then and slipping it to him when I thought the men didn't have eyes on us. He never ate it in front of me. I wondered, sometimes, if it was all he and his mother might eat that evening.

A few days after I'd given him some chocolate, he brought me a present in return.

'For you, Mister Edward!'

He came tearing across the dried mud, stumbling now and then, his arms filled with something plastic.

'I'm gifting you a very good Afghan present!'

The men near me shifted uneasily and cocked their weapons. No one liked surprises. No one liked sudden, dramatic approaches, even from kids.

A private, nearer him than me, stepped forward into Abdul's path, raised his gun and shouted: 'Stop!' The menace of his voice, and its loudness, brought Abdul to a dead halt. He looked at the private in alarm, then again at me.

'Thank you, Jenkins.' I patted the air with my arm, telling Abdul to approach more cautiously. 'Easy, Abdul. Slowly, slowly.'

He crept forward with exaggerated care, lifting the plastic contraption up above his head, as if he were raising his hands in surrender.

He said to the private, his eyes still on the weapon: 'It is only a kite. A fine Afghan kite. I am making it myself, see?' He sounded frightened. 'Maybe I make one also for you?'

Jenkins flicked his eyes to me, his lips pursed, then lowered his weapon.

'Watch how you move,' he told Abdul. 'It's not a bloody party.'

Abdul got past him and hurried to me. His face was pale. The multi-coloured strands of plastic, stretched over a flimsy wooden frame, shivered where his hands shook.

'Calm down.' I nodded to him. 'It's all right. Just come slowly and calmly next time, OK?'

'Yes, Mister Edward.' He turned slowly, as if he were showing off a fine new hat, the kite still high above his head. 'See how hard I am working? After sewing buttons, only.' He gave me a sheepish grin. 'I make very good kites. Baba teaches me, before he dies. First, fine bamboo, tied like this.' He ran a pointing finger down the criss-cross of the wooden frame. I saw the way he'd secured them in the middle. 'Then so many plastics, old ones, only, from thrown away bags.'

'Discarded,' I said. 'Discarded bags. It means the same thing, but it's better English.'

He looked worried for a moment, then practised the new word under his breath. 'So many plastics from discarded bags. Then the tail, see?' He ran his hand underneath it, letting the ribbons of plastic, tied one to the next, skim over his fingers. 'This is very important.'

I was becoming uncomfortable, aware of the fact Jenkins was glaring at us. 'It's great, Abdul, really, but—'

He lifted a hand to stop me, too far gone now to stop. 'This is the most best bit of everything. The rope.'

I blinked. 'The string? What's so great about the string?'

He held it up, pinched with care between two fingers. 'Glass,' he said.

I looked at him as if he were mad. It was clearly cheap string. 'What about glass?'

He lit up, excited to share his secret. 'First, I crush glass, like this, on stone. Then I am putting glue on rope…' He hesitated, remembered and corrected himself. 'I am putting glue on string, then putting broken glass.'

'Why?'

'For fighting!'

I shook my head at him. There were moments when I felt on the same page as the Afghan men I met, when we talked about how the burning sun made us sweat or about the taste of local freshly grown food. Then there were other times when I might as well have been on Mars. This was one of those times.

'Fighting what?'

He laughed at my stupidity. 'Kite fighting other kite!' He made his kite swoop and dive bomb through the air. 'Cut through other string and – poof! Kite dies.'

The troops around me were reforming, getting ready to move.

I shifted my weight. 'Look, Abdul, I'm going to have to go. But good luck flying it. Good job.'

He gave me a thumbs-up. 'It is your kite, Mister Edward, but I am flying it for you, OK? I'm not thinking you are good kite flyer.' He laughed to himself at the thought. Another thing these foreigners couldn't do. 'But I am very good. I am doing very good job for Mister Edward, yes please!'

I thought that was the end of it but, two days later, as dusk approached, I was jogging around the perimeter of the base with Johnson, sweat pouring down my chest, when I saw them.

'Hey!'

Johnson paused, panting, following my pointing finger. 'Can't keep up? You're out of shape, mate.'

The sky was darkening rapidly as the red sun fell. A flock of birds took off as one from a tall, broad-limbed tree and flew, wheeling, in a wide arc through the dying light. There, silhouetted, high over a Lashkar Gah suburb, were half-a-dozen kites, whirling and diving, swooping and rising, tails fluttering in graceful, sweeping flourishes.

As I watched, one, smaller than the rest, pulsating in the breeze with dozens of strips of multi-coloured plastic, swerved and launched a sudden controlled assault on its nearest opponent. A moment later, the rival, its string severed, fell tumbling out of the heavens.

I narrowed my eyes, following the triumphant kite as it rose, steadied itself, then headed towards its next victim.

'That's my bloody kite!'

Johnson, bending over, hands on his lower legs, twisted sideways to look up at me.

'You what?'

I didn't bother to answer him. I just stood there, sweat drying on my T-shirt, and stared, enthralled and absurdly proud. 'There. My kite. Beating the crap out of the big guys.'

Johnson shrugged, stretched and spat into the dirt. 'Are you coming or what?'

I couldn't tear my eyes from the battle going on in the skies. 'I'll catch up.'

Johnson shook his head and headed off, leaving me alone, watching the struggle playing out in the sky, knowing that a determined, scrawny boy, who rarely got enough to eat, out there on the edge of the city, saluting me in the only way he knew how.

CHAPTER TWENTY-SEVEN

LOUISE

Late on Sunday, I lie on the sofa, leg propped up on a cushion, and flick between the TV channels.

I'm restless. I keep thinking about everything that happened today. About sitting in the café with Ed over coffee. About being in the park, back in the wide world again for the first time since the accident, after what seems like forever. About watching Ed fly his kite with Mia. She likes him, even if Jo doesn't. That means something, doesn't it?

I hear Jo's voice again. *What do you really know about him, anyway?*

I switch off the TV. My body's heavy with tiredness but my mind won't stop. I pick up my phone from next to me and check it again, for about the hundredth time.

I look again at Toby's text from this morning.

Don't ghost me. We need to talk.

I mull it over. It could just be his way of getting my attention, in the hope we can still patch things up. But there are no kisses or hearts or declarations of love. Maybe he really does have something he needs to tell me?

I go into voicemail and listen back to the new message there. It's Toby from this morning, after I failed to pick up his call. He sounds very different from earlier in the week. Before, he was either angry, calling me every name under the sun, or pleading, begging me to pick up.

This message is careful and calm, as if he's in perfect control of his emotions. As if he's thought through in advance what he wanted to say and really means it.

> *I really hope you listen to this, Lou. I know you don't want to talk to me right now. And I'm trying to understand that. I really am. But I need to see you. There's something I need to tell you. Not on the phone. In person. Anyway, call me, will you?*

At the end, just as he hangs up, I hear something else behind his voice. I strain to make out what it is, then play it back and listen again. Is someone there, just audible, as he rings off? A soft voice. Little more than a breathy whisper.

I scroll down to his number and stare at it. He sounds in the message so much more like the man I once knew, the man I really liked. He's clearly trying. I wonder where he is right now and what he's so desperate to say. I lift my finger, about to press 'Call', then hesitate.

Maybe I shouldn't. Maybe I should stay strong and leave him alone, give him space. It's what I want, isn't it? A clean break.

I think again of that low whisper in the background. Another doubt creeps in. What could he possibly have to tell me?

I set down my phone and lean my head back on the cushions, letting my eyes close.

I must have dozed off, there on the sofa, when something startles me awake. A noise, near the door. A scuffing against the wood. I sit up at once, instantly alert, and strain to listen. It's just after eleven thirty.

Silence. Then a low creak. I blink. It could be anything. Just the woodwork settling as the building cools at the end of the day.

I shake my head. It's a person. Someone on the landing again. My heart races. The movements sound stealthy. Someone's creeping very carefully, determined not to be heard.

I bite my lip. Part of me wants to ignore it. I don't need this. If I'd done the sensible thing and gone to bed early, I wouldn't have heard a thing and be none the wiser. But it's too late. What if someone is there? I need to know. Otherwise, I'll never sleep.

I swing my leg down and hobble to the door. It's shadowy on the landing. I peer out at the fisheye view. Empty. Nothing's moving. I remember last time and the sense I had that someone was right there, against the door, crouching out of sight. The hairs on my neck bristle all over again.

I ease off the security chain, slowly slide back the bolt and reach for the handle. I raise a crutch high, ready to strike, then turn the handle, imagining someone on the other side, watching it rotate. I wrench open the door, then almost laugh out loud. No one. It's a small landing, nowhere to hide. Clear.

I'm a fool. A crazy, paranoid idiot. I grin into the darkness, weak with relief after the sudden surge of tension, ready to make fun of myself. What would Jo say? *Get a grip, will you?*

I'm about to close the door and lock up again when my eye falls on something. Something out of place. Down there, on the mat. A solid rectangle, slightly lighter than the surrounding shadows. I stoop to see. A brown A4 envelope.

That wasn't there earlier. I'd have seen it. I think again of the strange scuffing noise I heard. Maybe that was it? A thick envelope being dropped and grazing the bottom of the door, followed then by the soft creaks of someone who didn't want to be seen, someone creeping away, back towards the stairs.

I scoop up the envelope, then close the door sharply and slide the bolt and chain back into place.

I lean against the door. No doubting who it's for: my name is written in shaky capitals across the front. Someone using their other hand, maybe, trying to disguise their writing. Hand-delivered, no address, no stamp. It's bulky.

I turn it over. On the back, someone's scrawled, in the same untidy letters: *I know what you did.*

I make it back to the sofa and collapse heavily onto the cushions, then tear open the envelope and reach inside. I draw out a sheaf of papers. My stomach heaves. I don't need to look closely. I know them, I know them all. My hand goes to my mouth.

As soon as I can catch my breath, I fumble for my phone, bring up Toby's number again and this time, I do hit 'Call'. My hands are shaking.

I imagine him sitting up late at his desk, night after night, trawling the internet, searching. He must have dug deep, taken time to pore over old documents and scroll through newspaper archives.

He doesn't answer and it clicks onto voicemail. My mind is whirling. He didn't know a thing about this. I never told him. Who's he spoken to? Who tipped him off and spurred him to look?

I shake my head. Of course he isn't answering. He must still be nearby. Still inside the building or hurrying down the path. He won't take the call until he's got clear. I rush to the window, draw back the edge of the curtain and look out into the darkness. There's no sign of him. No sign of anyone. Just the darkness across the road, under the trees.

I try his number again. This time, he picks up almost at once, as if he'd been waiting.

'Lou?' His voice is careful. 'You got my message?'

'How could you?' I'm so shocked, so hurt, I can hardly get the words out. 'Why, Toby? All that effort, just to hurt me?'

A pause. 'Listen. I just—'

'What? You just what?'

He hesitates. 'Look, we need to talk about it properly. Not like this. Face to face.'

'But why, Toby?' I swallow hard. 'I know I've hurt you. I'm sorry. But this? Really?'

The line buzzes with static. Finally, he says: 'It wasn't just me, you know. It was her too. Right? I mean, I'm not saying—'

'What?' I struggle to breathe. Something swims into focus. 'What do you mean, *her*?'

'Well, you know.' He can barely bring himself to say her name. 'Rachel.'

My chest tightens. *Of course.* Toby didn't do this on his own. She did the digging. She put him up to it.

Toby sounds strained. 'It's late. We need to talk. But not right now. Not like this. How about—'

'No.' I shudder, trying to steady my voice. 'I'm sorry for what happened with us, really sorry. I've felt guilty as hell. Well, thank you. What you've done now has really helped. Because I don't feel guilty any more. I never thought you'd stoop this low.'

He tries to protest and I cut in, taking back control. 'Stay away from me. If you come round here again, spying on me, threatening me, I'm going to the police. I mean it. And that goes for her too. Goodbye.'

I end the call before he can reply, then send my phone skidding across the floor. I sit very still for some time, shaking, fuming, trying to calm down. Finally, I stuff all the papers back into the envelope and hide it away at the very back of a drawer.

I know there will be copies. Destroying this set won't end anything.

I just want them out of sight.

CHAPTER TWENTY-EIGHT

I wake with a cracking headache the next morning, not helped by the fact I've had so little sleep.

I lie there for some time, staring at the ceiling, head throbbing and sickened at the thought of what happened last night. It doesn't surprise me that Rachel's capable of being so cruel. I've heard the way her colleagues talk about her, the dark looks and muttering behind her back which Toby never seemed to notice. But Toby? I'm disappointed in him. I never imagined he'd agree to something like this.

When Ed arrives, I just put on a dressing gown to let him in, take the daily coffee he's bought me with barely a word, then retreat hastily back to the bedroom, out of his way. I don't want to see anyone, right now. I don't know who I can trust.

I'd been thinking over the weekend that I might try to work up a pitch on popular sites in Greenwich. Something I could write without too much hassle, getting quotes on the phone. I can't sit here forever doing nothing. Maybe Jo and Tanya are right. I need to stop thinking about the accident and move on.

But now, after last night, I lie back on the pillow, sip my coffee and listen to the dull pounding in my head. I can't face work. I really can't. Not quite yet.

I'm still lying there, only semi-conscious, when my phone rings. It takes me a while to come round and I only just reach it before it clicks onto voicemail. It's not a number I recognise.

'Hello?'

A woman's voice. 'Hello. Louise Taylor?'

'Speaking.'

'This is Detective Blakely.' Brisk as ever. 'How are you?'

'Fine, thanks.' *Bloody awful. My ex-boyfriend's trying to destroy me and my head's exploding, as if you care.* 'Any news?'

'Good news from forensics. They've found trace evidence.'

I push myself up to sitting. 'What does that mean?'

'They've recovered paint flakes from the frame of your bike. They were delivered on impact, so are almost certainly from the suspect vehicle. The analysis came through over the weekend.'

I hesitate. 'So, what does it tell us? Do you know what colour it was?'

'Indeed. It also indicates the make and model of the vehicle. And a guide to its age.'

'From a few paint flakes?'

'Absolutely.' She sounds smug. 'Dark blue Volvo S40 saloon. Possibly second-hand. It's been resprayed in the same colour at least once.'

'Wait…' I lunge for a pen and write all that down. 'So what happens now?'

'We'll circulate the details. We'll stay vigilant for vehicles matching that description. Vehicles involved in an incident.' She pauses. 'I don't want to give false hope, Miss Taylor. But it's definitely a positive development.'

She's about to end the conversation and say goodbye when I remember my own piece of new evidence and cut in quickly: 'Another thing, Detective. Something I've remembered. It was driving without its lights on.'

Her tone sharpens. 'What makes you say that?'

I fumble for the words, eager to convince her. 'I've been think-ing about it. Why was it so dark when it hit me? Why didn't I see it coming, see anything at all? Its lights must have been off. Even though it was pitch dark and pouring with rain. Don't you see? It must have been someone with something to hide. Even before it hit me.'

She doesn't give me very much in response, but I hope her sudden quietness means she's thinking it over. Then she makes some vague reference to amending my statement in due course and hangs up.

I stay in my bedroom all morning, nursing the headache.

At lunchtime, there's a soft tap on my bedroom door.

I hesitate, consider calling 'Hello?', then realise it might encourage Ed to pop his head round the door and see me lying on the bed. That feels way too intimate. We're alone together in my flat, a big strong bloke and someone who's... well, who's barely mobile.

I shout: 'Hang on!' instead, make it to the door and poke my head out.

He looks embarrassed about disturbing me. 'Are you OK?'

'Just a bit tired. Didn't sleep too well.'

'Sorry. I wondered if I could get you anything.' He seems concerned. 'I was going to microwave some soup. Do you want some?'

'I'm fine, thanks.'

I expect him to go but he carries on standing there, looking down at his paint-spattered hands.

'Is everything OK?' He hesitates. 'I hope I didn't, you know, on Sunday...'

I shift my weight. Standing is still not easy.

He takes a deep breath and raises his eyes to mine. 'I'm sorry if I did the wrong thing, coming round and everything. I didn't mean to overstep the line. I just thought it must be hard, shut in here, in the flat, day after day. That's all.'

'Of course.' I shrug. 'It's fine.'

He nods, unconvinced. I'm being odd and he knows it, he just doesn't know why.

'Pleasure meeting Mia.' He turns back towards the lounge. 'Great kid.'

Back in my room, the door ajar, I strain to follow the sounds. The low creak of the floorboards as he moves back and forth. The beep-beep-beep of the microwave. The opening and closing of cupboards and drawers as he finds what he needs.

I bite my lip and sit very still. I'm cold inside. How did Rachel know, anyway? Who told her? Or did she just start digging in the hope of dredging something up?

I put my hands to my face. She's merciless, I've always thought so. I can just imagine her sitting down with Toby and presenting him with the evidence.

I'm so sorry, Toby. I just thought you ought to know.

Did she shed a few crocodile tears, to hide her glee?

And now what? I start to shake. What are they going to do to me? Is Toby really so bitter he wants revenge? Surely he can't think he can use blackmail to make me go back to him? No. That's the last thing she wants. So what are they planning to do? To humiliate me, bring me down? They can, if they choose to. They're holding a loaded gun to my head.

I close my eyes and imagine Toby creeping to my door in the darkness and dropping that envelope, with its menacing message: *I know what you did.*

CHAPTER TWENTY-NINE

Soon after Ed leaves for the day, the buzzer sounds.

I freeze, tempted to ignore it. I'm not expecting anyone. My first thought is Toby. He said he needed to talk to me, face to face. Maybe this is when I find out what he and Rachel plan to do, what their threat really means.

It sounds again. I don't move. Finally, a text pings on my phone.

U there?

It's from Jo.

I hover at the door, listening to the distant sounds of she and Mia coming in through the downstairs lobby and then pounding up the stairs.

Mia's high-pitched voice bounces off the walls. She's shrieking something to her mother about school. I can't make out all the words, just enough to gather it's about some boy in her class getting into trouble. She sounds thrilled.

'Hi!' She runs right past me into the flat and gazes around at the lounge walls. 'Wow!' They're wearing their first coat of Willow. 'It's amaaaazing!'

'You like it?'

Jo, her face weary, reaches the landing a minute later. She's weighed down by Mia's school backpack on one shoulder and a bulky fabric bag beneath it in her hand. She smiles but I sense the effort. 'I brought supplies.' She raises the fabric bag a little. 'Few bits and pieces to keep you going.'

Jo doesn't open the café on Mondays. It's her day for catching up with the accounts and batch cooking, and it's often more hectic than the days she opens.

We hug. Her cheek's cold against mine and she smells faintly of traffic fumes and the outside world. She takes my arm and helps me to the sofa.

'I wasn't expecting you.'

'Sorry. Meant to text earlier but – you know.' She drops Mia's backpack off her shoulder onto the table. 'Mia, can you get your maths out?' She peers at me more closely and frowns. 'You OK? You're pale.'

'Am I?' I shrug and change the subject. 'How was school, Mia?'

'Good.'

Jo heads for the kitchen with her bag to decant whatever she's brought into the fridge, calling to Mia as she goes to settle down please and get started and not to touch the walls in case the paint's still wet.

Mia rolls her eyes at me, then, once her mother's out of sight, does a quick handstand against the door.

I smile and reach for her bag. 'Which book do you need? This blue one?'

She bangs her feet to the floor, sighs, then trails over and gets out her pencil case. She kneels up at the end of the coffee table, opens her maths book listlessly and chews the end of her pencil.

I say: 'Tricky?'

She nods, miserable.

Jo comes back with a piece of home-made brownie on a plate for me and two cups of tea.

'Did Mia tell you?' She glances down at Mia, who's doing a good job at looking engaged in her homework, even though the end of her pencil hasn't yet come out of her mouth.

'What?'

'We stopped off on the heath on the way over.'

I bite into the brownie. 'Not exactly on your way.'

'I know.' Jo gives a meaningful look at Mia, who's still pre-tending to work. 'We wanted to see it for ourselves. Where you came off your bike.'

'Where I was knocked off it by a speeding car with no lights, you mean?'

'Anyway.' Jo sips her tea. 'We think we found the right place. Just after the pull up from the village, yes? There were loads of skid marks and the mud at the side was churned up.'

'Any bunches of flowers?'

'Hardly.' She gives me a look. 'You're not dead. Not that I'd noticed.'

Mia looks up. 'I took my magnifying glass, looking for clues. Mum got a photo of the skids. Evidence.'

Jo doesn't move to show me the photo. I sense she's not entirely on board with Mia's determination to crack the case.

'Did you find anything?'

Mia's eyes brighten. 'An old bit of cigarette nearby. What? Mum wouldn't let me touch it. They could've tossed it out of the car after hitting you. It might have their spit on it.'

Jo says: 'Saliva.'

'And I found some old bits of plastic, all muddy. They could've come from their car too. If they go round hitting people, they probably drop litter as well.' Mia shoots Jo a sour look. 'She wouldn't let me touch those, either.'

'Filthy. Looked as if it'd been there for weeks,' Jo says. 'Mia, what're you supposed to be doing, right now?'

Mia turns back sullenly to her sums.

I say quietly to Jo: 'The police have got something on the car. Dark blue Volvo S40. I googled it. Sort of mid-range, four-door, bit nondescript. They say it was probably an old one.'

'Is that like Daddy's? That's dark blue.' Mia has forgotten she's not supposed to be listening. 'Is he a suspect?'

Jo says quickly: 'Don't be silly, Mia. There are thousands of cars like that.'

I nod. 'It is popular. But, even so, it's a good clue, Mia, isn't it?'

Her eyes shine. 'It might help us catch them.'

'Let's hope so.'

Jo gives me an annoyed 'Don't encourage her' look. 'We'll leave that to the police, won't we, Mia?' she says, firmly. 'We don't know who these people are. They might be dangerous.' She switches the focus back to Mia's maths.

Later, Mia traipses off to the toilet before they leave and I seize my moment alone with my sister.

'Toby came round last night.'

She hesitates. 'And?'

'He dumped a load of photocopies on the mat. He's threatening me. Can you believe it? I told him I'll call the police if he tries anything.'

I want her to be shocked. She always sticks up for Toby. Now maybe she'll see him for what he is, see the blame isn't all on my side.

She frowns, not understanding. 'Photocopies? Of what?'

'What do you think?'

Something in my expression makes her stop and think, then realise. 'But why? That's ancient history, Lou. You know that.'

I shrug. 'Makes no difference.'

She blinks at me. 'But he already knew, surely. I mean—'

I shake my head. 'Not from me, he didn't.'

'Didn't you ever…?' She stares. 'I know it's a big deal for you, a huge deal, but isn't that exactly why you should have told him? How could you keep it a secret from him, all this time?'

'It's not something I talk about.' I bristle. 'Anyway, apparently I didn't need to. He and that woman at work, Rachel, they've dug up a load of dirt. Not just newspaper cuttings. He's got hold of the police report, somehow. The coroner's report.' My eyes fill and I look away.

'Oh, Lou.' Jo takes a step towards me and lays a hand on my arm.

I blurt out: 'What if he rakes it all up? What if he goes around telling people?'

Mia comes skipping back from the bathroom, ears pricked. 'Telling people what?'

CHAPTER THIRTY

Another night with barely any sleep.

I lie in bed, restless, watching the play of shadows on the ceiling and listening to the intermittent hum of traffic outside. Now and then, I contort to reposition the pillow under my plaster-cast leg, trying to get comfortable.

I remember what Jo said about my need to be on the road all the time, never letting myself stop and think. Maybe she's right. Maybe I'm frightened of having time on my hands. Frightened of what thoughts might come.

In the silence, memories rise and fall. The flashbacks of the accident have given way to something far worse: flashbacks to that day, nearly twenty years ago, when I was still a teenager.

The crying.

The deep shadows in the house.

The scream.

Before that, I still had my life ahead of me. I was still intact. I still had hope.

I know what will happen if Toby stirs it all up again. I don't think I can live through it all a second time. The accusations. The hatred. The blame. Worst of all, the weight of the guilt.

I think about Ed and what he said about losing hope for his life and I start to sob, twisting my face into my pillow.

If I could just go back. If I could just change one thing. The one thing that would change everything that followed.

*

On Tuesday, Ed arrives early, as always. I stumble out of bed to open the door. I'm past caring how I look.

I get a sense anyway in his expression when he sees me. He takes a single glance, then hands me my coffee without looking me in the eye. I drop onto the sofa to drink it, wrapping around the sides of my dressing gown to cover my legs.

'Can I get you anything to eat?' His voice is gentle.

I shake my head and, as soon as I can face the effort of getting on my feet again, I stumble back to the bedroom and close the door.

He goes out at lunchtime. I don't blame him. He probably needs a break from the atmosphere in the flat. He doesn't come to tell me; I just hear the door close, then his footsteps fade on the stairs. I go through to the lounge and poke around in the kitchen for some bread and butter, a cup of tea.

He's in the middle of putting a second coat of paint on the lounge. Not much smell from these modern paints, just a hint of fresh chemicals. The traffic below whooshes a little louder than usual. He's unlatched a window at the front, letting in air and noise.

Inside, the silence is intense. Another few days and he'll be gone. I think about his cheeriness on Sunday when he surprised me with the wheelchair, when we sat quietly in the café eating pastries. Do I bore him? Have I chased him away?

When he comes back, he has to press the buzzer to be let in. I open the front door for him and he arrives on the landing, looking wary. 'Sorry.' He averts his eyes, no doubt taking in the fact I'm still not dressed. 'Did I wake you?'

'No.' I shrug. 'About time I got up.'

He brings something out from behind his back with a flourish. A big bright bunch of autumn flowers. He gives me a sheepish smile. 'Don't be annoyed. I just thought they might go well with Willow.'

It's such a sudden, unexpected kindness, on top of everything else, that my eyes fill. He reaches out, awkward, and pats my arm. 'You OK?'

I sink onto the sofa and he sits beside me, a careful distance apart. My breathing is ragged as I struggle not to cry. My head throbs.

Eventually, I say: 'I'm so sorry. You must think—'

He interrupts. 'You don't know what I think.' There's a pause. 'I'd like to tell you, though. I'm no good at explaining. I'm really not.' He hesitates. 'But I can try?'

I look at the flowers, lying on their side on the table now, in their cellophane shroud, quietly dying.

He takes a deep breath. 'I'll stop any time you like. OK? Just tell me. I know this is weird. The last week, well...' He breaks off and hesitates for a moment. 'I don't know where to start.'

I sit very still, my hands clasping each other in my lap. I don't know if I want to hear this. Whatever's coming, it won't be good. Maybe he knows. Maybe Toby's already started spreading the word, blackening my name.

'I haven't been in a relationship for years. By years, I mean, like decades.' He starts talking again, speaking rapidly, his eyes on the edge of the table. 'I couldn't do that to someone. I know what I'm like. I know I'd start to get close to someone and then stop. I can't let anyone in, you see. Not really. They can't really know me without knowing what I did. And if they found that out, they wouldn't want to know me. So, I'm stuck.' He sighs. 'Does that make sense?'

He doesn't risk looking at me and I'm not sure if he realises when I nod.

'But it's different with you. I know we hardly know each other. It's been a week. That's nothing. But I feel something. A connection.' He takes a deep breath. 'Maybe I'm making a right idiot of myself. Believe me, I've tried to convince myself NOT to do this, NOT to say anything. But I think we're two of a kind. We've both screwed up, royally in my case. And we're broken. Damaged. And because of it, we can't live our lives the way we want to. We're not the people we were meant to be.'

I can't breathe. *How does he know?* That's exactly what it's like. No one's ever understood that before. No one's ever put it into words. Is he really the same, or is he just saying that? Is he trying to trick me and if so, why? My hands grip each other so fiercely my knuckles blanch.

Finally, he tips his head a fraction to look at me, looking as if he needs some kind of response. 'Do you have any idea what I'm on about?'

I just nod, my mouth tight.

He blows out his cheeks and flicks his eyes back to the table. 'I thought so.' He nods too. 'That's not even the weirdest part. There's more.'

He doesn't speak for a while. Blood pounds in my ears.

'Since I met you,' he says at last, 'I've started feeling I might get a second shot. I don't understand it. I don't know why. I just feel it.' He pauses. 'You know what I said the other day? About going back and having the chance to do it again, to get it right this time? I pray for that every single day. And now, this past week... well, I feel as if it might be possible.' He lifts his hand, batting off possible questions. 'I know it's crazy. Trust me, I never thought I'd be sitting here talking like this. I've never been big on miracles. But I sense it. I really do.'

I don't know what to say. I think about how strange everything has seemed since the accident, since Ed first appeared in the flat. The way the past has come back to life in my head. The way his words about going back and putting things right have resonated through me ever since he spoke.

'It is crazy,' I say, finally. 'Completely. But I feel something too.'

It feels as if a bomb has just exploded in the room. We sit there in silence, letting the dust settle. All I can think is: *Now what?*

'Anyway, I'd better get cracking.' Ed jumps up and takes the flowers into the kitchen. The tap runs. He must be putting them in water. When he reappears, his manner is brisk and he won't look at me. 'Hoping I can get the second coat done today. You like it?'

I just nod. I don't feel much like talking about the decorating. I've got too much else on my mind.

CHAPTER THIRTY-ONE

I distract myself by trying to shower – my broken leg stuck out sideways – then get dressed. All the time I'm going through the motions: my insides feel clamped in a vice, my hands shaky. I feel exposed, as if someone's finally peered into my soul and seen the darkness there. Everything Ed described fits me to a tee: the stopping short of getting really close to someone, that endless paradox: how can I be genuinely close to anyone unless they know what I've done? But how could anyone love me once they did?

I go through to the bedroom and brush my hair, then sit on the edge of the bed, looking at the patch of grey sky framed by the window, lost in thought. I think about Ed. What did he do that makes him feel the same?

I think about the other things he said and frown. What did he mean about feeling it might be possible to have a second shot, since he met me? Can it be true that he's starting to feel differently about his life after a week?

I think how much courage it must have taken him to sit down and talk to me like that, to take a risk and lay his feelings on the line.

I clasp my hands and rock myself and let my feelings come bubbling to the surface. I know the answer because I feel it too. I don't know what it is or what it means, but there *is* a connection between us. It's not just an attraction, although that might be true too; it's more like a sense of being kindred spirits.

I shake my head. I don't believe in soulmates. I can't imagine he does either. What did he say? *I've never been big on miracles.* He's not the touchy-feely type. He's an ex-soldier, for heaven's sake.

Already, the daylight is starting to ebb. The trees' bare branches loom black and austere against the darkening clouds. Another couple of hours and he'll leave for the day. He mustn't. Not like this. I can't let him go without showing him I understand. Maybe it's my turn to take a risk.

I steady myself, then go and retrieve the envelope, buried at the back of a drawer.

In the lounge, Ed's worked his way around the room and is finishing off the last wall. 'Hardly worth getting dressed.' He smiles at me over his shoulder. 'Bedtime soon.'

'How's it going?'

'Pretty good.' He doesn't pause, roller in one hand and paint tray in the other. 'Nearly done.'

I sit on the sofa and watch, the envelope large on my lap. My heart's racing. I try to relax into the easy rhythm of his movements, stretching and rolling, stretching and rolling. The muscles down his arm tighten and slacken as he works.

It's not too late to back off, I think. *I don't have to do this.* Maybe I should think about it some more? It's a big step. My hands are sweaty on the paper. After all, I hardly know him.

The roller gives out a faint pulsing squish as it turns across the last section of the wall. He's nearly done for the day. I feel a sudden surge of panic. *What am I thinking?* I should just forget it, shove the envelope under a cushion and say nothing.

I hesitate and think of the silence after he closes the door behind him. If I do nothing, what will he go away thinking? He might wish he'd never spoken. He might think I'm offended or upset or that I just don't get it.

And what about tomorrow? What then? Maybe neither of us will have the courage to speak about it again. And the day after?

What if he ends up finishing the job and leaving and that's the end of it?

He runs the roller over the wall a final time, then stands back to check his work. 'I'll look again in the morning,' he says, 'when the light's better.'

He heads through to the kitchen and clatters in the sink as he washes his tools. When he comes back, wiping his hands on one of his cloths, he stops, looking at the way I'm sitting, tense shouldered, hunched, waiting.

'How are you doing?' Then he hesitates. For a moment, I think he's going to row back, to say: 'Look, about earlier, I'm sorry, just forget it—'

I plunge in before he has the chance. 'Remember my ex?'

He hangs the damp cloth to dry and starts packing away the paints. 'How could I forget?'

'I think he's going to dredge it all up again. What I did.'

He looks up sharply, picking up on how shaky my voice is. He frowns, then comes across and sits by me, giving me his full attention.

I carry on. 'I never told him. I never tell anyone. But he's found out. Well, I think someone else, someone he knows at work, a woman… I always thought she had a thing for him. I think it's her, actually. I'm guessing she's done some digging and showed him what she's found.' I pause, trying to get the words out. 'What if he rakes it all up again?'

'How?'

'I don't know. By telling everyone. On Facebook, maybe. Twitter. He's got a friend who's a news reporter. He might take it to him.'

He stares. 'But why? Why would he do that?'

'Revenge?' I shrug.

'Wow.' He looks stunned. 'That's pretty brutal.'

I lift the bulky envelope from my lap. 'He dropped this on my mat late on Sunday night. Making a point, I suppose, that he's got evidence.' I hand it to him. 'Maybe you should read it. If you want.'

I'm trying to sound casual but I'm not fooling either of us. He sits there with the envelope in his hands as if he doesn't know what to do with it. Finally, he says quietly: 'I don't know.'

I feel myself flush. 'You don't have to, if you're not interested. Obviously. I just thought…'

'Of course I'm interested. I just mean, are you sure?' He looks down at it again. 'Are you sure you want me to know?'

I swallow. He's right. I think of all the friends, all the ex-boyfriends who never knew a thing about it because I never told. 'It's right, what you said. About not being able to live your life. Not becoming the person you're meant to be. I'm like that too.'

He nods, his eyes on my face.

'It *is* crazy. I've known you a week. But, on this anyway, I trust you more than people I've known half my life. I hope I'm not wrong.'

He just says quietly, 'You're not. I get it.' He turns over the envelope and sees the message on the other side: *I know what you did.* 'Nice.' He breathes out noisily. 'That his writing?'

'Hard to be sure. Could be. Looks like he used his left hand, so it didn't look like his.'

Ed nods, then pauses. 'Look. I don't know if I can do the same. Tell you about what I did.' He looks at me. 'Are you OK with that?'

Something inside me shifts and gives way. Had I hoped he'd trust me with his secret the way I was trusting him with mine? I suppose I had. 'That's OK,' I lie. 'It's not a tit-for-tat kind of thing.'

'OK then.'

'OK.'

Silence.

I make a pathetic attempt at a tight smile. 'If Toby does follow through, you might know soon enough anyway.'

He slowly opens the envelope and peers at the bundle of printed documents inside.

I can't watch. I get to my feet, hobble back to my bedroom and shut the door. I sit on the bed, hands clasped, looking at the heavy sky and imagine him drawing out the papers, unfolding them and beginning to read.

CHAPTER THIRTY-TWO

LOUISE

2001

Mr and Mrs Collins had lived next door to us since I was about six.

We had a tall, narrow terraced house in a residential street, tucked back from the main road. It was a good walk from the centre of Greenwich and from the river too, and it didn't really lead anywhere, apart from to a network of cul-de-sacs across the far end. So there was never much traffic. The only people we saw, walking or driving up and down it, were each other, and the occasional delivery driver or workman.

Jo and I grew up knowing almost every family in the street, at least by sight, especially those with children around the same age as us or with a friendly cat or dog we could stroke and try to teach tricks.

In the long summer holidays, when our parents ran out of ways to entertain us, we played with other children in the road. We all dashed in and out of each other's gates, running up the neat paths and knocking on the doors to ask, politely – we were all well trained – *Excuse me, but is so-and-so playing?* Most of the time, they were.

Looking back, I suppose Mr and Mrs Collins were only in their late twenties when they moved in. That didn't seem young to me. They were just grown-ups. I was more interested in whether they had children to play with or an interesting pet, and disappointed when there was no sign of either.

Mr Collins was mild-mannered and funny and always stopped for a quick chat if we were hanging around the front garden when he came walking up the road, home from work. Once we got to know each other, and our parents too, he often carried something for us in his pocket – a lollipop or sometimes, disappointingly, liquorice which I didn't like but was too polite to say so. Whatever it was, he produced it with a flourish and presented it with a grave bow, as if he were a suitor proffering a rose.

Mrs Collins was more tight-lipped. I'd find her sometimes sitting in the kitchen with my mother, chatting over a cup of tea. I don't know what they talked about but they always broke off and looked round when I came trailing in, complaining about Jo or just wanting attention.

I didn't feel comfortable with her, not the way I did with her husband. She made me feel I was interrupting something and not really welcome, even though it was my home and my mother.

I didn't like the way she said: 'Well, hello there, look who it is!' Or sometimes: 'Look out! Here comes trouble!' It was embarrassing. I couldn't imagine her saying that to Jo.

My mother said it was just her idea of a joke and not to think anything of it, but Mrs Collins's tone was so bright it was brittle, and she had a way of smiling that didn't reach her eyes. I wondered if she knew about the lollipops her husband gave me. I had the feeling she didn't, and might not approve.

I got on with the business of growing up and gradually the world tugged at me more and more with its netball and tennis teams, its after-school clubs, friends and, eventually, boyfriends, and I went months at a time without talking to anyone else in the street, even the Collinses.

By the time I was sixteen, I'd almost forgotten they were still there. I'd packed them away, along with the liquorice and lollipops, into the memories of childhood. Until I came home from school one evening, my backpack heavy with homework, and found Mrs Collins sitting there in the kitchen with my mother, just like the old days.

She twisted round when I walked in and gave me a beaming smile – much better than the tepid ones from childhood. My mother grinned too and motioned to the pot of tea between them on the table. She looked as if she'd only just got home. 'Want a cup? I've just made it.'

I didn't really. I was tired and was more inclined to stomp upstairs, put some music on and crash on my bed before dinner. But it was so unusual nowadays to see Mrs Collins in the house that I sensed something significant had happened. And besides, I liked the fact my mother was inviting me to join them at the table, treating me as an adult.

Jo had been away at university for two years by then and I was gradually emerging from her shadow, starting to see myself as a person in my own right and not just Jo's shy little sister.

'Well, look at you!' Mrs Collins looked me up and down, taking in the school skirt, rolled up at the waistband to make it as short as possible, and the ribbed grey tights, ending in shoes with a tiny, rebellious heel. 'What happened?'

I was confused for a moment, wondering what she meant, what was wrong. The old sense of embarrassment washed over me. I picked up a mug and drifted across to the table with it to pour myself some tea.

Already my mother was saying: 'She's shot up, hasn't she? They're both tall. They've got my mother's legs.' She raised her eyebrows to Mrs Collins and glanced meaningfully at me as I sat down between them. I wasn't supposed to notice but I knew exactly what it meant: *Is it OK to tell her?*

'Mrs Collins has got some exciting news,' my mother said. She was cluing me in to be politely delighted: I recognised the signal.

Mrs Collins smiled. 'I was just telling your mum. Mr Collins and I are expecting a baby.' Her hand crept up to rest quietly on her stomach.

I knew that protective gesture from TV shows, although her stomach still looked perfectly flat to me. I had the sense she was milking the moment.

'Congratulations!' I tried to sound sincere, but I didn't really care. She seemed so old to me – she must be nearly forty – that it was all a bit gross. 'Is it a boy or a girl?'

My mother jumped in. 'Too early to know yet, Lou. When did you say you're due? Mid August?'

Mrs Collins beamed. 'August the eleventh. Although first babies are often late.'

My mother, who'd had two of her own, sat patiently and let Mrs Collins tell her all about pregnancy in a slightly patronising tone.

Afterwards, once she'd finally gone and, delayed by her visit, we hurried to get the dinner on, I said: 'Why's she making such a big deal of it, anyway?' I was jealous, I suppose, that she'd taken so much of my mother's attention.

My mother, pouring boiling water onto a pan of frozen peas, said: 'It is a big deal, having a baby.' She smiled to herself as if she were remembering. She lit the gas and put the pan on the hob. She looked thoughtful as she reached for a lid, then started to chop the carrots I'd just peeled.

She paused after a while, knife in the air, and turned to me: 'Most people get pregnant straight away. Sometimes even if they're not planning to.'

'Yes, Mum. I know.' I rolled my eyes. I'd already had this cautionary talk at least a hundred times.

She waved the knife to suggest she hadn't finished yet. 'What I was about to say is that some people find it really hard. They might really, really want to have a baby and it doesn't happen. There might be no obvious reason.'

I blinked, taking this in. 'And that's what happened with Mr and Mrs Collins?'

She nodded. 'It's very private, Lou. People don't like to talk about it. But that's why this baby's so special for them. They've waited a long time for it.'

I carried on thinking as I set the table, considering how strange it was that they lived right there, on the other side of the wall and yet, for all this time, I'd known so little about them.

They called her Cara. The first time I saw her, she was only a week old. Her face was red and wrinkled like a cracked vase. She barely opened her eyes. Mrs Collins sat on the sofa by the Moses basket, looking exhausted but regal, while Mr Collins fussed over her, offering everyone cups of tea and glasses of water and chocolate biscuits.

My mother, who always knew how to say the right thing, asked Mrs Collins about the birth and made sympathetic noises. I gathered that she'd had a hard time, without understanding what that meant.

Later, my mother was invited to scoop Cara out of the basket, swaddled in muslin cloths and a pink blanket. She cooed and made faces and Mrs Collins looked on proudly, as if she was the most beautiful baby ever born. After a while, my mother asked if I'd like to try and showed me how to hold Cara, supporting her head, then passed her across.

She was no weight at all. If I'd closed my eyes, it might have been an empty blanket. It was hard to believe she was a real person, that before long she'd take her place in the pack of children on our road, rushing in and out of gates and knocking on front doors to ask if so-and-so was playing. Then she sneezed, a sudden explosion, that made her open her eyes and look up at me in surprise. I laughed.

'Bless you, Cara!' My mother smiled too.

Cara was blinking up at my face, trying to focus. *I'll look out for you, little Cara*, I thought, looking right back into those vague, watery eyes. *I'm on your side.*

I had no idea how very wrong I was.

I started in my final years of school that September, when Cara was a few weeks old. It was a revelation and a rite of passage that pumped me full of my own importance. I was no longer required to wear school uniform and was allowed to hang out in the common room between lessons, chatting and drinking coffee. I'd signed up to help with the school magazine too, intoxicated by the thought of seeing my name in print.

I didn't see much of baby Cara. I heard her sometimes, crying late at night when I was studying or reading, and saw the bags of dirty nappies sitting by their bins when I hurried past to school. Once or twice, I passed Mrs Collins in the street when she walked out with the buggy. She had developed a harried look, her face drawn, but she also seemed happier. It felt as if the woman I'd known before had walked around wearing a suit of armour, protecting herself from the world, and now it had fallen away, revealing her to be soft and human, like the rest of us, after all.

One evening, my mother came upstairs and tapped on my bedroom door. She looked sheepish, apologising for disturbing me when I was working. In fact, I was struggling with an essay and glad of the interruption. 'Could you do me a massive favour, Lou?' She looked awkward about asking for my help. 'Are you around on Saturday night?'

'*This* Saturday?' I made an exaggerated show of considering. My latest boyfriend had just dumped me so I was actually at a loose end that weekend, but it was a sore point. 'Why?'

'It's just that Mrs Collins is desperate for a babysitter. It's her husband's work Christmas party and she really ought to go. She's hardly been out since Cara was born.' She paused, watching my face. 'I'd do it myself but I'm having Mrs McKenzie round.'

I hesitated. 'I don't know anything about babies.'

'That's OK.' My mother looked encouraging. 'I'll go through it with you. You'll be fine. I'll be here. Mrs Collins is a bit stressed about leaving her. She wants it to be someone she knows.' My mother waited, watching while I decided. 'She's a very sweet baby. And once she settles, she mightn't even wake up. You could get on with your work.'

I pulled a long-suffering face. But my mother so seldom asked me for a favour. She so seldom had anyone around.

'OK.' I nodded. 'I'll do it. But on condition you talk me through what to do.'

She brightened. 'Thanks, love. She'll be so grateful.'

CHAPTER THIRTY-THREE

LOUISE

2001

Mrs Collins didn't seem grateful. She seemed a bundle of nervous anxiety, all dressed up in heels and a slinky dress which didn't do her post-pregnancy figure any favours, topped off with too much make-up and a cloud of spicy perfume.

I stood at her side in Cara's bedroom and listened as carefully as I could while she twittered on about bottles and nappies and cream, and that was before she got started on the first aid box and how to use the baby thermometer. She gave me sharp, sideways glances every now and then, as if she didn't trust me and was looking to catch me out.

I did my best to look alert, but the truth was I'd had a headache and sore throat all day and what I'd really wanted to do was stay at home and veg out in front of the TV. When I'd dropped a few hints to my mother about 'coming down with something', she'd clamped a cool hand on my forehead. 'Maybe – a slight fever.' She frowned. 'But you can't let them down, Lou. Not at a few hours' notice.'

So here I was, dosed up with paracetamol, trying to focus on Mrs Collins's reedy voice. Being in Cara's bedroom was like standing inside a womb. The walls were painted pink and covered in stencils: a frieze of dancing princesses above the picture rail, pink fairies and cartoon bunnies dotted around the walls.

Cara lay on her back in her large wooden cot in the far corner, a gently turning mobile of moon and stars suspended over her head. She was fast asleep in a sleepsuit, her legs bent at the knee and falling outwards from the hips, her arms stretched above her head as if someone had just yelled, 'Hands up!'

'I've just fed and changed her.' Mrs Collins was still going on. 'I'll be back by eleven for the next feed. If she wakes before that—'

I tuned out, looking down at little Cara. She already looked very different from the scrawny, red newborn I remembered. Her limbs had thickened and her cheeks were podgy. Her chest rose and fell as she breathed.

Mr Collins put his head around the nursery door and winked at me, then caught his wife's eye and tapped his watch.

Mrs Collins said: 'You're sure you'll be OK?'

I smiled. 'Fine.'

Downstairs, she pointed out the baby monitor in the lounge, then the tea and coffee and the biscuit tin. Mr Collins hovered all the time, clearly concerned they were late.

I stood at the front door as they finally left. She turned back again when they reached the gate and opened her mouth as if she'd thought of yet another piece of advice to dispense but was interrupted by Mr Collins, who grabbed hold of her arm and hurried her off.

It was odd to be alone in someone else's house. It was almost the same layout as ours but better kept. My mother had bought our house after Dad left, with money from her parents, and she struggled to maintain it. There were always damp patches appearing on walls and cupboard knobs coming off in your hand. I didn't mind. I thought it was bohemian.

Theirs was pristine, the walls freshly painted and the kitchen modern and shiny. I trailed a hand over the countertops as I went to put on the kettle and wondered what Mrs Collins had really thought of us when she came through to sit at our stained kitchen table and drink tea with my mother. I shrugged and made myself a coffee, then checked out the biscuits. I didn't much care what they thought. I wouldn't swap my lovely mother for all the posh kitchens in the world.

I popped up to check on Cara, still sleeping like, well, like a baby, then settled downstairs with my coffee and biscuits. I opened up my schoolbooks, mostly for show, then found the TV remote and fell to flicking through the channels, lolling back against the cushions, my head fuzzy.

I was near the end of a cop drama, not one I usually got the chance to see, when Cara started wailing through the monitor. I wasn't pleased. It wasn't just that they were about to reveal the identity of the murderer, it was also the fact I was drowsy and my head ached and it was an effort to move. I sighed, muted the TV with its screams and wailing police sirens, and traipsed upstairs, hoping she'd soon be back to sleep.

Cara's face was purple with rage. Her arms reached for the ceiling, her fists opening and closing. Her cries were high-pitched and piercing. I reached into the cot and lifted her out, remembering to support her bony head with its wisps of fine, downy hair, then sat on the nursing chair and tried to rock her. She screamed, head thrown back, back arched.

'It's all right, Cara,' I said, using the calm sing-song voice I'd heard my mother use with her. 'There, now. It's OK.'

She drowned me out. It was hard to believe such a tiny body could make so much noise. Half the street must be able to hear. My heart raced and I struggled to stay calm, to remember what to do.

I ran through the checks. Her nappy seemed clean and dry. She didn't seem too hot or cold. It was too soon for her to be hungry again, surely? I eased her into a new position, upright now, and held her close to my chest, trying to stroke the length of her tight back. She kicked and fought, furious. She butted me in the chin with the top of her head. A flailing hand grabbed at my hair.

I managed to heave myself to my feet and started to pace up and down the room, murmuring in her ear, wondering how long this was going to last, how long I could stand it.

I walked her out onto the landing and through to the bathroom, just for a change of scene and temperature. The screams exploded off the tiled walls, twice as loud. I tipped her forward in my arms, a hand cupping her head, and showed her the mirror, the revelation of the two of us, her blotchy, crinkled face cheek to cheek with my weary one. She blinked her wet eyelashes for a second, distracted and trying to focus, then screwed up her face and went back to bawling.

Time hung, suspended, as I walked around the house, struggling to quieten her. Nothing seemed to work. She seemed oblivious, whether I rocked her gently or tried to jig her about, dancing with her in my arms.

I stomped her up and down the stairs, in and out of bedrooms. The wailing was relentless, a siren that I simply couldn't switch off. My head throbbed. 'Stop it, Cara!' My voice rose. 'Stop crying!'

Maybe she'd never stop. A wave of hot panic swept over me. Maybe there was something really wrong with her? I wondered about calling my mother for help.

I carried Cara through to the lounge and sat down heavily on the sofa, holding her against me with one hand while I reached for their phone, sitting in its cradle on the side-table. My fingers were just closing around the plastic when the world shifted and changed. It took a moment for me to realise what was different. A tightness eased in my head.

I abandoned the phone and sat up to look. Cara had stopped crying, as abruptly as she'd begun. She was staring at the flickering pictures on the TV screen, red-rimmed eyes round and staring. Her mouth hung slightly open. The silence settled over us like falling snow. She hiccupped, her eyes never leaving the television.

As I looked, not daring to move, the blotchiness started to drain from her skin. Her eyelashes hung with drying beads. She was transforming before my eyes from a nightmare vision of hell back to baby Cara. I let out a low, steady breath.

'You want to watch some TV?' My gentle voice was back, coaxing. I groped for a tissue in my pocket and wiped off her sloppy nose, her cheeks. Maybe it was over. Maybe she was finally settling. 'We can do that. No problem.'

I eased myself backwards, holding her steady on the length of my chest in her sleepsuit, her ribcage against mine, until I was leaning back against the cushions, half sitting, half lying. Cara's head turned to the side, her eyes stubbornly locked on the screen. The cop show had ended. It was a soap, now. Nothing there to upset her. Just a parade of miming ghosts, gesticulating and talking, a procession of people driving silent cars across the screen.

I twisted round to look at Cara's face. Her eyes were heavy, drooping, starting to close, however much she fought it. Gradually, they fell shut. Her breathing deepened as her body softened into sleep. The pudgy legs that had kicked with such passion lay still, the hands that had balled into fists relaxed, the miniature fingers uncurling.

I felt a soft glow of satisfaction. I'd done it. I'd survived.

I closed my own eyes, my hand on her back, trying not to move a muscle, frightened of disturbing her sleep. I let go of the tension in my shoulders, giving way at last to the dull throbbing in my head.

CHAPTER THIRTY-FOUR

LOUISE

2001

The scream was high-pitched and terrifying, like nothing I had ever heard in my life, then or since. A female cry of absolute horror.

My eyes snapped open. For a second, I was lost, shaking with shock but disorientated. What had happened? A nightmare? Where was I? My body, crammed onto the short sofa, was stiff.

Someone flew at me. Mrs Collins, sharp nails outstretched, made sudden, scrabbling movements at my side. A flash of snowy-white sleepsuit, bony fingers plucking her sleeping daughter from beside my body, against the back of the sofa.

Cara. I blinked, remembering. I opened my mouth to explain but I couldn't speak. I wanted to tell her: *It's OK. She wouldn't settle, that's all, so I brought her down here. I must have dozed off.*

The room was suddenly airless. Her second scream broke the quiet again, this one longer and more desolate. Mrs Collins was clasping her daughter to her face, as if she were consuming her.

Mr Collins stood behind her, in the doorway, transfixed. His hand, in the act of loosening and removing his tie, still held it, raised, in a noose around his neck. His movements seemed slightly uncoordinated, as if he'd been drinking.

I sat up, sick to the stomach, my hairline prickling.

'What?' Mr Collins came back to life. He strode to her side and she angled Cara towards him, for him to see.

'Look!' Her voice was a screech. 'Look at her!'

Mr Collins touched Cara's cheek with a cupped palm, then wrenched open the front of her sleepsuit and started to pound frantically on her tiny chest with the heel of his hand. Cara's arm fell to one side and hung limply.

Her features were perfect. Those long eyelashes, the delicate, paper-thin eyelids, the fine, wispy hair. But her skin had a waxy pallor.

I stood up and took a step towards them. 'She was asleep,' I stuttered. 'I don't—'

'Ambulance.' Mr Collins shoved past me as he ran from the room.

Mrs Collins clasped Cara to her, as if the warmth of her body, the fierceness of her love, could somehow revive her. She started rocking, not a soothing movement but a storm-tossed, desperate one.

I took another step towards her, still not understanding. She was just asleep. It was a mistake, surely? I'd held her. I'd settled her.

I touched Mrs Collins's shoulder. 'Maybe—'

She shook me off as if my hand had scalded her. 'You killed her!' she screamed. 'You killed my baby, you wicked, wicked girl!'

CHAPTER THIRTY-FIVE

LOUISE

PRESENT DAY

I pretend to be asleep.

Ed taps softly on the door and whispers my name. 'Come on. I know you're there.' A low shuffling as if he's shifting his weight. A long pause. Then another rap on the wood. 'Come out. Please. Talk to me. Louise.'

I think: *Which day did he start calling me Louise?* I don't remember. My name sounds different when he says it. His voice is rich and gentle. I imagine him sitting in the quiet of the lounge and reading over those printed papers. What have I done, letting him see them? I can't face him again.

Outside, the sky is darkening. It's almost five. He should have gone by now. I lie on my side and strain to listen for the sound of his footsteps and the low click of the door, closing behind him. I wonder what he thinks of me now. I wonder if he'll tell anyone. If he'll bother coming back to finish his work. I imagine again the emptiness without him. The silence.

I hide in my bedroom for as long as I can. Six o'clock. Then seven. The darkness is dense, pressing against the window. I'm thirsty and hungry too. I wonder what he's doing. Out with friends, perhaps, eating and drinking. Will he tell them about me, the paranoid baby-murderer with the broken leg? Now he'll understand why I wonder if the driver might have hit me on purpose. Now he'll know why I deserve to be punished, even after all this time.

I lower my heavy leg to the floor and heave myself to my feet, swinging on my crutches to the bedroom door and opening it. Quietness. I don't bother putting the light on. My eyes have slowly adjusted as the gloom has deepened.

The curtains still stand open and the flat is silver with shadow and reflected shards of streetlight. I head towards the lounge, making my way to the kitchen, when a large, dark shape suddenly rises.

I scream. One of my crutches clatters to the floor and I grope for the back of the sofa to steady myself, heart pounding.

'Louise! Are you all right?'

Light floods the room. I blink, trying to focus. 'Ed? Why're you still here?'

He's at my side, his hand under my elbow, taking my weight and guiding me to the sofa to sit.

'I couldn't leave.' He looks wretched. 'Not without seeing you.'

I look away. I don't want to hear what he thinks. I remember it all too well.

The women whispering at the far end of the supermarket aisle who break off and glare when they catch sight of me. The lies about me in the local papers, bolstered by mean-spirited quotes from people who barely know me. They make me sound cruel and careless, painting a picture of a person I don't recognise. One of the nationals runs a piece before the inquest, mistakenly writing I was eighteen, instead of sixteen, and hinting that I'd taken 'substances' that night. All I'd had was paracetamol, of course, but the implication was there, that I was smoking dope or snorting cocaine or who knows what.

At school, someone writes 'Baby Killer!' on my English book. A bloodied sanitary pad appears in my locker. A boy shouts down the corridor after me: 'Look out! It's Loony Lou!' The name sticks.

I quit work on the school magazine. I'd had enough of seeing my name in print. Even now, I won't write news.

I got through it all by keeping my head down and hiding away in the school library.

Now, I sit in silence, my face hot, waiting for Ed to pass judgement.

'It wasn't your fault.' He sits beside me. His leg is warm down the side of mine. 'It's all there. The coroner's report. The inquest. It's tragic, but they say it's not clear why she stopped breathing. Young babies just die in their sleep, sometimes. Look, it says right here: Sudden Infant Death Syndrome. It just happened to be on your watch.'

'It was my fault,' I say, dully. 'Everyone thought so.'

'It wasn't. It wasn't anyone's fault.' He shakes his head. 'I read the police report. The medical report. I went through all the evidence.'

'She didn't believe me.' I shudder. I remember the screams. The sight of Mrs Collins's face. White. Stricken. Wretched. 'I should have put Cara back in her cot, safely, on her back. I didn't mean to fall asleep. I didn't feel well. And I was just so glad she'd stopped crying.' I pause, my voice a whisper. 'I didn't know.'

Ed lets out a small groan of frustration. 'Of course you didn't! But listen, she might have died anyway, even in her cot. Look at the coroner's verdict.' He reaches out and taps the papers with his forefinger. 'Don't you see? That's what the diagnosis means. Unexplained.'

I sit, rigid, wishing he'd just go.

'This stuff?' He picks out one of the newspaper reports and holds it up. I see it and look away. I don't need to read the screaming headline. It's seared on my memory. *Did Teen Babysitter Kill Baby Cara?* The picture of a sleeping Cara alongside, swaddled in a baby blanket, is heart-breaking. 'Garbage.' I feel his eyes on my face. 'You've carried this, all these years.' He sighs. 'Listen to me, Louise. It wasn't your fault.'

I say very quietly. 'She thought it was.'

'Who?'

'Mrs Collins. Her mother.'

He gets to his feet and paces about the room. 'Maybe, at the time. She must have been out of her mind with grief. People say and do strange things when they're in pain. Cruel things, sometimes. They can't help themselves. They're hurting so badly themselves, they want someone else to hurt too. But it was a long time ago. Half a lifetime.' He plonks himself abruptly beside me again and takes my hand in his. His palms are large and warm. 'What happened to her?'

I shrug. 'They moved away. Out of London. They couldn't bear being in that house, afterwards. And the gossip. People were sorry for them, obviously. Too sorry. Everywhere they went, people pitied them. I don't think they could stand it.'

I remember my mother coming back from the funeral, her face pinched. She'd said it was better I didn't go and I was glad – I don't think I could have got through it. My mother stood there in my bedroom, looking out of the window at the trees and pulling off her black leather gloves, finger by finger.

'They waited so long,' she'd said, more to herself than to me. 'She was their miracle baby.'

I'd known at once what she meant. Cara was their only chance of a family. No child can be replaced but, for them, the loss was complete. Without her, they'd never be parents. She had been their one shot.

Now, I say: 'They weren't likely to have had another baby after her. Everyone knew that. They'd had problems.' I shrug. 'Mrs Collins was only a year or two older than I am now, I suppose. It seemed ancient to me, then.'

He says: 'Maybe you should find her. Go and see her? It might help.'

I give him a cold look. 'See how sad and miserable her life's been? How's that going to help, exactly?'

'Maybe you can do something for them. They'll be, what, retirement age now?'

'I suppose so.'

'I could help you track them down. If you like.'

I look at him. *He hasn't given up on me. Quite the opposite. He wants to help.*

'I know where they are,' I say. 'They wrote to us after Mum died. They didn't blame Mum, you see, just me.' I think of the plain, cream paper Mrs Collins used. Thick parchment. Her neat handwriting, as uptight as she was. 'Jo's got it in a file somewhere, with all the others. We thought Mia might like to see the letters someday, when she's older. They're full of stories about Mum. About things she did for people.'

'Well, I think you should get in touch.' His tone is thoughtful. 'Tell them how you've felt, all these years. How desperate you've been.'

'She'll probably be delighted.'

'Maybe.' He frowns. 'Maybe not. Maybe she's old and wise enough now to know she shouldn't have blamed you. To tell you she forgives you and lay it all to rest.' He leans forward for a moment, quiet, head bowed, as if he's deep in thought or prayer. After a while, he straightens up abruptly, stirred back to life. 'Right. Here's what's going to happen.' He gives my hand a final squeeze and lets it go. 'I'm going to go into the kitchen, rummage in the fridge and cook us something. Have you got a bottle of wine?'

I nod. 'There's one in the cupboard, near the cooker.'

'Good.' He nods. 'I think we could both do with a glass. I'll replace it tomorrow.'

He pulls himself to his feet and moves into the kitchen. Cupboards open and bang closed. Saucepans clang as he pulls one out and water splashes into it. The gas hob fizzes into life.

I wonder what he's found. 'What are you making?'

His head bobs to the door. 'Wait and see.'

My shoulders ease and fall.

It's been crippling, this weight I've carried for the last twenty years. It's still there. It's a burden I'll carry until I die. But, I realise, as I listen to the stirring and chopping, the hiss of rising steam, that for the first time in my life, someone's sharing it.

Later, after we've eaten, Ed asks permission to re-arrange the furniture. I shrug. He turns the sofa around, to face the bare window, then turns off the light. We sit together, side by side, looking out at the latticework of branches against the sky, and drink our wine. The threads of light from the street gleam along the freshly painted walls.

'You think you're unlovable, don't you?' he says. 'That if someone knows about all this, they'll hate you. Run a mile.'

I don't need to answer. He knows.

'It wasn't your fault.' He hesitates, knowing I can't agree. 'I'm not going away. You know that, don't you? When the job's done, I mean. I'd like to see you again. Cook you dinner, maybe at my place?' He pauses, looking for a response. 'If you like.'

I manage to nod. 'I'd like that.'

Some tension in him relaxes, as if we've settled something. He sips his wine. There's a breeze getting up. The tree branches rattle like bones.

After a while, he says: 'You know, he may not be planning to do anything with those papers. Your ex. Maybe he just wants to get your attention.'

'Toby?' I consider this. 'Pretty weird way of going about it.'

He hesitates. 'You mentioned there's a woman?'

'Rachel. I think she's put him up to it. He says they're just friends. A group of them go for a drink together now and then, after work.' I think about the times she's gone a step further and

invited him to a barbeque or a picnic at the weekend, always
when I just happen to be overseas for work. 'I don't trust her.'

He nods, taking this in. 'What about him? He seemed pretty
angry the other day.'

I think of the way he burst in and tried to take a swing at Ed.
'He's been acting pretty weird.'

'You said something about him spying on you?' He paused,
watching my face. 'I don't mean to pry. I mean, if you—'

'You're not. You're right.' I realise my eyes are scanning the
quivering mass of shadows on the far side of the road. I do it
all the time now, instinctively, checking to see if Toby is there,
hiding, watching me in the darkness. 'I think he comes round
some nights. To keep an eye on me.'

He frowns. 'Have you seen him out there?' He cranes forward.
'Have you seen him this evening?'

I shake my head. 'Not exactly. Sometimes I think I catch a
glimpse of him, if he moves. But I'm not sure. That's his game,
I think. I sense him more than see him.'

'It's out of order. You know that, don't you? Trying to frighten you.'
He hesitates. 'I'd never do that to you. However much you hurt me.'

I consider this. He's thinking about the two of us, then, and the
future and how it might end. 'That's the thing, though. Everyone
thinks that in the beginning. You never know how you'll be. Put
people under enough pressure and they crack.'

'I don't crack.' He stiffens and goes suddenly quiet. I wonder
again what he did in the past and if he'll ever feel comfortable
enough to tell me. If I'll change my opinion of him if he does.

His thoughts drift. I know because after a while, he harks back
to that same old theme. 'Imagine if you could go back. Live that
awful evening all over again and set it right.'

I close my eyes. For a moment, I see myself carrying that
impossibly light bundle back up the stairs, placing her gently in
her cot, keeping her safe, watching her sleep. If only.

I open my eyes again. 'It's not possible, though, is it? What happened, happened. I can't set it right.'

'I wonder.' He doesn't look me in the eye, just gazes out at the darkness and murmurs. 'I really do.'

CHAPTER THIRTY-SIX

The flat feels too quiet once he's left.

Jo picks up as soon as I call. 'I was getting worried.' She sounds tired and out of sorts. 'Did you switch your phone off? I've been trying to get hold of you.'

I think of Ed, cooking us both dinner and how comfortable he makes me feel. How safe.

'Sorry. I dozed off.'

A pause. 'Are you OK?'

I hear disapproval in her voice. I don't need this. 'Yep. Just really tired. Must be the medication or something.'

'What did you do today? You been out?'

'No.' I hesitate. 'Nothing much.'

'Are you pitching for work?'

'A bit.'

'Good.' She sniffs. 'It's your leg you've hurt, not your arms.'

In the background, water's splashing. She's at the sink, doing the washing up. I imagine her hurried movements, the phone clamped between a raised shoulder and her ear. Mike's probably in the lounge, half-asleep, watching the news.

'I'm trying.' I don't know how to explain how I'm feeling. We never talk about Mr and Mrs Collins and Cara and what I did. It's been a taboo subject in our family for so many years. I'm not sure she ever really understood. She wasn't around when it all happened. 'Anyway, how was your day? Was the café busy?'

'Steady. Lunch was poor, then a rush around four o'clock. The tea and cake crowd.'

I nod to myself. She has trouble finding staff. The good ones don't stay long. As soon as she gets them trained, they move on to the cafés and restaurants down by the river where the tips are better. 'Anyway, sorry, it's late. I should let you go.'

But Jo hasn't finished yet. 'You need to keep busy, Lou. Sort out your bedroom or something. Clean out some drawers. You need to take your mind off the accident. You're brooding.' The crash of dishes as something on the draining board slides and topples. 'Maybe you should go out tomorrow? You can't stay inside all the time. It's not good for you.'

'You're right.' She isn't, but I don't want a fight, I haven't got the strength just now. I have another go at changing the subject. Sometimes, with Jo, that's the only answer. 'How's Mia doing?'

She sighs down the phone, sending me a mini hurricane. 'That's another thing.'

Oh.

'I've had an email from her teacher. Apparently, she's going round the playground, offering sweets to the other kids, to anyone who can find her one of those dark blue Volvos.'

I smile and try not to let it show in my voice. 'She's trying to help find the car that knocked me over. It's a game, that's all. She's playing detectives.'

'I know that.' She sounds curt. 'The teachers told her to stop but she just carried on doing it on the sly. You should see the email.' She's takes a deep breath, trying to calm herself. 'When we see you at the weekend, just don't encourage her, OK? Tell her you've stopped looking now or that you don't want to think about it any more. I don't know. You think of something. Please.'

'OK.' I think she's getting worked up over nothing, but there's no point saying that. 'I promise.'

'Thank you.' The acoustic changes as Jo moves about in the room. She'll be tidying now or folding laundry or whatever else she does. 'I don't know where she thinks she's getting all these sweets from, anyway. They're not even allowed sweets in school. And I never buy them.'

I take a deep breath. 'So, what about Sunday? You and Mia come over after lunch, if Mike's busy? We could go to the café on the corner? Give me a change of scene.'

She hesitates. 'We'd love to see you. Obviously.'

'But?'

'Well, maybe you could come to us? I'm sure Mike'd drive you over.'

'Really?' Mike usually spends Sunday afternoon dozing in front of the TV. Seeing me isn't usually top of his list of fun things to do.

'Don't be like that.' Jo, always the diplomat. 'I'll be baking anyway, for the café. We can eat some rejects. Anyway, I'm sure he'd love to see you.'

I'm not convinced, but I bite my lip. I've learned not to pry too much about my brother-in-law.

'OK. If you like.'

CHAPTER THIRTY-SEVEN

Ed finishes up in the flat on Wednesday.

He moves with steady deftness, packing away his dust sheets and carrying his equipment – rollers and brushes, trays and tins – down to the van.

I sit on the sofa and watch it all. I'm awkward all over again. He must be embarrassed, now he knows so much about me. I wonder if he's glad he's going. If I'll ever ask him to come back in January and do the rest of the flat.

'Like it?' He comes to stand near me, and we look together at the wall.

I nod.

'Good choice, even if I say so myself. It's really freshened the place up.'

He heads off again, carrying another load, and I wait, stomach tight.

He bounds back up the stairs and reappears in the doorway. 'So, I've been thinking.' He's all nerves again, hardly able to look me in the eye. 'This weekend.'

I hesitate, wondering if he's going to suggest coffee again. I hope so. I need to know he isn't just moving on, now the work's done.

He takes a deep breath. 'How about that dinner on Saturday night? My place. I'll cook for you.'

I hesitate. I can just imagine what Jo'll say if I tell her.

He says: 'I'm not that bad, you know. Never poisoned anyone yet.'

I smile. 'I'd love to. That's assuming I can…' I gesture to my leg.

He shrugs. 'Not a problem. I'll come and get you. I kept hold of the wheelchair, just in case.'

'The wheelchair? Marvellous!'

We both laugh, the tension between us dissolving at once.

I think about him all week.

Some evenings, I get as far as reaching for the phone, thinking I should cancel.

Jo's right. I know next to nothing about him. Maybe he's already got a girlfriend and he's just messing me around, spinning me a yarn. Why would a guy like him be on his own?

Besides, it's too soon. I'm still getting over Toby. I need to get used to being alone and not rush into anything.

Then I find myself thinking about him. About the flow of his muscles as he works. About his eyes. About how safe he makes me feel. How understood. About this weird connection between us that neither of us can explain.

So I never quite make the call.

On Saturday evening, he appears at my door with the wheelchair.

His voice, the smell of his leather jacket, his smile. I feel like a schoolgirl going out on a big date, all nerves and elbows.

We agree I'll try to manage on crutches and tell him if I need to switch to the chair.

Outside, the air is sharply cold and smoky with mist. Dragon breath, we used to call it when we puffed out clouds as children. I stand on the pavement and draw it in deeply. It feels as if I'm rejoining the real world at last, after a long time away.

'Nice and steady.' Ed is there at my elbow. He seems even more solid in the open air, the kind of man you want to grab hold of in a storm. 'Take it slowly.'

I swing my crutches and we set off down the pavement with Ed pushing the empty wheelchair beside me. I haven't got the breath to talk. The crutches settle into the familiar bruises under my arms.

He leads me onto the high street. Christmas lights are strung across the road. Shop windows glow with Christmas displays, flashing trees and heaps of brightly wrapped boxes sprinkled with artificial snow. I realise with a jolt how close we are to the holidays – just over two weeks away now.

We head down towards the river, then away from the docks and the Cutty Sark, over Deptford Creek, past the new residential development of Millennium Quay, with its clean lines and rows of balconies with their thin slices of river view. We progress slowly, stopping now and then so I can catch my breath.

'Nearly there.' He doesn't fuss, but his eyes steal covert glances, making sure I'm managing.

He turns me inland again and down a narrow alley between two converted warehouses. One looks modern, the brickwork recently sandblasted; new, metal-framed windows have been fitted in the stone and the façade is edged with brightly coloured plastic drainpipes.

The other warehouse is its neglected twin. The size and shape are the same, as if they were built a century or so ago as a pair, but this second building is rundown. The brickwork is stained black with decades of urban grime. The pipes and gutters are broken and mossy. Ed unlocks a side door and, inside, in semi-darkness, he hoists me up a metal staircase, his hands clasping my upper arms. The crutches clang on the steep steps and the sound echoes hollowly.

It crosses my mind as he unlocks the door at the top, two storeys off the ground, that this is a strange, secluded place. I think of Jo's warnings about how little I know about this man. My heart pounds. My phone bounces against my hip and I wonder if I'd even get a signal in here, if I needed one.

The door opens into a cavernous loft space. Ed flips on the lights and I stand, dazed, looking around. It's vast and smells of wood-smoke and brick dust.

The walls aren't plastered. They show the same bare brickwork as the exterior, just less weathered. The space is dominated by a broad sofa and two worn armchairs, loosely arranged in front of a wood-burning stove which is fitted into the far wall. Ed crosses to it, takes a thick cloth and pulls open the glass front, then stirs up the fire, adding two blocks of wood from a basket on the hearth.

He gestures to the sofa and I drop onto it, shattered by the walk. I look around, panting, taking it all in, as he goes to a kitchen island at the other end. I hear him fill a metal pan and set it on the hob, then the sudden pop and flare as he lights the gas.

A worn wooden crate sits by the side of the sofa, covered with piles of books and a storm lamp. The bookshelves are makeshift, planks of knotted, uneven wood bracketed into the wall, over-flowing with books of all sizes. A free-standing metal staircase leads to a mezzanine level, jutting out from the wall. The corner of a mattress, draped with a trailing sheet, is just visible there. Two giant stereo speakers are angled high in the walls, set on either side of the wood-burning stove, peering down at me from wall-bracket perches. In another corner, tucked away behind a wooden chair, his plastic-bag kite lies at rest.

A large photograph of a stark landscape, clipped into a cheap plastic frame, hangs near it. I narrow my eyes and try to make it out. It's a drab, desolate world of rock and wiry scrub, with a line of austere jagged mountains rising in the distance. The range is sharp with fissures which throw deep pointing fingers of shadow. The sky is cloudless but heavy with orange dust and mellow with a fading, burning sun.

I consider it, trying to guess. 'Is that Iran?'

'Afghanistan.'

He doesn't expand and I don't ask. I remember how much he seemed to know about my supposedly Afghan rug, the Tree of Life.

I focus on the rising smoke of the fire, the sudden darting flames as the wood takes, spits and cracks. Behind me, the water boils. Ed moves with quiet efficiency around the kitchen units, making tea. He comes over to set a mug beside me on the wooden chest and settles in the armchair to my side, close enough to talk but far enough away to give me space. I watch his hand as he lifts his mug to his lips and remember the feel of his fingers on mine. I look away.

'What a place.' I'm suddenly awkward. 'I didn't know Greenwich had flats like this.'

He smiles into his tea. 'Well, it doesn't. Not officially. On paper, this building's abandoned, ripe for development. They're waiting for planning permission. Have been for nearly a year. The developer's a mate of mine.' His smile broadens. 'A good mate. I get the feeling he's slowing things down, if you see what I mean. Keeping a roof over my head.'

I look around, considering. There are no normal windows, just a single skylight, set at an angle over the mezzanine shelf, framing a vast rectangle of black sky.

'Did you do all this yourself?'

'Pretty much. With the help of a few mates who know more about building than I do.' He gestures to the lines of the roof. 'It was a grain silo, back in the day. We just sealed it off, put in the staircase and the stove, bunged in the kitchen.'

He curls in his armchair, side on to me, facing the fire. We sit like that for a long time, sipping our tea, watching the flickering shadows, neither of us speaking. It seems easy to be quiet together. As easy as if we've known each other forever.

My eyes fall closed and, for a moment, I feel as if I'm floating, warm and comfortable, looking down at the two of us. I don't want anything else to happen. I don't want it to become complicated. I fear the way all this will end.

He's the one who finally breaks the silence. 'Louise?'

His voice is shy. I open my eyes.

He's staring fixedly at his hands. 'I don't know how to put this…'

I hold my breath. I think: *Maybe, whatever it is, it's better you don't say it. Please. Don't spoil this.*

He's struggling. 'I don't understand what's going on.' He hesitates. 'I mean, I know the score. We're both people who don't get involved with anyone. Not really. Who make sure we don't get too close.' He bites his lip. 'I'm not even sure I can explain.'

'Is this because of what you read?' I manage to say. 'What you know about me, now?'

'Partly.' He pauses. 'I still don't think you were to blame. You must know that. It was tragic and I'm sorry. But it makes no difference to how I feel about you.'

A piece of wood on the fire stirs and spits sparks.

'Look,' he says. 'You don't know me very well. But I'm a solid guy. I don't go in for weird stuff, mumbo-jumbo.' He shook his head. 'None of this makes any sense to me.'

I blink. I'm not sure what he's talking about.

He leans forward, lowering his voice as if he's afraid of being overheard. 'Since I met you, something's happened. I can't get my head round it. I just feel it's possible. I don't know why or what it means. A parallel universe or something? I have no idea.'

I wait, feeling my heart banging in my chest. I can't speak.

'Tell me I'm not going crazy.' He looks at me, his face flushed. 'Have you felt it too? That the worst day of your life is somehow closer again? That you can almost close your eyes and feel yourself back there. That it's possible we could both have another shot at getting it right.'

I hesitate. 'It's always in my head,' I say. 'And it's true I've been going back over it all recently, stuck in the flat with this.' I point to my plaster cast. 'But it's not real. It's a memory. A very vivid one. A flashback. My mind playing tricks on me. That's all.'

He sits very still, watching me. 'It's more than that, at least for me.'

'A second chance?' I say. 'To go back in time and do it again? Sorry. That's impossible.' My cheeks feel flushed, perhaps from the fire. 'Of course, I'd love it to be true,' I add. 'You're right. We're two of a kind, aren't we? Both of us damaged by what we've done. But we can't go back, Ed. That's a fantasy.' I pause. 'I'm not sure it's helpful to keep thinking like that.'

He gives me a long, sad look, then gets to his feet and goes back to the kitchen to cook. His mellow, old-fashioned music hums through the speakers. Frank Sinatra croons a sentimental love song.

After we've eaten, he comes to sit close to me on the sofa. He smells of musk and washing powder.

He reaches out a hand and strokes stray hair from my cheek, tucks it behind my ear. 'Whatever you say, I feel different since I met you. I feel better.'

I don't answer. I take another sip of wine, then set down my glass on the table and turn to him. His eyes shine in the low light. They reflect the orange glow of the fire as it cracks and shifts. I check myself for feelings of guilt about Toby, of uncertainty about getting involved with someone new so soon, of anxiety about this man I barely know. Then I lean into him and we kiss.

Later, we lie together on the floor in front of the fire, wrapped round in a rough, grey blanket. Army-issue, he says. I wonder where it's travelled and what it's seen. My broken leg is propped on a cushion on the floor. My healthy one is bare, turned outwards and snaked lazily between his. My head is cradled by the firm flesh below his shoulder, my cheek against his skin, drowning in its smell.

I'm relaxed, close to drifting into sleep but he seems tense suddenly, thinking of something.

He lifts his head and rests his chin on his hand, his elbow bent, his eyes close to mine. 'I want to try,' he says. 'I want to tell you. I'm not sure I can.'

I prop myself up too, alert. 'You don't have to.' I'm frightened of what he might say. Of the way I might feel about him, once I know his secret. 'Just because I told you, you don't—'

'It isn't that.' He blinks. His eyelashes are so long. I smile to myself, dreamy. 'It matters to me, Louise. It's everything we've been saying. We can't move forward until you know.'

I hesitate. I'm supposed to encourage him to open up and talk, but I'm not sure I want to. I don't want to risk it. I don't want anything to change.

'If I try, will you hear me out? It's a long story.'

I wrap the edge of the blanket around me and lie against him and we settle together, his arms embracing me, my head on his chest. His heart thumps hard as he starts to talk. I can't look him in the eye and I sense he feels the same. I keep very still and don't interrupt.

'It was in Afghanistan,' he starts, 'in Helmand Province. A place called Lashkar Gah.'

CHAPTER THIRTY-EIGHT

EDWARD

AFGHANISTAN, 2007

All in all, Abdul was a good kid.

Having tried to shake him off at first, I soon found myself looking out for him. He always came bounding out to find me eventually, breathless sometimes, apologising for being late – he'd been busy with this errand or that chore. Catching sight of his eager, beaming face searching me out – that wasn't such a bad feeling, you know? In the middle of a godforsaken war. I wouldn't say I looked forward to seeing him, exactly, but it was one of the better parts of the routine. Let's just say that innocence and hope in the future, like his, weren't that thick on the cracked, hard-baked ground.

I could never get him to explain how he knew I was there.

He shrugged: 'I am just knowing,' he'd say, as if it were a stupid question. 'All are knowing. You are Britishers.'

It was true. The kids always appeared within minutes of us showing up in town. That part was weird. And if they knew, by some process of osmosis, of bizarre Afghan signalling, surely the bad guys knew too.

Then one of the men put a spanner in the works. I never found out for sure who dobbed me in – Jenkins? – by having a quiet word with Johnson, who then felt obliged to have a quiet word with

Captain Miles but, first I heard of it, the two of them cornered me one evening outside the deserted cookhouse, gesturing me over to join them as they sat opposite each other at a scrubbed wooden table, making the most of the bad coffee.

'Just been getting an update from Johnson.' Miles seemed relaxed. His green army-issue T-shirt was stained with salty sweat patches, a reminder of the heat of the day. Already, now the sun was down, the air was blowing cold, the dust scouring sunburnt skin. 'Sounds as if the trips into town are going well. Major Hopkins is pleased.'

'Glad to hear it, sir.' I climbed onto the bench beside Johnson who had his head down, looking at the tabletop. 'Johnson's got a way with kids. Heard his nickname, sir? Beckham.'

Miles allowed himself a smile. 'Need to vary the routine, though. I was just telling Johnson. It seems safe enough down there – mostly, they're on side. But we're getting reports. Once darkness falls, it's a very different story. Lot of families getting night letters. And that's just the ones we get to know about.'

I blinked. 'Night letters?'

Johnson turned his head. 'From the Taliban. Death threats and stuff, you know. If they think someone's got too friendly with the police. Or with us.'

'Keep at it,' Miles said. 'Just don't get complacent, will you? Make sure you keep the enemy on their toes.'

I nodded. Something in the hunch of Johnson's shoulders bothered me. We were mates now, Johnson and I. Not best buddies – we were too different for that – but we'd been through a lot together. I knew him well enough to know he was uneasy, just not why.

Miles took a mouthful of coffee. 'This lad. Abdul, is it? What's that about, Spencer?'

Something in his tone made me start. The atmosphere was suddenly more tense. This was what the conversation was about,

I felt it. The rest had been leading to this. Johnson didn't look me in the eye.

'Not sure what you mean, sir. He's a decent enough kid. He's desperate to get some sort of scholarship to study in England. He asks me to correct his English. That's it.'

Miles pursed his lips. 'Do you encourage him?'

I pulled a face. 'I don't encourage him or discourage him, sir. He comes by for a chat, that's all. He's a bright lad. Keen to learn. Might be a terp for us, some day, if he keeps it up. His old man was a copper.'

Miles shook his head. He pulled back his shoulders, shook the dregs of his coffee into the dust and made to leave. 'Not a good idea, Spencer. I know you mean well. But you need to set an example to the men. Treat them all exactly the same. No favourites. Keep your wits about you.'

He nodded goodnight and headed off, leaving me staring after him. He was a mild-mannered man. From him, that felt like a telling-off.

I turned to Johnson. 'What was that about?'

He shrugged, heaving himself up from the bench. 'He's right. Dial it back a bit. The men don't like it.'

I splayed my hands. 'Come on. He's a swotty kid, trying to practise his English. What's the big deal?'

'Just cut the teacher's pet crap, all right? It's dangerous.'

CHAPTER THIRTY-NINE

EDWARD

AFGHANISTAN, 2007

Soon after that, Abdul disappeared.

It took me a while to register. For a day or two, when we headed into town for a kick-about, I felt oddly alone, just standing there, weapon ready across my body, scanning the dirt road for sudden movements in amongst the passing pick-up trucks, the battered, windowless buses, the ancient bicycles. No small wiry lad came bowling across the mud to seek me out. I realised, absurd as it sounds, that I missed him. He wasn't much company, he was just a kid, but I liked him. I liked his bright eyes and enthusiasm, his quirkiness, his hope. And he'd chosen me. I was his foreign friend.

I tried not to think about it, not to look out for him. Maybe he'd got bored. I wasn't as much fun as Johnson. I looked at him now – getting them all in a line and setting up some new game. The kids adored him. All I did was wait on the sidelines and keep watch.

I tried to shrug it off. Maybe Johnson and Miles were right, anyway. Maybe I needed a bit of distance. After all, if the lads had been gossiping about it, some of the locals might've noticed too. There were eyes everywhere.

By the end of the second week, when there was still no sign of him, I starting asking a few of the other kids if they'd seen him around, if he was OK.

They shrugged and looked vacant, avoided my eye.

'No, mister.'

'Sorry, sir.'

Something in the way they hastily turned away worried me. I caught one of the bigger boys by the arm. 'Abdul. You know Abdul? Skinny lad. This tall.'

He didn't struggle but his eyes, looking back at mine, were deliberately blank, his expression too carefully guarded. They knew something, these boys. Something they wouldn't tell.

I bent down to the boy's eye level. He glanced past me to his friends, already running off. 'Find out for me, would you? Ask around. I'll bring you chocolate. You like chocolate?'

He didn't answer, just twisted out of my grasp and ran after his friends.

That night, Johnson and I sat outside the cookhouse together, drinking coffee. He was gloomy.

'I wouldn't mind,' he kept saying, 'if there was some point to it. But what the hell are we doing here?' He gestured to the neat path running from the cookhouse to the nearest barracks, edged with white-washed stones. Beyond it, a patch of ground had been turned over and rows of vegetables were being cultivated, edged with rows of flowers. That and the ablutions block were the only places that weren't permanently dusty.

Johnson looked disparaging. 'What is it, a vicarage bloody garden? "What did you do in the war, Daddy? I grew sodding carrots."'

I swallowed down a mouthful of coffee. 'I'm worried about Abdul.'

He twisted to look at me. 'That boy? For God's sake, Spencer. What's with that?'

I shrugged. 'Where's he gone? It's been ages. You know what it's like here, as soon as we pitch up, half the town knows about it. He always comes running.'

'Stop jiggling the table, will you? Get a grip.'

I stretched out my legs and tried to keep still.

Johnson narrowed his eyes. 'Leave it. Someone's probably told him not to be so bloody friendly to foreigners. They're not our pals. Hate to break it to you. Most of them are trying to kill us.'

I didn't answer. I couldn't help worrying. Abdul had told me what happened to his father.

I thought about the way the other lads' eyes slid away from mine, the studied blankness in their faces. They knew something, something they couldn't tell.

The thought sat in my stomach like a stone, sickening me: What if he's in trouble and it's because of me?

Another week passed.

There were rumours of a redeployment, up country. Gereshk, maybe. Even Sangin.

Johnson cheered up, a fresh glint in his eye. 'Bandit country,' he said, standing next to me in line for food, grabbing an apple, a bread roll and portion of butter, waiting for bangers and beans and a sloppy dollop of mash. 'Eat up, mate. It's all MREs up there. This'll seem like the Ritz.'

He was gearing up, all bravado. Nerves, too, mixed in with the adrenalin. I sensed it in him. He was dying to see some action and make his folks proud at last. Make himself proud.

I thought about the MREs – Meals Ready to Eat – that laughable description of the stodge in sealed plastic that passed for food in the field. I'd finally get to use the kit I'd been lugging around –mess tin and cutlery and all that. The only use they'd had so far was during training.

I thought back to the heady rush I'd felt when I'd first caught sight of Afghanistan. This alien world of bleak, austere beauty, the jagged mountains, stripped of life. I couldn't find the same thrill now, not any more.

On patrol through the centre of town, round the bazaar, past the newly painted school, my eyes turned to every running boy, checking for Abdul. My mind jumped, seeking him out in crowds.

I was distracted. I knew it, and I wondered if my men knew it too. It was dangerous.

Captain Miles summoned all four lieutenants one evening, after dinner.

'Lid on it, men,' he said, 'but it looks like we're moving on soon. Can't say too much just yet. Make the most of Hotel Lash while you can.'

Johnson craned forward, all schoolboy excitement. 'Can you say where, sir?'

Miles smiled. 'Not yet. Just make sure the lads sort their kit. They've got lazy, sitting around here. Check everything. Anything missing, broken, get to stores. Not a speck of crap on anything, weapons especially. We'll need them in full working order.'

'Yes, sir.' Johnson was like a puppy straining at the leash. 'How long've we got?'

Captain Miles shook his head, as if to say: *Nice try*. 'All in due course.'

On the way back to barracks, the two more-seasoned lieutenants grumbled to each other as they cleared the Afghan dust from their weapons.

'Bloody SA-80s. Dangerous pieces of shit.'

'Can't wait.' The other scowled. 'Cold meatballs in the middle of the bloody desert.'

Johnson piped up cheerily: 'That the food or your crown jewels?'

'Bugger off, Johnson.'

He just laughed. Nothing could dampen his spirits. He was so damn up for an adventure.

CHAPTER FORTY

EDWARD

AFGHANISTAN, 2007

Kit inspection would have to wait.

The next morning, Johnson and I took our units on routine patrol into downtown Lashkar Gah, as we had so many times before. This was different, though. Johnson was joshing everyone, exuberant, buzzing. The men, too. They knew as much and as little as we did but, like Johnson, they were bored of sitting around on their arses and eager to get on with their war.

We parked the Snatches on a dirt road, at the back of a compound, and Johnson and I set off with the men. He was up front, directing them with hand signals as we walked in single file; I took the rear, the radio on my shoulder squawking static.

The bazaar was heaving that day. Johnson led us round the back of the stalls, avoiding the press of the crowd. *Never get hedged in. Keep an escape route.*

The air smelled of batter frying in cheap oil, of fresh bread, of pyramids of oranges, sweating and spoiling in the heat. I hadn't slept much the previous night, revved up about the deployment, and the sharp brightness of the sun didn't help the headache brewing behind my eyes.

Johnson slowed at the corner and took a few of the boys to check something out. I waited, scanning the road. I was just by a carpet shop, owned by an old guy who was sometimes good for a bit of information. He emerged from the dingy interior and stood there, watching what was going on.

The tight stream of people – hunched women in faded *burqas*, men in baggy cotton tunics and Afghan caps – flowed round us. The carpet man spat to the side, then grinned at me. His teeth were stained: black with tobacco and decay, dull red with chewing betel nut. The crowd around stank of stale sweat. Maybe I did too.

Johnson squawked a clear on the radio. I was turning, signalling to the men with me to move on again, when an approaching motorbike slowed, then swerved in, unnaturally close, coming right for me. The carpet man shrank back.

Two lads were astride the bike. The front one, driving, faced forward, his head wrapped in an Afghan cotton scarf. The second, perched behind, twisted in my direction to eyeball me. A defiant stare, a challenge in itself. Then he grinned, a mean smile, goading me. His chin sprouted a young, thin beard and his hands, behind him, clung to the motorbike's metal frame.

They were almost past me when I realised. Squashed hard between them, shorter and only just visible, sat Abdul. He looked pinned there, his arms stretched back as if his hands were tied. Our eyes met, just for a second. He looked terrified.

I spluttered into the radio to say I was in pursuit, motioned to the men to follow and set off at a run down the road after the motorbike. Johnson came on the radio at once, asking what the hell I was doing. I didn't answer. My mind was everywhere. They'd clearly frightened the hell out of Abdul, those thugs. It was a message to me. They were taunting me, asking me what I was going to do about it.

The bike had to switch and swing its way through the shoppers and hawkers, through the chaotic oncoming traffic. It wasn't easy to keep up with it, but I did.

At the next corner, Johnson was waiting. He stuck out an arm to stop me.

'What the…?' He looked furious. 'For God's sake!'

'They got Abdul.' My blood was boiling.

He kept his voice low. 'They're messing with you. Can't you see? Get a grip, can't you?'

I tried to push him away and get past, my eyes still on the motorbike, but he grabbed hold of me.

'Stop.' He put his body in front of mine, in my face, forcing me to look at him. 'Calm down, mate. Nothing to do with us. Got it?'

'What? They're going to beat the crap out of him. He's a kid.'

'He's not your kid.'

'Do what you like.' I spat out the words. 'I'm going after him.'

I don't know what it was. Something broke in me. All those hot, dusty patrols, the boredom laced with tension, the sense always of eyes watching, of lurking danger. Abdul was the only one, the only person in this godforsaken town who'd bothered with me, who'd tried to reach me, person to person. A scrawny fourteen-year-old, who looked about ten. The kind of kid who always got pushed around by bullies. The kind of kid I'd been, years ago.

Well, this time, they'd picked on the wrong one.

I shoved Johnson aside and broke into a run, sweating hard in my uniform, weighed down by body armour and kit.

The bike weaved on. The road out of the market was bounded on the right by a high mud wall, the perimeter of a large compound. On the left, rows of shops, cement and mud-brick boxes selling car parts and groceries and cheap plastic toys from China. The lad on the back of the bike kept twisting back to laugh at me. I couldn't wait to pull him off. I'd bloody lamp him.

Johnson squawked in my ear, telling me to wait, some line about giving me cover. I didn't respond. If I stopped, I'd lose them. I was on my own with this one. It was all I could do to keep them in sight.

The youth on the back lifted his hand and waved at me, still smirking. The bike curved left, disappearing into a narrow street. A few moments later, a sudden series of cracks. Gunshots.

I broke into a run. Johnson started squawking again. I didn't listen. I reached the corner.

The motorbike lay on its side in the street, abandoned, engine cut, wheels still spinning uselessly. No sign of Abdul or the youths. The street was oddly quiet. Deserted.

I cocked my weapon, then headed toward the motorbike, blood pounding in my ears, every sense screaming. Halfway down, across from the bike, a battered wooden door stood ajar. I hesitated beside it, listening. Then my lip curled. That smell. The metallic tang of blood.

'Wait!'

I turned. Johnson, on the corner, came charging towards me. Two of the men appeared behind, taking up positions, weapons ready, to cover us.

Johnson was red in the face from the run. 'For God's sake, Spencer. Don't be a bloody idiot!' He put a hand on my arm. 'What if it's a trap?'

I nodded at the open door. 'I'm going in.'

He swore, shaking his head at me. He'd never seen this side of me. The bloody-minded side.

'All right.' He blew out his cheeks. 'But steady. I've got your back.'

It was dark inside. I went in hard, weapon raised, blinking as my eyes struggled to adjust to the gloom. I sensed something move and wheeled, turning my gun on it. A dark cloud of flies, agitated. Bile rose in my throat.

Abdul's small body was crumpled, deathly still on the dirt floor. He was thickly coated in the blood which still spilled from the gaping bullet wound in his chest. It flowed down his side and pooled along the ground, sticky, congealing and buzzing with flies. His pallid face, eyes sightless, mouth gaping, was half turned towards the doorway, almost as if he were looking for me.

I was too late.

I gagged. A sound erupted behind me. The crack of rapid gunfire bounced off the walls. Deafening. I threw myself to the ground, twisted round, trying to figure it out.

A moment later, more rounds. SA-80s this time. Our boys. The flies rose a second time from Abdul's body.

Shouts blared on the radio, calling for back-up. *Medic. Man down.*

I jumped up and hurled myself to the doorframe, gun pointing out into the street.

Johnson lay on his side in the dust, blood spurting from a ragged wound in his neck, staining the ground. I ran out and pressed the heel of my hand into the hole. Warm blood pumped through my pressing fingers, fountaining, staining my skin red.

One of Johnson's men joined me in the dust, fumbling in his pack for a trauma dressing, tearing off the plastic with shaking hands. Another stood over us, shouting into the radio, giving our location, trying to find the nearest medic.

I grappled with a roll of gauze, securing the dressing as tightly around his neck as I dared. Then, arms shaking with shock, I started CPR.

Even as I pounded, counting a steady beat in my head, another me was detached, watching from above, numb. It saw my own frantic, useless efforts to save Johnson. It saw the crumpled body of the Afghan youth, the one who'd taunted me from the back of the bike, lying a little further down the street, shot by Johnson's men after he'd opened fire. Sun glinted on the muzzle of the gun by his hand.

Johnson's skin was pallid and clammy and already cooling. I just kept pounding. I couldn't stop. He'd been the nearest thing I had here to a mate. He'd been a better soldier than I'd ever be. A smarter one.

He'd finally got what he wanted. He'd seen action. Now he would indeed make his family proud.

But how could I live knowing that if it hadn't been for me, both he and Abdul would still be alive?

CHAPTER FORTY-ONE

LOUISE

Ed lies very still when he's finished telling me his story. His body is rigid with tension.

I lift my head from the cushion of his shoulder and move to sit up. I want to see his face, to try to read his eyes. He just tightens his arms around me and keeps me where I am. His heart hammers, the pulse resonating through his bones.

I ask: 'What happened, after that?'

He shrugged. 'We went up country, just the same. I got through the tour. Quit the army, first chance I got.'

I frown. 'And then what? You came to live here?'

'Not straight away.' He pulls a face. 'Drank too much, for a while. Burned through my cash. A few mates tried to put me straight. They're the ones who got me into painting and decorating.' He shrugs. 'It's not a bad living. Plenty of work.'

I try to imagine him adjusting to the civilian world, after all that. 'Didn't the army give you any… you know, help with adjusting?'

He gives a hollow laugh. 'Shrinks? I had a few sessions. They went through the whole PTSD thing. I didn't buy it, frankly. It wasn't all about poor little me and my poor little feelings, you know? I wasn't the one who died.' He pauses and waits until he's calm again. 'He was a good man, Johnson. A good mate. Say what you like, I know what happened. It was my fault. He tried to tell me. I didn't listen.'

I try again to get him to look me in the eye, but he twists away.

'You did it because you cared about that boy. What was his name? Abdul?'

'I made him a target, don't you see? Johnson was the only man who did the right thing. Warning me. Then covering my back, even though I didn't deserve it. And look where that got him.' He pauses, remembering something. 'His men knew what had happened that day, but they didn't grass on me. I saw the report. They pretended they'd all gone deaf, dumb and blind when they were called in to answer questions. But they knew, all right.'

I wait for a while, running my hand over the smooth, hard muscle of his chest. Finally, I say: 'You were in the middle of a war. Johnson was just unlucky. Very unlucky.'

'Try telling his family that.'

We lie quietly. The fire is cooling, the wood falling away into ash. I'm desperately sad for him. I think of the way he carried this burden for so many years, of the fact it nearly suffocated him. But I feel something else too, something more selfish. Relief. I realise now how anxious I've been about his past. I was worried he'd killed someone with his own hands, beaten up another man or even a girlfriend. How could I have carried on getting closer to him, knowing that? But this, I can understand. This I can forgive. It was poor judgement. Stupid, even. But he wanted to save the boy. And he was in the middle of a war, for heaven's sake. And he wasn't the one who pulled the trigger.

'That's why we've found each other.' I struggle free of his arms at last and prop myself up on my elbow. 'Other people don't get it. The guilt. The fear. But we do. We both do.'

He struggles to look at me. 'It's not the same. You were just in the wrong place at the wrong time. I really was responsible. They both died because of what I did, Johnson and Abdul.'

I shake my head. 'I was responsible too. If I'd only told them I didn't feel well. They'd have been put out, but they'd have found someone else. Or if I'd taken her back upstairs and put her down properly…' I trail off. 'I think you're too hard on yourself. You cared about him.'

He runs a hand through his hair. 'It's late.' He kisses the tip of my nose and starts to move. 'I should call you a taxi. I'll come back with you, just to make sure you get in OK.'

'No.' I lift a hand to pull him down again. 'I want to stay.'

He frowns slightly. 'I'm not sure that's a good idea.'

'Please.'

For a while, he doesn't speak. Blood beats in my ears, waiting. I don't want to leave him.

'Louise. I don't think I can love you. Not the way I want to. I don't think I can love anyone.'

'I know.' I hesitate and try to think how to convince him. I sense all the other times I've thought exactly that, the times I've pulled away from someone who loved me and crawled home to be alone in my own space, to keep myself separate from them. 'But we can try. Both of us. One step at a time.' I hesitate. 'If you want to.'

He has to carry me up the metal staircase to his mezzanine mattress, my broken leg trailing, stiff and useless. Now the fire's died, the flat's rapidly cooling. We wrap our arms around each other under the heavy duvet and hold on tightly, clinging to each other as if our lives depend on it.

CHAPTER FORTY-TWO

'What happened to you?'

My brother-in-law frowns as soon as I open the front door of my flat to him. It's Sunday afternoon and, instructed by Jo, Mike has driven over to pick me up and take me back to their place for tea and cake. I'm hoping he won't realise I've only just made it back to the flat myself.

'What?'

'Are you hung-over?' He sniffs, disapproving. 'You look shattered.'

I shrug that off. 'Come inside a minute, will you? I'm nearly ready.'

He stalks into the lounge, his eyes darting from one surface to another as if he's looking for evidence he can somehow use against me. I have to bite my lip to stop myself saying something acerbic. We do our best to rub along, Mike and I, but it isn't easy.

Uninvited, he pulls up a chair and sits down. 'Actually, I'd like a word.'

'No problem.' I pull an exaggerated grimace as I hobble across to the sofa and perch heavily on the arm.

I can't help myself. Mike and I just bring out the worst in each other. Always have.

His jaw is set. 'First of all, let's be clear about something. My car isn't an S40. Right?'

'I never—' I open my mouth to carry on when he lifts a hand to silence me.

'Second, the Volvo S40 is a very popular car. And dark blue is a very popular colour.'

I roll my eyes. 'Fine. I get it. What's your point?'

He glares at me. 'Mia and I were down at the police station yesterday morning.'

'What? Why? Jo never—'

'Jo doesn't want you to know. She doesn't want to upset you. So I strongly suggest that what I'm about to tell you, you keep to yourself.'

I nod, waiting.

'As I think you're well aware, Mia's been playing detective. Asking about everyone's cars. Make and model, as well as colour. Writing their details down in a notebook if she thinks they might be the one that hit you. Jo's told her to stop, but she's obsessed.'

I squirm, remembering what Jo told me about Mia getting into trouble at school for offering sweets in the playground. 'Well, she's very—'

'Just listen, will you?' His voice is loud. He's taller than I am, and heavier. 'On Friday, she wrote out a long list of "suspects".' He mimes ironic inverted commas round the word with his fingers. 'Most of them, people we know. Then she took the phone into her room while Jo was busy and called emergency services.'

'She didn't!'

'She read them all the names on her list and told the operator to pass them on to the police "working on Auntie Lou's case".'

I swallow hard. 'I'm so sorry. But I don't see—'

'Just listen, would you? The police phoned Jo about it. That's why I took Mia down to see them in person. To apologise.'

I imagine Mia, shoulders hunched, lip trembling, being marched down there by her father.

'She's only—'

'We're lucky they're not taking it further. They could. Wasting police time. Making false accusations.'

'Surely they realised—'

'Jo says I mustn't blame you.' He glowers at me. 'I don't want a long debate about it. I'm merely asking you not to encourage any more of this nonsense. Right? For some reason, Mia listens to you.'

We sit, glaring at each other across the room for a while.

Finally, I decide it's pointless getting into a row. I force myself just to say: 'Fine.'

We drive over to their place in silence.

I stare out of the passenger window and try not to care. I let myself think about Ed instead. I hug close the memory of being with him, just a few hours ago. My body still feels relaxed and languid. I think about eating breakfast in bed together, about the feel of his arms around me, about his lazy smile.

Ed. Edward Spencer. I find myself smiling too and put my hand to my face to hide it. I feel different. Changed. For the first time in decades, I feel a surge of hope for the future.

It's frightening, but exhilarating too.

I stare out at the blur of passing shops and parked cars, at the bus pulling in at the next stop and the ragged crowd of people pressing forward to get on.

I imagine Ed in his strange flat, cooking in his kitchen, listening to his old-fashioned music. Nothing else seems to matter any more. Just him.

He makes me feel alive again. He makes me feel as if it's really possible, after all this time, after all this pain, to love someone wholeheartedly and be loved in return.

And I can make him feel the same. I know I can.

CHAPTER FORTY-THREE

Ed pops around early on Monday to bring me fresh bread for lunch. He kisses me, then puts up the lounge curtains for me, knocks in fresh picture hooks and rehangs the pictures. Finally, he comes back to kiss me again, then decamps with his tools.

He's in demand, apparently. His delayed job is back on and two new clients have called him in the last few days, saying they're happy with his estimates and want him to start as soon as possible.

I potter happily around the flat all morning, drinking coffee, listening to the radio and thinking about him. I think about texting him to see how the new job's going, then decide against it. I don't want to be clingy.

By the evening, time's starting to drag. I'm not expecting to see Ed again for a few days, maybe not until the weekend. A lot's happened. Neither of us has said as much, but I suspect he needs some space and the chance to take this slowly and carefully. But I'm restless without him. I can't settle to anything, rattling round the flat on my own. Maybe Jo's right. Maybe I do need to get back to work.

I compose a careful email to a section editor suggesting a short piece on An Insider's Guide to Greenwich, written from a local's perspective. It might find a slot in the New Year when everything's still quiet.

I've just completed a balletic shower, one leg stuck clear of the water, and managed to wash my hair, when the door buzzer sounds.

My stomach instantly knots, and I smile at myself. There's only one person I want that to be: Ed. Maybe he's decided to head over, even though we haven't planned anything. Maybe he's missing me as much as I'm missing him.

I wrap a towel around my wet hair and poke it into a turban, then put on my dressing gown.

'Hello?'

The image on the camera is blurry as the person below moves back and forth. A man, but I can't make out the features. Dark hair.

I say: 'Who is it, please?'

A man's voice, broken up by the static. 'Lou. It's me.' Ed.

I press the button, then hobble through to my bedroom to pull on some clothes and give my hair a frantic rub with the towel. I'm reaching for a comb when there's a rap at the door.

I peer through the spy hole and my heart sinks. It isn't Ed, after all. It's Toby.

'Come on, Lou.' His voice is pleading. 'Let me in. Please. I just need to talk to you.'

I hesitate. 'I don't want to see you. I told you.'

He puts his mouth to the doorframe. 'I won't stay long, Lou. I need to talk to you.' He pauses, listening. Neither of us move. He's so close, his breathing's audible, slightly laboured, as if he ran up the stairs. 'You owe me that, at least. Don't you?'

This is absurd. How did we get to a situation, after more than two years together, that Toby's standing on the other side of a locked door, begging to be let in?

I open up.

He comes in slowly, carefully keeping his distance from me as he passes and heads for the lounge. I think of the heavy envelope he left at my door and the cuttings inside.

I close the front door and hobble after him. He's standing behind the sofa, waiting, his hands gripping the top as if he's taking his place on the back row of a family portrait. As soon as he sees me, he starts gabbling. It sounds like the incoherent ruins of what might once have been a rehearsed speech.

'Where were you on Saturday?' He peers at me as if he'll be able to read the answer if he looks hard enough. 'I came round on Saturday night. The curtains were open and it was all dark. You weren't here, were you?'

I take time lowering myself to the arm of a chair, resting my leg. 'That's not your business, Toby.' I snatch quick glances at him, feeling myself blush. 'You've got to stop spying on me.'

'Why won't you see me?' His lips contort and for a moment I think he's going to cry. Then his gaze softens as he looks me over. 'I love you, Lou. Don't do this.'

I shake my head. Threatening someone isn't love. Is that what he's here to do, to warn me what he might do now, how he might expose me? 'I'm sorry.' I take a deep breath. 'It's over. That hasn't changed.'

'Something's happened, hasn't it? You look different.' His eyes are on my face, trying to figure me out. 'Is it because I punched that guy? I'd never lay a finger on you. You know that, don't you? I just want to sort it out.'

'There's nothing to sort out, Toby. If you've got something to say, say it. If not, leave.' I struggle back to my feet and make a move towards the door. He doesn't follow. I start thinking. What do I do if he refuses to go? I could call the police, but what exactly am I going to say? I should never have let him in.

Unless he threatens me or hurts me, I'm not sure he's committing an offence. I hesitate, thinking. I could call Ed, but I don't want to make things worse. Toby's jealous enough already.

'Look. I should have told you.' Toby's started gabbling again. 'That's what this is all about, isn't it? I'm sorry. I really, truly am. It was a one-off. A mistake. I was a fool. Tell me what to do. Tell me how I can make it up to you.'

I lean heavily against the back of the chair and turn to stare at him. 'Stop, Toby. Please. I really—'

He raises a hand. 'I'm not asking who told you. I don't need to know. I have my suspicions, but never mind. That's it, isn't it? That's what's upset you?'

I have no idea what he's talking about. He's gazing at me with such an embarrassed, hang-dog look – a little boy who's been caught sneaking chocolate. For a moment, his words hang there between us, in the quietness. Finally, I say: 'Sorry about what, Toby?'

He takes a moment to reply. Maybe he's calculating, wondering if he's got it wrong, after all. 'Come on, Lou. Don't make me spell it out.'

I narrow my eyes. Something falls into place: an unease I've felt around him in the last few months. Around his oh-so-casual mentions of her.

'You slept with Rachel.' Not a question, a fact.

He spreads his hands, fending me off. 'It didn't mean anything! Not to me, anyway. You know what she's like. She wouldn't leave me alone. And you were away all the time.' He sees my expression and adds hastily: 'That's no excuse. I know that. But come on, give me a break. It was just that one time.'

'When?'

'Does it matter?' He looks thrown, anxious. This isn't going the way he'd planned.

'Yes. It matters to me.'

A long silence. His eyes are fixed on his hands, again gripping the back of the sofa. 'August. You were in New York. She asked me to go to a barbecue with her, no big deal.' He trails off. 'I guess I had a bit too much to drink.'

'August.' I close my eyes. All those months ago. I cast my mind back. He met me from the airport when I flew home. A surprise.

Standing there in the arrivals hall with a big bunch of flowers. I should have guessed something was up.

'You're only telling me now because you think I've found out.' I think of the anguish I've felt since I first told him I wanted to break it off. The gnawing guilt. 'I trusted you. I really did.'

He looks crestfallen. 'I told her it could never happen again. Never. I said it was a mistake. That I love you. Ask her yourself if you don't believe me.' He waves a hand towards the windows.

'What? She's here?'

He shrugs. 'She drove me over. She was the one who said I should talk to you about it. She knows how much I want you back.'

I shake my head. She wants to make sure I know what happened. Of course she does. She wants to make sure I don't relent and patch things up. I can just imagine the way she's been popping round to comfort him, offering him a hankie and sympathetic advice.

'It was just that one time,' he says again.

I remember Jo saying she heard a woman's voice when Toby called her. I remember Toby's voice message on my phone and the whisper in the background.

I say: 'That's why she started digging. That's why she put those cuttings together. She wanted to make absolutely sure we didn't patch things up.'

'What do you mean?'

'Oh, please.' I turn away. I can't bear to look at him any more. 'You need to go. Good luck, Toby.'

He looks startled. 'That's it?'

'That's it.'

He frowns. Again, that sudden flash of anger in his eyes. The same as the day he burst into the flat and attacked Ed. The same as the night I cycled over to his place and he turned on me: *You'll regret it.*

Now, he stabs a finger at me. 'You know what? I'm done.'

He storms past me without another word.

A moment later, the front door slams.

CHAPTER FORTY-FOUR

The next day, Tuesday, I imagine Ed driving to his new job. He'll have set out dustsheets, taken down the curtain rails and taped over the window furniture, the same way he did here, all that time ago. I smile to myself, remembering the way I watched him work. The careful, methodical strokes. The old-fashioned music in his ears. It's too late. I'm usually so cautious in a new relationship. Not this time. This time, I'm already sunk.

I shake myself back to life and check my emails. I've got a brief reply from my boss, promising to look over my ideas once she's done the round of morning meetings. That's good. I need distracting. It won't be long now until I can get this stupid plaster cast off and go back to the office.

I make a coffee and sit by the window. It looks fresh out. Weak, wintery sunshine shines along the bare branches. When my phone rings, I dive on it, thinking it's bound to be Ed.

'Louise Taylor? It's Detective Blakely. Can you talk?'

I know her voice by now. I try to hide my disappointment. 'Yes, of course.'

Her voice is clipped. 'I'm pleased to tell you I'm calling with good news.'

'Really?'

'There've been some rapid developments.' Her usual officiousness is underpinned with smugness. 'Late on Sunday, we received a report from the public of a vehicle driving erratically, without lights. It matched the description of the vehicle which we believe hit you. One of my officers tracked down CCTV footage and was able to identify the registration. We were able to make contact with the owner.' A dramatic pause. 'The suspect has confirmed that they were also responsible for the collision on November the twenty-third. And that they failed to stop or subsequently report the accident.'

'They confessed they hit me?'

She carries on. 'He attended the police station this morning to be formally charged with those offences. We made a decision to detain.'

'What does that mean?'

'The suspect will be held in police custody overnight and produced before a magistrate's court tomorrow.'

'Tomorrow?' I'm struggling to catch up. That's fast. I imagine a faceless stranger sitting in a poky cell. Serves them right.

'As they are expected to plead guilty, the magistrate is also likely to pass sentence at tomorrow's hearing.' She pauses. 'You have the opportunity to submit a VPS if you wish. A Victim Personal Statement. This describes what impact the accident has had on you, practically and emotionally. I can send over guidelines.'

I hesitate. 'Does it make much difference?'

'The magistrate will take it into account.' Her voice becomes fainter as if she's turning away from the phone slightly. I imagine her at a desk in a busy, open-plan office, the kind I've seen in cop shows with massive whiteboards bristling with photos and criss-crossed with long, black lines.

'Do I have to read it out in court?'

'You have that option, but it isn't necessary. A written submission can be just as effective, sometimes more so. In that case, you're not required to attend. But of course you may choose to.'

She ends by saying she'll email me the VPS guidelines and the details of the hearing, and rings off.

I sit for a moment, stunned. Just a few days ago, I was still afraid, wondering who hit me and why, if they might try to hurt me again. Now it's over. They've been caught. I'm safe.

I call Ed first, then Jo, leaving them both voicemail messages with the news, then power up my laptop, and start drafting my – what did she call it? – my VPS.

I feel flushed as I start setting it all down, writing about everything from my lost earnings to the physical pain and the anguish. I want to understand how someone could hit me and then leave me in the darkness at the side of the road, not knowing how soon I'd get help. I want to understand them, I really do… and, as well as that, I want justice.

CHAPTER FORTY-FIVE

I wish I hadn't come to court.

It isn't the effort and cost of getting here, although the taxi wasn't cheap. It isn't even the difficulty of doing it all on crutches, standing in a queue forever until I can finally hobble through security, have my bag checked, find out from the desk which courtroom I need to attend for the session and head towards the lifts to take me there. It isn't even how long it takes – the endless waiting for proceedings to start, as if time hangs suspended.

It's the memories. The smell of cheap wood varnish and stale air. The soulless, boxy corridors, set with narrow, reinforced windows, that all look the same. The rows of shabby chairs with stained padded seats and metal arms.

It gives me flashbacks to the coroner's inquest, all those years ago, when I was sixteen. Mrs Collins, her cheeks gaunt, bursting into tears and pressing her face into her husband's chest once she heard the verdict. The sickening twist in my gut as I clutched my mother's hand, knowing they'd been cheated, that justice had not been done, that I deserved to be blamed and to rot in jail.

Once they finally open up the courtroom, I head inside. It's a large, light, rectangular room, carpeted and modern, dominated by a raised section at the far end with a long wooden table and high-backed chairs for the magistrate and other officials. Directly beneath, there's a sunken pit of individual desks and chairs, separated from the rest of the court by a low wooden barrier.

The body of the room is filled with single, long desks, positioned to face the magistrate. To one side, set apart, there's a small, narrow area which is partitioned off by see-through walls. Bulletproof glass, perhaps. There's a single row of seats inside. I imagine the defendant being led inside, flanked by guards.

An usher directs me to one of the flip-down seats along the edge, side on to the magistrate and facing the defendant's enclosure. Two young men and a middle-aged woman take seats together at the back and chat in murmurs as we wait.

I fold my hands in my lap and gaze around at the quiet, almost empty chamber. I feel a sudden surge of anxiety, as if I might unexpectedly be called upon, as if I might myself be guilty. I think of Mrs Collins, broken, burying her face in the lifeless body of her baby.

I shake myself. It's all right. No one expects anything of me. I'm just an observer. I'm glad I did as Detective Blakely suggested and submitted a written statement. No one need know I have anything to do with all this. Not even the defendant.

Officials file into the courtroom and take up positions towards the front. They seem relaxed, speaking in low voices, as if dispensing justice were incidental to their day.

The usher moves to start closing the public doors to the corridor. I look over the other observers. The three, who clearly know each other well, produce notebooks and pens. Journalists, perhaps, or law students.

A movement in the background draws my eye. It looks like a late arrival – a woman, partly obscured by the doors as she pauses out in the corridor to have a word with the usher, trying to slip in before he closes them.

She hesitates at the back of the court and I only see her clearly as she turns to look round.

Tanya! I sit up straighter in my seat and raise my hand to show her where I am. A wash of relief breaks over me. I hadn't realised just how alone I feel here, how vulnerable. Now I've got an ally, after all.

She spots me and manages a nervous smile before she hurries across to join me. She's wearing the same, tired old jacket and flat boots. She reaches down to touch my arm. 'You OK?' she whispers, all concern.

'Kind of.' I must look far from OK. 'Thank you for coming.'

'No problem.' She slips into the seat beside me.

I say, realising: 'I should have called you, shouldn't I? To tell you they'd caught him. I'm so sorry. Really. It happened so—'

She waves away my apology. 'It's fine. I heard they'd made an arrest.'

She looks tired. She cranes forward, gazing round the court as if she's assessing every detail. I imagine how busy she must be, with a husband and maybe children and her victim support work too. She must have made a real effort to find time to come to court for me. I feel a rush of gratitude.

I lean in to ask her a question about the procedure. 'So what do the—'

The usher intones: 'All rise.'

I heave myself to my feet, steadying myself against the flipped-up seat as the room bursts into life. Doors open at either end of the magistrate's bench and a woman in a skirt suit, her hair a neat salt and pepper bob, sweeps in and takes her place in the central chair. Attendants slip into place around her.

She tells us to sit and Tanya reaches out to lower the flip-seat for me so I can drop back into it with less of a struggle. I try to catch her eye to say thank you but she's preoccupied, her eyes still darting around the courtroom. I wonder if she recognises people here. The police officers, perhaps, or the court staff. She must attend a lot of hearings.

As the proceedings start, I gaze around too, trying to take it all in. My eyes stop abruptly on the glassed-off box.

It's no longer empty. A man has appeared in the seat nearest the front of the chamber. He sits with his head bowed, a uniformed officer at his side.

I stare. My breath quickens.

As I look, he raises his head and looks me straight in the face. His face is stony as he registers the sight of me, then tips his chin quickly down again, eyes on his knees.

My heart pounds, the room tilts and for a moment, I think I might fall. I grasp at the empty seat beside me and concentrate on breathing hard. The magistrate's clear, educated voice sounds somewhere far away, issuing instructions.

I can't focus.

I slide my eyes back to the defendant and look again.

There's no question about it. I'm not hallucinating.

It's him. Edward Spencer. Ed.

CHAPTER FORTY-SIX

I don't remember much about the actual hearing. I have little idea how long it took or what was said. It all passes in a haze.

I sit with my eyes fastened on Ed's face, willing him to look across at me again. I want to see some emotion there, something that makes sense to me. Remorse. Guilt. Embarrassment, at least.

He knows I'm there. Of course he does. But he won't even acknowledge me with his eyes. Somewhere, in the background, the process continues. The magistrate's voice runs on, interspersed now and then with the voices of other officials.

At some point, Ed is poked to his feet and confirms his name and address, hears the charges against him read in open court and enters his plea: Guilty.

I can barely focus on what's happening, right in front of me, in the courtroom.

All I can think about is Ed. *It's impossible. It can't be him. It makes no sense.* My hands tremble as doubts flood in. Is he really a painter or was that just an excuse to come to my flat, to befriend me? That whole story about Afghanistan and being haunted by his dark past – was that real or lies? I shake my head.

I sit forward, trying to relieve the sudden cramp in my stomach.

The magistrate passes sentence, directs the court, then gets to her feet and sweeps out of the room.

Ed is helped to his feet by the uniformed officer at his side and led away.

A spell breaks in the courtroom. Around us, the mood shifts and becomes more relaxed. The officials chat in low voices as they gather together their papers and stow them away. Only Tanya and I are stock still, rigid with tension.

I turn to her and manage to say: 'Did you know?'

Her face gives me the answer. It's pinched and pale with shock. She shakes her head and offers her hand and I grasp it. We stay there, clutching each other, unable to move, even as the court starts to disperse.

A young man in a suit pauses as he passes by, heading back to the main doors to the corridor.

'You two OK?'

My body's shaking so much I'm worried he can see.

He looks at my plaster cast and lowers his voice. 'Was it you? The cyclist?'

I nod.

He gives me a sympathetic look. 'Well, I know it doesn't put the clock back but three months custodial isn't bad, especially for a first offence. He's in for a shock.' He pauses, misunderstanding our distress. 'Did you think he'd get longer? Didn't anyone talk to you about tariffs?'

He shrugs and moves on. Already, the room is clearing. The three observers close their notebooks and pull on their coats.

Tanya extracts her hand from mine and twists to face me. 'I had no idea.' Her voice is husky with emotion. 'I don't know what to say. I'm so sorry. Obviously if I'd had the slightest…'

She breaks off and bites her lip. She looks as desolate as I feel. I think of the way she'd vouched for Ed when we first met.

She continues: 'You can report me, if you want to. I'll understand. I should never have…' She stops, breathing heavily. 'We've known him for years.' Her face is so stricken, it's pitiful. She ploughs on, reaching for a professional tone. 'I can send you the link, if you like. For the form. You actually should report me, OK? You really should.'

I imagine what might happen if I do raise a formal complaint against her, the internal investigation she'd face, suspension in the meantime and who knows what bureaucratic punishment for failing to stick to protocol.

I shake my head. 'You weren't to know.' My lips are so dry, I can hardly talk. 'I just can't believe it. It's not possible. Not Ed.'

Around us, the room has emptied. An usher approaches us, discreetly hovering, eager to clear the court.

'I know.' Tanya gets to her feet and reaches for my arm, to help me up. Her hand shakes. 'I can't believe it, either.'

CHAPTER FORTY-SEVEN

Mia sits on the floor of my flat, her arms wrapped around her knees, her shoulders hunched. 'There's no WAY.' Her face is blotchy with tears. 'You've got it all wrong.'

I sit beside her and try to put my hand on her arm, but she wriggles angrily out of reach.

'I'm as shocked as you are,' I say. 'But it really is true, Mia. I was right there, in court. He admitted it. I'm so sorry.'

Jo hovers in the background, making us both dinner. She's left it to me to break the news to Mia. I'm not enjoying it. I'm trying hard to set a good example and act like an adult when really all I want to do is sob and rage as much as Mia.

She wails. 'Why didn't he just tell you the truth? You'd have forgiven him, wouldn't you, if he'd said sorry? Why did he pretend? He LIED to you.' She hesitates, remembering. 'He got that wheelchair and everything. Acting like he was your friend. We flew his kite.'

I pluck a tissue from my sleeve and wipe her eyes. She looks so betrayed.

'I know, Mia.' I sigh. I don't understand it any more than she does. 'It's awful.'

Jo bustles through with our cups of tea and hands Mia a glass of warm milk. She sips it, her face miserable.

They've called in to see me on their way home from school to find out how it went today. I'd expected to have good news – not this. I'd warned Jo by text what had happened, but Mia's still absorbing the shock. She looks pitifully young, in her school uniform, to have her heart broken.

She turns big eyes to her mother. 'I could write to him, Mummy. I could ask him. Pleeease?'

Jo frowns. 'I'm afraid not, Mia. I don't think that's a good idea.' She doesn't look me in the eye.

I can just imagine Mike's face. *Something else to blame me for.*

Jo continues: 'We were all taken in by him, Mia, not just you. He was charming, wasn't he?' I know what she's thinking: *Don't say I didn't warn you.* She has the grace not to say it out loud. 'But what he did was very wrong. He's broken the law and that makes him a criminal.'

'He's not a criminal.' Mia gets to her feet and storms off to my bedroom. 'He's my friend.' She bangs the door behind her.

Jo raises her eyebrows to me. 'Sorry. Seven going on seventeen.'

I hesitate, thinking about Mia. This is all my fault. 'Shall I go after her?'

Jo settles beside me on the sofa. 'Leave her to cool off. She'll be OK.'

'I'm sorry.' I take a deep breath. 'You never trusted him, did you? You were right.'

Jo pulls a face. 'I didn't want to be.'

'Mike'll have something to say about it. About the fact I introduced him to Mia.'

She doesn't answer. We sit quietly for a moment.

'It was such a shock.' I think of the moment I looked up and saw him there, in that stupid glass box. 'I couldn't believe my eyes. He saw me. I know he did. Then he just wouldn't look at me.' I run my hand in front of my face. 'Like a mask.'

Jo frowns. 'I still don't get why he came to work here. You'd think he'd keep his head down.'

'I know.' My mouth trembles on the lip of the cup. 'Maybe he didn't realise who I was until he got here. Why would he?'

Jo looks around the flat, thoughtfully. 'You haven't missed anything, have you?'

'What, you think he was a thief too?'

She shrugs. 'I don't know. I'm just saying.' She hesitates. 'How did you get his name, again?'

'From Tanya. Victim Support.'

She frowns. 'Does she know what's happened?'

'She was with me. In court. She was as shocked as I was.'

'She should be. And embarrassed.'

I blow out my cheeks. 'She said I ought to make a formal complaint against her. For recommending him in the first place.'

She pauses, reading my face. 'Are you going to?'

I shake my head. 'You should have seen her face. Honestly, she was gutted. He's a family friend.' I hesitate, remembering her awkwardness when we first met. 'And I like her. I don't want to drop her in it.'

Jo nods, clearly losing interest in Tanya. 'Well, whatever else, he did a good job with the flat. Have you paid him?'

I shake my head. 'Not yet. He said he'd email me an invoice.'

Jo snorts. 'Doubt he will now. Not where he's gone.' She gets to her feet. 'Think of it as compensation. A free makeover. I'm just sorry I didn't get him to do the café too.'

She takes our empty mugs back into the kitchen and the water runs as she washes them up for me. She comes back and stops to look me over. 'You look really rough, Lou. Are you all right?'

I don't know what to say. *No, I'm really not all right.* But that isn't what people want to hear, not even a sister. She's got her own problems.

'Is it the fact you feel taken for a ride?' she says. 'Or did you really like him?'

I shrug. 'Neither.'

'Don't lie. I know you too well.' She peers closely at my face. 'I don't blame you, either way. He's an attractive bloke. And he seemed so credible, right?'

I nod, miserably.

'Just as well you didn't—' She stops dead and narrows her eyes. 'You didn't, did you? I mean…'

'Stop it, Jo.' That's not a question I feel like answering. She never needs to know about Saturday night. Especially not now. 'I liked him. A lot. I almost can't believe it was really him.'

'Lou, he confessed, for God's sake. He's in prison. What more do you need?' She looks sorry for me. 'He's a con artist. I'm sorry, but he is. You know what Mum used to say: if it's too good to be true…'

'Right.'

Jo gathers up their coats. 'Look, we'd better go. Are you sure you're OK?'

'Fine. I hope Mia's not too upset.'

She sighs. 'She's got to learn. You can't trust everyone.' She pauses, on her way to my bedroom to get Mia. 'She'll get over it.'

I watch her coax her daughter out of my room and into her coat, ready for home.

As Jo heads for the door, Mia twists away from her and darts back to me for a hug. She buries her face in my hair and murmurs a hot-breath whisper: 'I'm sorry, Auntie Lou. I liked him too.'

CHAPTER FORTY-EIGHT

I feel as if I'm the one who's been imprisoned.

The flat never seemed so small. The walls press in on me, suffocating. Every time I look at them, so freshly painted, I think about Ed. I can almost see him, steadily working there, his back strong. Already it seems like a different time.

Everything I remember about him, the conversations we had, the days we chatted as we got to know each other, building trust – now all of that seems horribly recast. All that time, he must have known he was the one who'd hit me.

I thought he was so kind, bringing me coffee in the morning, getting hold of that wheelchair to take me out. What was going on in his mind? Remorse? Fear that he'd be caught? Did he somehow think that if he helped me out, if he distracted me, I'd be less likely to lean on the police to find him?

I hardly eat. I wake feeling sick to the stomach. Betrayed.

For the rest of that week, I force myself to sit at my desk and try to concentrate on researching the Greenwich piece. It's a struggle. When I try to write about the docks, the naval history, the Observatory, I think about looking out over the park with Ed that day, chatting about the view. I remember how light I felt. How happy.

One by one, all our conversations play back in my head. I wonder now if any of it was true. His story about Abdul and Johnson and his time in Afghanistan – was that a lie? Was he even in the army?

I try to imagine where he is, what he's doing at the same moment I'm standing in the kitchen, making myself a cup of tea or settling down again at my desk. I've never been inside a prison. All I see, when I think of him, is an austere Victorian building with metal stairways joining open landings, small cells with hard bunks and little else. I shake my head.

At the weekend, Jo and Mia make a point of distracting me, stopping by as much as they can. No one mentions Mike and what he's had to say about it all. It helps to see them but once the door closes again, the silence presses down on me once more. One or two friends call but I don't pick up. They'll probably think I'm travelling anyway – I usually am. I don't want to speak to anyone. I can't explain what's happened. I just don't know where to start.

I go to bed early but I can't sleep. It's nine days to Christmas and Greenwich is rowdy with office parties. The steady dull thud of music resonates from nearby pubs and bars. Now and then, all through the evening until the small hours, knots of people, young and drunk, shrill and shrieking, spill out down the street, bubbles of giddy noise floating past.

Finally, despairing, I get up and hobble around the flat, too stressed to ignore it all and get to sleep. I pour myself a glass of wine and drink it off, fast and without pleasure. Then I go to the drawer and dig out the envelope of printouts from the back. I stumble to a chair and sit with it in my hands, utterly miserable. *I let him read it. I shared my greatest, most terrible secret. I let him in.*

I turn over the envelope and look at the wobbly writing on the outside. That threatening message: *I know what you did.* I blamed Toby and Rachel. I was determined to believe it was them.

I swallow hard. Maybe this was Ed too, all along. He must have been the one who dug the dirt on me, trying to frighten me so I'd keep away from the police and not keep up pressure on them to search for the man who hit me. To search for him. I trusted him. How could I have been so wrong?

I take out each sheet of paper, one at a time, and tear it into tiny scraps, then bury the lot at the bottom of the recycling where no one will find it.

Back in bed, I can't get comfortable. I think about his flat, dark and empty now, and the mattress bed overlooking it where we slept wrapped around each other. The feel of his skin. The smell of his body.

I wonder if he also thinks about that night, lying in his cell, or if that was just another lie.

I want to forget him. I need to forget him. But I can't, not yet.

CHAPTER FORTY-NINE

'Can you hear me?'

Monday evening, the end of another long, empty day of sitting at my desk, trying to concentrate enough to work.

The voice is a breathy whisper, barely audible on the phone. My heart stops. 'Who is this?'

It comes louder: 'Auntie Lou! It's me, Mia!'

'Are you OK?' Tension falls out of my shoulders. 'Why are you whispering?' I check the time. It's nearly nine o'clock. 'Why aren't you in bed?'

'I am!'

I press the phone to my ear, realising how distorted she sounds. Muffled. 'What's wrong?'

'I'm under the duvet.'

I smile to myself, imagining Mia burrowed down her bed with the phone. It must be a new game.

'Listen,' she says again, her tone dramatic. 'I can't talk long. Mummy might hear.' She pauses for effect. 'I've got news!'

I take another sip of coffee, happy to listen to her. 'What sort of news?'

'There's a girl at school. Katie. She says a family in her street's got a car just like the mystery car. The exact same colour and everything. Katie says maybe they did it.'

I shake my head. 'Mia, you've got to forget that now.' I love this little girl. I don't want her getting into any more trouble with Mike. 'Anyway, it's not a mystery car any more. Remember? The police found it. It's Ed's car. He told them in court that it was him.'

'I know, I know, but wait.' Her voice rises in excitement, then she pauses and softens it again. 'Katie says it's gone. Disappeared, just recently. Maybe it's evidence and they've hidden it? She took a picture of their house with her mum's phone.' She hesitates. 'It cost me one pack of sweets for all that about the car. She wants another pack if I want to see the photo.'

'Mia, you must stop this.' I can just see Jo's face if this gets out at school. It won't only be emails from the teacher, it'll be complaints from this other girl's mother and the unknown family in her street too. And Mike's bound to blow a fuse. 'Katie's very kind. I know you're both trying to help. But these people might be really annoyed if she thought Katie was spying on them and accusing them of something they didn't do.'

'But why's it disappeared?' Mia sounds disappointed with me. 'That's super suspicious!'

'There are lots of reasons their car might not be there. They might have sold it. Or it might be in the garage, getting mended, especially if it's old.' I hesitate. Mia doesn't answer. 'Look, just tell Katie the case has been solved now. She'll understand. I'll buy you some sweets next time I see you, to pay you back. You can take some for Katie too, if your mum says it's OK. Deal?'

The phone crackles. It sounds as if Mia's moving about under the duvet. A moment later, I catch a hurried: 'She's coming!' before the line goes dead.

I sit quietly, drinking my coffee, smiling to myself as I imagine the scene in Mia's bedroom. Jo, popping her head round the door, and Mia, dashing to lie down, then screwing her eyes tightly closed and breathing hard, doing her usual poor job of pretending to be asleep.

She's a good kid. I'll make it up to her over the weekend. Maybe we can invent a different detective game together, one that doesn't involve anyone getting knocked off their bike and doesn't get her into trouble with her mum and dad.

CHAPTER FIFTY

As the week drags on, I go back to researching pieces for next year and trying to fix some travel dates. I need to get back on the road just as soon as I can get this cast off. Somewhere sunny, ideally. Somewhere far away.

On Wednesday night, I force myself to stay up until three in the morning, working up a pitch for Peru until I finally have something worth offering. I crawl to bed feeling glad I've managed to press send, imagining trekking through the jungle to Machu Picchu once I'm healed.

I'm slow to get going the next morning, groggy from lack of sleep.

When the downstairs door buzzes, my first thought is that it's a parcel for someone else. I bring up the image on the security camera. A woman, certainly. But she's pacing back and forth, making the picture even more blurry than usual.

'Hello?'

She stops and turns back to the camera. Her voice isn't distinct enough for me to catch what she says but I know who it is now.

'Jo?' I blink, confused. It's just after half past nine. I'm halfway through a strong coffee, not quite awake. 'Come on up.'

I buzz her in and wait at the open door, staring out at the empty landing, listening to her feet pounding up the stairs. This isn't right. It's Thursday. Jo should be up to her elbows in food in the café kitchen, cooking up a vat of soup of the day and prepping salads and veg and making heaven knows what else. She opens at ten.

As soon as she appears, she hurries straight past me into the flat, then rushes wildly around it, dashing in and out of my bedroom, peering into the bathroom, then coming back into the lounge where I'm now leaning against the back of the sofa. Her hair is dishevelled, her coat flapping open, her phone in her hand.

'Jo? What's going on?'

'You haven't seen her?' She looks into my face as if she's only noticing me for the first time.

'Who?'

'Mia!' She sounds impatient, as if I'm a fool not to know, as if I haven't been paying proper attention.

'Of course not.' I shake my head, frowning now. 'Isn't she at school?'

Jo looks so brittle she could shatter. She paces back and forth, checking her phone every few seconds. It's so unlike her. 'They called me. She's not there.'

I blink, trying to catch up. 'But you walked her in?'

'Of course.' She shakes her head. 'She ran in, as usual, into the playground. I didn't hang around long. She seemed excited. They break up for Christmas this afternoon. She was fine. Playing.' Her cheeks drain of colour as she remembers. A day which seemed so ordinary is suddenly horribly extraordinary. 'Her teachers say they never saw her. They left a message to check everything was OK. I always let them know, you see, if she's off ill.' Her legs seem to buckle and she sits with a bump on the side of the armchair. 'Oh, Lou! What if someone took her, before school even started? Snatched her. I should have waited. I should have watched her go into class with my own eyes.'

'No one does that. Don't be silly. And no one's snatched her.' I'm trying hard to sound confident but my body shakes. I hobble to the sofa and sit down hard too. 'What exactly did they say?'

'The message was just routine. But I phoned them at once, of course, and explained I'd dropped her off. They've talked to her class. Some of the kids remember seeing her before the bell went but no one knows what happened after that.'

I frown. 'Should you call the police?'

'We said we'd give it an hour or two. School's searching, in case she's somewhere there. Hiding, maybe.' She looks vacantly around the lounge again, as if she might have missed something. 'I just thought she might be here. Where else can I look?'

Her face is wretched. I know why she doesn't want to call the police until she really has to. That makes it real. That means Mia is officially a missing child, like the ones you hear about in the news. The ones whose parents make distraught appeals. The ones whose bodies turn up a few days later in a ditch.

Not Mia. Please God, not her.

I take a deep breath. 'Maybe she just slipped out of the playground. Is it possible?'

She shrugs. 'I suppose so. There's a lot of milling about, parents coming and going.' She checks her phone again, desperate. 'But why would she? She loves school. It's the last day of term today. It'll be fun. It makes no sense.'

I take a deep breath. 'It couldn't be anything to do with playing detective again, could it?'

She frowns. 'What do you mean?'

'Well, she just seemed determined to carry on. To clear Ed's name. I told her to drop it.'

Jo stares. 'You mean that business with the car? She stopped all that.'

I swallow hard. 'Don't be angry, but I'm not sure she has.'

I tell her about my phone chat with Mia from under the duvet a couple of nights ago.

Jo gets to her feet again, agitated, and paces around the room like a caged animal. 'She promised! Mike made her. He's going to be livid.'

I can hardly look her in the eye. 'I'm sorry.'

Jo tuts. 'She's so stubborn. She just really took to Ed.'

I can hardly breathe. I introduced Mia to Ed. I encouraged her to like him. I had no idea how manipulative he'd prove to be.

Jo shakes her head. 'I remember going to check on her. I'd no idea she was talking to you, though. She just said she was talking to her babies, you know, all those soft toys she has in bed with her.'

'Maybe it's nothing to do with that, anyway.' I'm sick with guilt. I should have taken it more seriously. I should have texted Jo and told her. Maybe none of this would have happened. 'I told her to forget about it too. I really thought she would.'

Jo focuses on her phone. 'What was the girl's name, did you say? Katie?' She pounds on the keys, searching her contacts, then makes a call.

'Hello? Liz? It's Mia's mum. Have you got a second? So sorry to bother you. I've got a bit of a situation.'

As soon as she starts to speak to Katie's mother, her voice changes. Suddenly she's composed, her personable, professional self, back in control. It's an act, but I'm the only one who knows that. Her hand, gripping the back of a chair, is white-knuckled.

'Of course. No, I understand.'

I can't catch the voice at the other end. Jo bides her time.

'Of course you would! I know. I'd do the same, if I saw Katie on her own.' Jo nods as if the other woman can see her. 'It's just that she mentioned something about a family in your road. It's a game she and Mia have been playing, sort of detectives. Did she? You don't happen to remember which house? Number seventy-two? Right.'

She gestures to me to write that down.

'Well, that's London for you. I know. There are only a few in our street I know to talk to. What's the name of your street again?'

Finally, she rings off. The two of us look down at the scribbled address.

I reach for my keys and crutches and look for my shoes.

'No harm checking,' Jo says. 'Katie's mum's not at home at the moment. She's at work.'

CHAPTER FIFTY-ONE

The taxi driver slows as we count down the numbers.

It's a modern road of small houses, with tiny front gardens and narrow paths, mostly in semi-detached pairs. It's clearly on-street parking only and we have to crane to see through the row of cars and vans.

'That's it! If you could just pull in here?' Jo bends low to see past me through the window. 'That's Katie's house, over there. I've dropped Mia here once or twice for parties. I doubt she'd find it on her own, though.' She points a little further along on the far side. 'Look, that's seventy-two.'

We hesitate, not sure what to do next. I have the sense that Jo wants to keep busy, keep dashing from place to place, to feel she's doing something and put off the phone call to the police which is starting to feel inevitable.

'Shall we watch for a minute?'

The taxi driver clicks the meter on to waiting time and I try not to focus on the steadily mounting bill. Jo leans right over me, her hand on the seat between us, and scrutinises the houses.

Katie's house has a path down the side, leading to the back. From the car, I can just make out a red plastic swing and slide set in the back. It looks as if it fills half the tiny garden. The house itself looks like a classic two-up, two-down, with a bay window. Nineteen-fifties, perhaps. Part of the post-war building boom. The curtains are drawn back, the rooms lifeless.

The house across the road, number seventy-two, looks much the same size and layout. I scan the road outside without success for a dark blue Volvo, then remember Mia's story that it's disappeared, anyway.

Jo unfastens her seatbelt. 'Let's go.'

'And do what?' I turn back to her.

She has a steely look, as if she's planning to kick the door in. 'Talk to them.'

'And ask what, exactly?' I put my hand on her arm, trying to get her to listen. 'Jo, even if they have got a car like Ed's, they've done nothing wrong.'

'You're missing the point.' Jo shrugs me off and reaches for the door handle. 'It's not about what we think, it's about what Mia thinks.'

I climb out of the cab with difficulty and get my crutches into position. As I do, the taxi driver pulls a battered paperback out of the glove compartment and settles down to wait.

The family at number seventy-two clearly don't like gardening. The patch at the front is a dense tangle of evergreen shrubs and bushes, and the path's crazy paving slabs are edged with grass and weeds. The narrow path snaking round towards the back of the house is blocked by a shabby, rusty gate.

Jo's already at the door, her hand raised to the bell. There's a bright Neighbourhood Watch sticker prominently displayed in the window and a No Junk Mail sticker over the letter box. Not exactly welcoming.

I whisper: 'What're you going to say?'

She shrugs. She doesn't look as if she cares. Whatever I say, it clearly won't stop her.

The bell chimes a three-note tune inside. For a moment, there's nothing but the silence as the final chime dies. My heart bangs in my chest. I whisper: 'Maybe we should—'

Jo, ignoring me, presses the bell hard, a second time.

Finally, footsteps sound. Light and quick down the stairs and across the small hallway to the door. It opens.

'Can I help you?'

I gasp.

The woman's expression changes as she sets eyes on me. Her cheeks flush.

Jo looks from her face to mine, thrown. 'You two know each other?'

'Tanya,' I manage to say. 'From Victim Support.'

Tanya blinks. 'How did you find out where I live?'

'I didn't,' I stutter. 'I had no idea—'

Jo interrupts. 'We're looking for my daughter, Mia. She's seven.'

Tanya tears her eyes from mine. 'What do you mean, looking for her?'

Jo says: 'She wasn't in school today. She's friends with a girl in your street. Katie.' She points back in the vague direction of Katie's home. 'Number sixty-seven. I just wondered—'

'I haven't seen anything. Sorry.' She shakes her head, frowning. 'I've been busy in the house. Have you called the police?' She seems to slip into Victim Support mode, even as we watch. 'Look, if you're really worried, lay it on thick when you talk to them. Tell them it's completely out of character, if it is. Stress how young she is. Don't let them tell you to wait twenty-four hours.' She nods sympathetically to Jo. 'Try to stay positive. Most missing children turn up safe and sound. They really do.'

We turn to head back down the path, dejected. My head's still reeling from the shock of seeing her. The crutches chafe under my arms and I stop on the crazy paving to shift their position a little. Jo stops too to steady me.

We're moving off again when she lets out a cry. Colour drains from her face and her eyes widen. I turn to peer in the same direction and see it at once.

The polished toe of a black school shoe is just visible, poking out from under a thick leafy bush. A shoe that looks very much like Mia's.

CHAPTER FIFTY-TWO

When we hold back the leafy branches and force Mia to crawl out of her hiding place, it's hard to tell which of them is more angry, Mia or Jo.

I'm just relieved. *We've found her. She's safe.*

I lean against the gate, suddenly exhausted, playing the spectator as I so often do, while the two of them fight.

'How could you, Mia? Do you have any idea how worried I've been? I thought you'd been kidnapped or murdered. How could you be so selfish?' Jo's shaking with emotion. Fury, but probably relief and embarrassment too. 'You're in so much trouble.'

'What's the big deal?' Mia pouts. 'It's just end of term stuff today. Assemblies and badges and everything.'

I can see she's upset, but trying hard not to admit it. Her eyes glisten.

'*What's the big deal?*' Jo echoes in disbelief. 'What do you think you're doing here, anyway?' As she speaks, she roughly brushes down Mia's duffel coat. It's spattered with fragments of leaf and burr, dark with slime. Her hair's much the same.

Her plastic binoculars, designed for junior bird-watching but rarely used for that, are just visible through the toggle gaps in her coat.

'She was being a detective, weren't you, Mia?' I say. 'Keeping an eye on the house.'

She gives me a grateful look and nods silently.

'From a bush?' Jo isn't relenting. 'How did you get here?'

Mia shrugs. 'I got the bus.'

Jo shakes her head in disbelief. 'But how? How did you even know the way?'

'Katie told me.'

Jo crouches down to her, large adult face to Mia's small, forlorn one. 'You're going straight back to school. You need to say a very big sorry to the teachers. They're all looking for you. Everyone's been very worried.' She straightens up and pulls out her phone. 'I should call them.' She adds in a mutter: 'God knows what your father'll say.'

Mia turns to me, miserable. 'I really need the toilet.'

'Can you hang on?'

She shakes her head.

I lift my eyes to Tanya who's standing in the doorway, watching. She nods at once and opens the door wider to invite us inside. We troop in behind her, stamping mud off our feet on the mat. Tanya points Mia to a door further down, off the hall, then turns back to us. Jo is staring blankly at the stairs, already on the phone to school, telling them Mia's been found. I'm struggling to stay upright on my crutches without leaning against the hall wall.

Tanya pushes open the door to the lounge. 'Have a seat, if you like.' She hesitates. 'I do need to go out soon, though. I'm running a bit late.'

Jo is preoccupied, falling over herself to apologise to whichever member of staff is at the other end of the call and promising to have Mia back in school within the hour.

I limp in ahead of her, sit down in a faded armchair and have a look around, without being too obvious about it. It's a cosy family room, but decidedly shabby. Winter sunshine, streaming in through the bay windows at the front, shows shiny, bald patches in the carpet. There's an old-fashioned gas fire in the fireplace which looks as if it needs updating. A tired artificial Christmas tree stands on a table in the corner, a poor imitation of the real thing. Christmas cards stand in a row along the windowsill.

A series of inexpensive china ornaments – a coy shepherdess, a cat, a plump bird – are interspersed with framed family photographs. They look as faded as everything else. A wedding portrait, showing a beautiful, flushed Tanya as a young bride, barely out of her teens, on the arm of a broad, handsome man, looking just as impossibly young. A snapshot of a newborn baby, swaddled in a blanket, eyes scrunched and closed. A stilted school portrait of a girl of nine or ten in school uniform, her hair in ribboned plaits, her mouth all teeth as she beams.

At the far end, another framed picture of Tanya with the same man, the groom, looking only slightly older. They're bronzed and relaxed, in shorts and T-shirts, standing against the lush green of a tropical landscape, leaning into each other and grinning.

Jo ends her call and joins us, apologising all over again, this time to Tanya. 'I'm so sorry. It's some game she's been playing, thinking she's going round solving crimes. She doesn't know when to stop, sometimes. I'm so embarrassed. Really. She's never done anything like this before.'

'It's partly my fault,' I say. 'She wanted to help me, to find out who knocked me off my bike. You know how upset I've been.'

Tanya looks surprised. 'But we know who it was.'

I hesitate. 'I know,' I say. 'But she liked Ed. She can't quite accept it.'

Jo says: 'Anyway, we're so sorry to—'

'Where's the car?' Mia's voice, high-pitched and clear. She's reappeared in the doorway, back from the downstairs toilet.

Jo twists around. 'Mia!'

Tanya, unruffled, smiles at Mia. 'Actually, we don't own a car.'

Mia frowns. 'Katie says you do.' She takes a tiny notebook from her coat pocket and flips over the pages to check her notes. 'Is it a dark blue Volvo S40?'

'That's enough!' Jo hurries over and takes Mia by the shoulders. 'You're being very rude.' She says again to Tanya: 'I'm so sorry.'

Mia, defiant, calls over her shoulder as she's marched away: 'Where were you on November the twenty-third, the night of the accident?'

Their footsteps sound on the path outside as Jo hurries her back towards the street and our waiting taxi. Jo's voice is too low for me to catch what she's saying but her tone is fierce.

Tanya reaches forward to help me to my feet, then follows me as I cross the hall to the front door. She's so close her breath is warm on the back of my neck.

'I'm so sorry.' I hesitate, wondering if she believes me. 'I had no idea you lived here.'

'That's OK.' She nods after Jo and Mia. 'I'm just glad you found her.' She pauses, watching them thoughtfully as they cross the road, mother and daughter, hand in hand.

As I leave, she adds: 'That's all that matters, really, isn't it? Keeping our kids safe.'

CHAPTER FIFTY-THREE

It's a strange Christmas.

I'm too exhausted to care. It's only Mia's exuberance that galvanises me into making any effort at all. She's been counting down through her advent calendar with increasing hysteria about the prospect of getting presents.

The last Saturday before Christmas, Jo brings Mia over to hang out in the flat with me. Mike's working, marking books and catching up with admin. Jo's planning to run the final shift at the café, then dash around the shops, stocking up on everything from food to presents. Knowing Mike, she'll be buying her own, too. His idea of a thoughtful gift is usually an apron, and she's already got dozens.

It's frosty out. Mia and I make hot chocolate and settle together in the lounge, crunching through biscuits. I'd ordered some packs of coloured, sticky paper online and we cut them laboriously into strips and start making paper chains to decorate the flat.

As we work, Mia chatters in an endless, life-affirming stream about anything and everything. When she gets restless, she sings and dances for me, arms twirling, feet stomping, hips gyrating and I applaud. Her handstands steadily improve and she's started work on a ragged, bunny-hop cartwheel.

We're just finishing a sandwich lunch when the door buzzer sounds. Mia and I look at each other.

It's far too soon for Jo, and I'm not expecting anyone. 'Did your dad say anything about coming for you?'

Mia shakes her head and jumps up, already halfway to the door.

I call after her: 'Check who it is first, won't you? Don't just let them in.'

Her voice drifts through from the hall, excited, as she speaks to someone on the intercom. Whoever it is, she seems to know them.

'Who is it?' I'm slow, still reaching for my crutches and struggling to get up.

She calls back: 'It's a surprise!'

I'm only just hobbling across the lounge when I hear Mia open the front door and squeal. A man's voice, low, says something about Christmas, asking Mia about presents. It takes me a moment to realise who it is.

'Toby? Is that you?'

He appears in the doorway, smiling but uncertain. It's barely two weeks since we last saw each other and that visit ended with him storming out and slamming the door.

'Am I interrupting?' He glances past me, checking out the lounge, as if he's not sure who he'll find here. Still spying, then.

I lean heavily on my crutches and we face off for a moment, weighing each other up.

Mia, oblivious, leaps round him like an excited puppy. 'Did you hear?' She's thrilled to have news to share. 'They caught the man who knocked Auntie Lou off her bike. And it was Ed, all the time! The painter!'

'I did hear.' He nods down at her, then lifts his eyes to me. There's a question there but I'm not sure what it is.

'He's doing time,' Mia says. 'That means he's locked up in prison.'

Toby smiles. He pulls a small packet out of his pocket and hands it to her. 'Would you give that to Auntie Lou, please?'

Mia's eyes widen. 'Are you her boyfriend again?'

I interrupt, embarrassed: 'Toby, what's this? You shouldn't have.'

He shrugs. 'Don't take it the wrong way. It's just' – he hesitates – 'look, I bought it weeks ago. They can't take it back, that's all. It seemed stupid to throw it away.' He gestures to the present. 'You'll see when you open it.'

Mia scampers across to me and helps me to sit down again.

I sit with the package in my lap, not sure what to do. It's expertly wrapped in plush paper with a ribbon.

Mia says: 'Can she open it now? Or does she have to wait til Christmas?'

'I think she should open it now. Don't you?'

Mia nudges me, all eagerness. 'Well, go on!'

It's a silver bracelet, engraved with an elegant *Louise*. Not my style, to be honest, but very kind. I can see why he can't take it back. I lift it out of the box and put in on. 'It's very pretty, Toby. Thank you.'

He hovers awkwardly, keeping close to the door, still in his coat.

'Do you want a coffee?' I point at the table. 'We were just on lunch.'

'That's OK.' He pauses. 'We're on our way out, actually.'

We. He says it self-consciously, knowing I'll notice.

Mia looks up, finally sensing the tension.

Toby says: 'So, Merry Christmas. Best of luck, you know.' He nods emphatically. 'No hard feelings, eh?'

I manage a smile. 'Happy Christmas. And thank you. It's lovely.'

He shrugs. 'Well, I couldn't think what else to do with it.'

Mia sees him out, then dashes across to the window to wait for him to reappear on the path below. I sit quietly, thinking, looking at the way the light glances off the shiny silver surface of the bracelet.

'There he is!' She raps on the window and waves, then presses her nose against the glass. 'He's getting into a car. A big one. I didn't know he had a car.'

I hesitate. He's always hated driving. 'Is it a taxi?'

Mia, still staring down, considers. 'No. He's sitting in the front but on the other side. Someone else is driving. They're just pulling out now. Oh, it's a lady, I think. Yes, a lady's driving.'

Of course, it is. It'll be Rachel. I don't move. Too late and, anyway, I refuse to give him the satisfaction of trying to look.

Mia turns back to me, her eyes wide and confused. 'Auntie Lou?' She's hesitant, wary of how I'll react to what she's about to say. 'I'm not sure what kind of car it is,' she says, quietly, 'but it's dark blue.'

I say at once: 'Stop it, Mia.' We look at each other, both thinking hard. 'You've got to stop this. Seriously. Besides,' I go on, 'it's not a mystery any more. We know who hit me. And he's in prison. Case solved. Right?'

Mia pulls a face. 'That's what Mum says. I just can't quite believe—'

I nod. 'I know. Me neither. But it's true.' I put the bracelet back in its box and set it aside. 'Now, let's finish these decorations, shall we? And about the car... just don't mention it to your mum or dad, OK?'

CHAPTER FIFTY-FOUR

Two days later, it's Christmas Day.

I wake early and lie quietly in the grey morning light, thinking. I feel very small and alone in the bed. I imagine Ed in a bare prison cell with some thuggish cellmate. I wonder if he's awake right now, if he's thinking about me, as I am of him.

I feel different since I met you, he said. *I feel better.*

Did I tell him I understood? That I knew exactly what he was saying because I felt the same way too? He made me feel hopeful. He made me feel I could be someone better, someone else. Was it really all a lie, just an act designed to con me? How could my instincts be so wrong?

By the time I manage to wash and dress and have breakfast, I'm considering calling Jo to cry off coming to lunch, after all. I don't want to spoil their day and, in my current mood, that's exactly what I fear I will do. Then I think of all the work Jo's poured into planning and cooking and imagine Mia's disappointment, and berate myself for being so selfish.

I wonder where Toby is and what he's doing. Maybe he's with Rachel.

Last year, Toby persuaded me to spend Christmas day with his family down in Hampshire. They're kind people and always welcoming but I felt trapped there, committed to three nights in his parents' house in the middle of nowhere, with hearty walks in the drizzle each day and board games or charades in the evening.

It was all made worse by the forced jollity and his big brother's endless jokes about Toby finally finding the right woman and settling down.

I wouldn't rather be there. I really wouldn't. If Rachel's gone with him this year, good luck to her.

As soon as Jo opens the door to me, still in her fluffy dressing gown and slippers, hair sticking out in clumps, I'm glad I came. I'm enveloped in her warm, damp hug, then, a moment later, Mia, the human tornado, barrels into our legs.

'I've got SO MANY presents!' she screams, hair flying everywhere. She grabs my hand and pulls me off to see what Father Christmas has brought in a room still littered with scraps of ripped wrapping paper.

Even Mike manages to look welcoming as he kisses me on the cheek and pours me a glass of Prosecco. Jo seizes the chance to get dressed while Mia, too excited to concentrate on any one thing, rummages through the debris as if the floor were a lucky dip and picks up one present after another to brandish in my face. 'Felt-tip pens. Look, thin and thick ends. FORTY colours! And chocolate coins. And this is a book. And another one, about a lost puppy. And a new nightie, see, it's got a sparkly unicorn on…' She rattles on, flushed and happy, and I wonder how on earth I ever considered being anywhere else right now.

Later, after a large lunch, Mike falls asleep in his chair, his paper hat tipped forward over his eyes. Jo puts a DVD on for Mia. Jo and I sit together at the back of the lounge with coffee, far enough away from the screen to talk in low voices without spoiling the film but on hand in case Mia needs back up for the scary bits.

I nod over at Mike and mouth: 'Is he OK?'

Jo nods and whispers: 'Just tired. What about you?'

'I'm fine.' I shrug. I thought I was doing a good job of acting cheerful. Mia's lying on her stomach in front of the screen, chin resting on her hands. 'Mia seems happy.'

'I should hope so. She gets far too much.' Jo tries to sound stern, but she can't help softening as she gazes across at her daughter. 'Anyway, don't change the subject.' She turns back to me. 'She said Toby came round.'

I shrug. 'He'd had a present for me. A bracelet.'

Her eyebrows shoot up.

'Nothing like that. He had it engraved ages ago, so he had to give it to me. That's all.'

'Were you nice to him?' She sighs. 'Please tell me you were.'

'I was, actually. I offered to make him a coffee, but he couldn't stay.'

I'm not getting into the whole Rachel thing with Jo, not yet. I still haven't told her about his last visit and his confession about last August.

She frowns. 'He's obviously still keen. Maybe it's not too late? Maybe you should think about it.'

I shake my head. 'It's very much over. You're the one who keeps telling me to move on.'

'Not from him!'

'I'm fine. Honestly. I'm glad.' I pull a face. 'I think I knew, deep down, that it was never right.' I point to my plaster cast. 'Two or three weeks and I get this thing off and life'll start getting easier again.'

She frowns, unconvinced, and turns her face back to the screen.

I wonder what happens in prison on Christmas Day. I wonder if they get turkey and Christmas pudding and if it's edible. I wonder if they're allowed to do something out of the ordinary, like see a film, or if it's just another dull day, no different from any other.

Most of all, I wonder how he is. I wonder if he's coping. I wonder if he's thinking of me.

'Do you like the helmet?' Jo leans across, whispering again. 'I can give you the receipt if you want to change it. Mike wasn't sure.'

I reach down and pat the new cycling helmet by my chair, their gift to me. 'Love it,' I say. 'Can't wait to use it.'

Mia laughs out loud at the movie – an unselfconscious bark that makes us both smile, first at her, then at each other. Jo, my kind, exhausted big sister, reaches over and gives my hand a quick squeeze, then our eyes turn back to the film.

CHAPTER FIFTY-FIVE

A week into the new year, a young doctor at the hospital announces that my leg's very much on the mend. He celebrates the new X-ray as if I've won the medical lottery, then cuts me free of the cast.

The skin underneath is white and wrinkled and, for a while, it feels alien to me, as if I'm walking around with someone else's dead leg.

I hand back the crutches and get used to having a stick, then walk with no support at all. A fierce physiotherapist sets me exercises and I do them religiously and slowly develop the muscles again.

Now the compensation has come through, I buy a new bike and start getting ready to ride it.

The offer of a trip comes up. Five days in Prague in March, with a two-night river cruise. I say yes, then fire off emails to a couple of section editors to see who might take it.

I'm concentrating better. I can feel a change, losing myself in work to make up for the lost weeks before Christmas, ready to get out on the road again.

Jo and even Mia seem pleased with me. They think I'm getting over the accident, I can tell. They think I'm recovering from 'all that unpleasantness', which is the nearest Jo comes to mentioning Ed. They think I'm getting back to normal.

I don't disillusion them. But however hard I try not to think about Ed, not to remember, he's always there. He's in my head as I pass the café where we ate pastries, when I buy a takeaway coffee. Every time my phone beeps with a new message, my heart leaps, just for a fraction of a second, with stupid hope. He's there with me every time I put the key in the lock and step into my flat to see the freshly painted walls.

At night, I lie in bed and watch the shadows flicker on the ceiling.

I imagine him in a prison cell, lying on a hard bunk, listening to another man snore. I count off, as I imagine he must, how many weeks he's been there, how many days. How many more still lie ahead.

I think of him so intensely, I can almost sense him thinking of me.

Once or twice, as I drift finally into sleep, I'm startled awake by his voice. A low, gentle tone, whispering my name.

I sit up, wide-eyed, and stare into the empty darkness, struggling to understand how I can feel so close to him when he's far away; when he's, anyway, not the man I thought I knew.

CHAPTER FIFTY-SIX

It's Mia who helps me back into the saddle.

I've been cautious about trying out my new bike. My leg's still stiff. The muscles aren't back to normal and I don't want to rush it. But Mia, never one to accept an excuse, doesn't stop nagging me. As soon as we hit a patch of chill, dry weather at the end of January, she's on the phone, ordering me to meet them in the park for a maiden ride on my new bike.

'You've got to try it out!' she keeps saying. 'And your helmet! Aren't you excited?'

Mike's got work to do so Jo comes along and settles on a bench with her phone as if she were an old-fashioned nanny, leaving Mia to take charge of me.

'You can do it, Auntie Lou!' Mia sits astride her own bike, helmet half obscuring her face, and peers at me as I climb on. 'Don't be scared!'

For a moment, some bodily memory of the accident makes my legs shake. Then my feet settle onto the pedals and remember what to do and I start to press forward, feeling the old muscles engage again, enjoying the pleasure of moving.

Mia cheers and pushes off on her own bike to pursue me. We do a few circuits of the park, slowly at first, then speeding up as I gain confidence. As I cycle, my face chilled by the wind, it seems a further incremental move forward, as if another filament connecting me to the past, to Ed, has broken and fallen away, and that's both a blessing and a sadness.

Afterwards, when Mia and Jo finally say goodbye and leave me to go home, I cycle slowly down through Greenwich towards the river, then pause, leaning against the rail which edges the waterfront, to look out across the grey churn.

An icy breeze blows in from the Thames and whips my cheeks, my nose, the tips of my ears under my helmet. It freshens the stale smells of fried onions and coffee from the open-air kiosks behind me. Weak sunshine ribbons across the surface of the water, broken here and there by bobbing gulls and Canada geese.

Families, their small children trussed up in padded coats and woolly hats, saunter to and fro along the paved riverside path, off to visit the Cutty Sark or the museum or just strolling after lunch at one of the dockside restaurants.

I turn and start to cycle on, moving slowly past the pub on the corner, then the cafés and shops beyond. My eyes wash over the pedestrians. The families; the couples, gloved hand in gloved hand; the youngsters out with friends.

Then I pause.

A messy head of blonde hair catches my eye. A slight figure, wearing a dark, wraparound coat, is sauntering along the pavement towards me. She hasn't seen me. Her head is turned as she listens to the much younger woman at her side.

It's Tanya. Her face is relaxed, the cold giving her cheeks a natural blush. Her lips are slightly parted as if she's about to reply or perhaps laugh.

My eyes shift to her companion. She's a teenager, sixteen or seventeen, perhaps. A younger, funkier version of Tanya. She has the same neat features, the same sweep of natural blonde hair, but hers is streaked with blue and purple. Her face is transformed by dramatic, gothic make-up, unnaturally pale cheeks making a stark contrast with lips and eyes so dark, they seem almost black. A black ring glints in her nose.

As I look, watching them weave their way together through the crowd, then turn at the corner and disappear, the hairs along the back of my neck prick. My breathing quickens.

I cycle slowly off, preoccupied, shaken without knowing why. My body seems gripped by some instant knowledge that my mind can't yet reach. I shake my head, cycling slowly now, my legs falling into a steady rhythm as my thoughts swirl.

I think of the school photograph on Tanya's mantelpiece of the smiling young girl with plaits. It must date back six or seven years, a wistful memory of her daughter when she was still a child and, by the look of it, a lot easier to parent.

I cycle back to the flat, frowning with concentration, trying to make sense of something, something that's bothering me.

Inside, I let the door fall closed behind me and start searching, throwing cards and papers aside as I look through piles of papers, my wallet, my desk.

I find it at last. The Victim Support business card Tanya gave me as she left at the end of that first visit, the one I stuffed into the back of a drawer and never bothered to retrieve.

I stare down at it, my hand suddenly trembling, my throat so tight I can scarcely breathe.

CHAPTER FIFTY-SEVEN

The prison looks exactly as I imagined: grim, dark and forbidding.

Two squat stone towers stand on either side of a vast wooden door, set in an arch. The door is the only feature that seems even twentieth century. Everything else looks as if it hasn't been upgraded – or cleaned – since the Victorians built it.

It takes me twenty minutes of searching to find the visitors' entrance. There's already a ragged knot of people, mostly women, gathered there: middle-aged women, dressed for the cold in thick coats, woolly hats and boots; younger women in sweatpants, their hair piled up on their heads, eyes heavy with mascara and eye shadow. They stand with their shoulders hunched, hands thrust deep in pockets or raising cigarettes to their lips.

Some stand in clusters, chatting in low voices. Most, like me, are here alone. There's a hardness about their expressions. No one's here for fun. One or two glance at me as I join them, registering the fact I'm a new face, that I'm different from most of them, that little bit better educated, more advantaged. They check out my shiny new bike. Nothing is said but I sense they're calculating what it's worth – more, I'm guessing, than most of them can afford for food each month. I keep my head down, keep my distance and wait.

Eventually, a scraping of metal signals movement. A guard unlocks the side door and checks off names on a clipboard list as the women press forward, jostling as they shove their way into line. The guard looks over the bike, then points me to a bike stand round the side of the building.

'Hope you've got a good lock, love.'

The stand is rusting. There's only one other bike chained there, its frame chipped and weathered, its front wheel gone. The street stinks of sour drains.

Inside the prison, the officers point me through the procedures, recognising me for the newbie I am. I fumble through my purse for change and work out how to stow my bag in a locker, then follow the other women into a shabby waiting area.

The chairs are institutional, with curved metal backs and seats. I grip the cool metal arms and try not to look at the other women, gathered in small groups, hunched forward, speaking in low voices.

An officer does the rounds, matching our IDs to our pinched faces. He does a second name check against printed lists. A large industrial clock, high on the wall, ticks through the minutes.

We wait.

My heart thuds. My knuckles whiten on the chair arms. There've been days I've almost forgotten what Ed looks like. I've wondered if I'll even recognise him. I wonder if it's right, if he's really agreed to see me. I wonder if he's changed.

Eventually, they beckon us to move forward and we file, one by one, through an airlock, then a metal detector arch. Finally, a cheery female officer pats me down with hard hands, checking I'm not concealing anything I shouldn't take in.

The visiting room looms ahead and we queue up at the entrance. From the little I can see, peering around the women ahead of me, it reminds me of an airport lounge. It has the same sterility, the same feeling of stale air and anonymity.

My turn. The guard checks me off yet another list, then nods me in. 'Table seventeen. On the right.'

For a moment, I'm afraid to move. I hover on the threshold, looking around. The walls are freshly painted in neutral colours

– beige and cream. Stark strip lights run overhead. A single leafy pot plant rises in one corner.

Then I see Ed. I know him at once – how could I ever have imagined anything else? His gaze hits mine then falls to his hands, clenched and resting lightly on the edge of the table. His jaw is hard.

I thought I was prepared. I'm not. The shock of seeing him takes my breath away. For a second, I feel disorientated, almost dizzy, then the room comes crashing in again, with its smells of floor polish and cheap disinfectant. I can't speak. I'm not sure what might happen if I unclamp my teeth and try to say something, if I'll laugh or cry.

I manage to cross the room and pull out the chair opposite his, lower myself into it. I say, stupidly: 'Hello.'

He shifts his weight and sits back in his seat, one leg crossed at the knee, holding himself apart from me. His cheeks seem more hollowed than I remember. Lack of sleep, perhaps. Or poor food.

He doesn't reply at first. Finally, he says quietly, without looking at me: 'You shouldn't have come.'

I want to reach out and touch him, to take his hand, but I know it's not allowed. I'm conscious of all the couples around the hall, meeting each other in tense huddles, their heads together in their own conversations. Guards stand along the walls, scanning us all, watching.

I sit forward and lower my voice, willing him to move closer. 'Ed. I needed to see you. I need you to tell me the truth. Please.'

He keeps his eyes low. His face is closed and sad, as if to say: *Come on, now, you know I can't explain, however much I'd like to.*

I steady my breath. 'I can't believe you did it.' I keep my voice to a whisper. 'But why are you here? Why did you plead guilty? Ed, I want to trust you. I really do. But I need you to trust me too. I need to know.'

He doesn't move.

I say, as calmly as I can: 'If it really was you, it means everything that happened between us was a sham. You must have realised from the start who I was, from the moment you saw me and heard me talk about the accident. Or did you know even before that? Was that why you came in the first place?' I swallow. 'Did you just pretend? You pretended to be kind because you felt guilty? Or did you take some perverse pleasure from seeing what you'd done to me?' I hesitate, thinking about being with him in his flat and the way he held me. 'I just can't quite believe it. If that's true, I need to hear it from you. Look me right in the eyes and tell me that's how it was. And I'll go away and leave you alone.'

A long pause.

Finally, he says softly: 'I can't do this.' He lifts a hand and rakes it through his hair. 'I'm sorry. You should go.'

My lip crumples and for a moment, I think I'm going to sob. I take a deep breath. 'Not yet.' I sound bolder than I feel. 'I've come a long way for this. I need some answers, Ed. You owe me that, at least.' I pause, finding the words. 'You've known Tanya a long time, haven't you? I know who she is, Ed. Tanya Johnson. She's your friend Adam Johnson's wife, isn't she?' I think of the unkempt garden where Mia hid in the bushes, the rusting side-gate and shabby lounge carpet, all ripe for replacement. A home without much spare cash. 'Was it true, what you told me? Did he really die in Afghanistan?'

A long pause. I fix my eyes on his face, trying to read him.

Eventually, he nods.

I only realise I'm holding my breath when it comes rushing out.

'So that's it, is it? That's why you came to live nearby when you left the army. To keep an eye on his family. Look out for them.' I pause. 'Or is Tanya more to you than that?'

He raises his eyes briefly to mine. 'It's not like that. I've just tried to help, that's all. It's not been easy for her, on her own. She's got the pension and she's always worked, but Victim Support doesn't pay much. She's struggled. Her daughter, too, growing up without a dad.'

I nod. I believe him. I imagine him going around at weekends, fixing things around the house, redecorating when she needs it. Paying back, year after year.

'Did she have your car?'

I lose him again at once, his eyes back on his knees.

'You've got the van for work, haven't you?' I carry on, insistent. 'You could manage with that. Is that what happened, Ed? You lent her your car. Because you felt sorry for her. Because she's a widow and you think that's your fault.'

He says at once: 'It is my fault.'

I nod. 'So you lent her your car just for a while, until she'd saved up enough to get her own. Only cars are expensive and she never gave yours back, did she? You just carried on paying the insurance, the road tax, never complaining about it, never asking for the money because you were happy to help. Happy there was something you could do to chip away at this enormous, life-long debt. Right?'

He shifts his weight awkwardly but doesn't answer.

I lean forward, getting as close to him across the table as I dare. 'Right, Ed?'

He says quietly: 'I can't talk about it. You know I can't.'

I'm right. I know I am. His unease says it all. My pulse quickens.

'Tell me about the accident, Ed. Go on. Which stretch of road were we on when you hit me?'

He shrugs. 'I don't remember.'

'But you must remember. Were we cresting the hill or out on the heath? There was a car coming towards us, on full beam. Was that what blinded you, what made it impossible to see me, until it was too late?'

His tongue snakes out and licks dry lips. 'Maybe.'

I shake my head. 'You're such a bad liar. There was no other car.' I take a deep breath. 'It was Tanya driving, wasn't it? That's what all this is about. Poor Tanya. She was driving and she got you to take the rap for her. How could you say no? She'd struggle to keep her job with a criminal record, wouldn't she? How embarrassing. The Victim Support star suddenly on the wrong side of the law.'

He shakes his head. 'Stop it, Lou.' He doesn't sound angry, just desperately sad. 'Please.'

I can't stop. I'm only just getting started. 'She knew exactly what she'd done. She wanted to cover her tracks. So she kept an eye out for the police referral when it came in for her team at Victim Support, she made sure she was the one who came to see me. I should have realised. Odd, after all, for a team leader, one of the few paid members of staff, to bother with house calls for a pretty trivial crime.'

He opens his mouth to speak, and I cut him off.

'It must have been a gift when I said something about getting a painter in. No wonder she jumped at the chance to give me your details. Why was that, Ed? Did she ask you to spy on me? Did she want to find out what I'd seen, what I knew and make sure I didn't press the police too hard? Is that why you made such an effort – sharing lunch, getting the wheelchair – to distract me?'

'It wasn't like that.' He twists in his seat. 'I'm not doing this.'

I blurt out 'Yes, you are. You owe me that much.'

He blinks, then says slowly: 'You've got it wrong. Tanya was working that evening. Training. Helping to run a course for new volunteers. It was nothing to do with her.'

For the first time, I'm taken aback. I say flatly: 'I don't believe you.'

He shrugs. 'Check for yourself. She was there all evening. Never left the room. There were plenty of witnesses, including a police officer.'

I hesitate, my mind whirling. I'm so focused on Tanya, so determined it was her.

'Then who—?'

Something comes to me, something that's always bothered me. The darkness when the car hit me. The fact that someone was driving in the dark and rain across the open heath with nothing more than weak sidelights. I'd put it down to stealth. Someone who was frightened of being seen. But what if it wasn't that? What if it was something else?

CHAPTER FIFTY-EIGHT

'The daughter.'

Ed winces, just the slightest movement, before he tries to hide it with a fake cough, hand to his face.

I think of the teenager's gothic make-up, the rebellious nose-stud, the slight swagger as she held forth to her mother, picking her way through the crowd.

'It was her. Wasn't it?'

A teenager, sneaking out in her mum's car without permission. Showing off to her friends. Trying to look cool.

'I bet she hasn't even passed her test, has she?'

A teenager who didn't quite know her way around the dashboard, who wasn't sure which lights were which and what she needed on a black, rainy night when she suddenly hit a stretch of road without streetlights, away from the brightly lit shops and restaurants.

'She's the one you're protecting. What's her name? Tell me that, at least.'

He says quietly: 'Ellie.'

I stare. A memory slides into my mind of the name that flashed up on his phone in the café, his hunched shoulders as he paced outside, returning her call. *Ellie.* I'd feared she was a girlfriend.

'Ellie. A young kid with her life ahead of her. That's why you're doing this.'

Ed raises his eyes and looks right at me. 'That's enough.'

'But Ed, you can't.'

He says quietly: 'Don't ever suggest again that I didn't tell the truth. That's perverting the course of justice. That's perjury. That way, we all end up in jail.'

I bite my lip. I look around at the cheap fixtures, the reinforced glass in the windows, the hostile faces of the watching guards. 'But how can you? How can you stand it?'

He shifts his weight to face me properly, square across the table, so close our knees touch.

'You know the only tough part about all of this?'

I can't answer, transfixed by his eyes.

'That day in court. Seeing the hurt in your face when you saw me in the dock.' His gaze doesn't falter. 'I never lied to you. I promise. I meant every word I said. About us. About how I felt about you. I had no idea what had happened when I came to your flat to meet you. None. I swear it. Can you believe me?'

I shudder. This is a man who must have lied to the police, who lied in court. But, despite everything I've learned, I do trust him. I nod.

He lets out a sigh. 'Maybe Tanya did have some ulterior motive in sending me round to you. I've thought that too. I don't know. But I never spied on you. I wouldn't do that. None of this has anything to do with the way I feel about you. That part was true.'

A guard, with a voice like a sergeant major, bellows out a warning: 'Last few minutes. Time to finish up.'

I want to reach out and grasp his hand. 'But it's not right. You shouldn't be in here.'

He shakes his head, weary. 'They should have locked me up a long time ago for what I did. I've got off lightly.'

I say in a rush: 'I'll come and visit every week. I'll write to you. Tell me what you need. And you'll be out soon. I'll wait for you, Ed. I'll be here.'

His forehead creases in a frown. He leans in so close that his breath is warm on my face. 'That's not going to happen.'

'But why—'

He raises a hand and interrupts me. 'Listen. We haven't got much time. I once said that knowing you makes me feel as if I can really change things. Do you remember? I don't know what it is with the two of us, this connection. But it's real. And in here, inside, despite everything, it's stronger than ever.' He speaks hurriedly, trying to get the words out before he's forced to leave. 'It's not romance. I don't mean that. And I'm not asking anything of you. How could I? It's something else.' He falters, groping for the words. 'It's a different kind of love. Transforming. Healing. And there's such power in it. It's the sort of love that answers prayers. It makes me feel that somehow, I don't know how, I really can change things. I really can live the life I wanted to live.'

The guard is making his rounds, breaking up the couples, calling time.

Ed scrapes back his chair. 'Whatever it is, thank you, Louise. You've changed me more than you will ever know. I'm sorry it has to be like this. I truly am.'

'Ed!' I try to reach for him, to grasp his hand, but he's already getting to his feet, drawing himself away from me.

As he's about to leave, he turns back and says: 'Go and find that woman. Mrs Collins. You must, Louise. Please.'

'But—' Even as I speak, he's joining the reluctant flow of prisoners, heading towards the heavy far door. His shoulders are broad, but his head is slightly bowed.

I sit very still, hardly able to breathe, and watch as the guards order them into line, then count them off the list. Finally, the door opens and they shuffle through, back into the body of the prison.

In all that time, Ed doesn't attempt to turn and look back.

CHAPTER FIFTY-NINE

I leave the prison in a daze and go to retrieve my bike.

I set off, trying to steady myself, and pour myself into pedalling. *Pump, pump. Left, right.* Mind and body straining to keep up.

The sunlight is thin, fading now, giving way to dusk.

My hands tremble on the handlebars. My leg, still weak, struggles with every incline. Ed is there with me, in my head, just as he always has been. He's a decent man. I know him. I understand now. He's sacrificed himself to give his best mate's daughter a second chance, a chance to straighten herself out. After all, it's all he's longed for: a chance to set right the biggest mistake of his life, the debt he's been paying back to Johnson's bereaved family ever since.

Around me, the traffic thickens. It's getting dark. Cars hover behind me, then suddenly overtake in a sweep of light, nudging me into the kerb as they flash past, too close.

My eyes blur as I cycle, buffeted by the wind. It was so little time together. There's so much I still need to say. I didn't even tell him I understood when he tried to explain about the connection between us. The power in it. What did he call it? *The sort of love that answers prayers.*

I'll go again, week after week, to see him. To tell him I'm here. That I'll still be here when he comes out. It's not that long. My stomach clenches as I remember his frown when I told him that. How could that not be what he wants?

Jo will be angry when she finds out I want to be with him. She just sees him as a criminal. She always will. Mia will be confused. But how much can I explain? I can't risk telling them everything. Ed's right. If the truth gets out, it'll make things far worse. Both he and Tanya will end up in jail, and who knows what they'll do about Ellie.

I concentrate on cycling. My leg's aching. It's still not used to so much exercise. I'm tiring but I'm nearly home. I imagine a hot shower, a good dinner.

The blackness intensifies as I pull painfully up the hill out of Blackheath and out onto the emptiness of the open heath. I lower my head and pedal as hard as I can. As the landscape expands, the wind blows up in a moment, snatching my breath and almost knocking me sideways off the road. There's a hint of rain in it.

I steady myself and battle on, piston knees, hands knuckle-white on the handlebars.

My focus on Ed is so intense I can almost feel him.

A car skirts around me, overtaking too fast in the darkness. I wobble, then steady myself.

All I hear is the wind, clipping my helmet, and my own breathing, blood pumping hard in my ears, beating time with my legs. I press myself forward. I've almost reached the site of the accident. My cheeks and chin are numb with cold.

One moment, I'm powering across the open expanse of heath, inside the wind and the rhythm of my own hard breathing; the next moment, the bike is skidding from under me, the ground rising.

I'm flying, soaring through open air, tossed, arms flailing in emptiness. I fall through darkness, blinded. Time stops. Everything hangs. Silent. Suspended.

Then the bubble bursts and I crash. My body, limp, pounds into cold metal, skids sideways, hits the ground with such force I can't breathe.

Bright lights pulse in my head. Pain explodes everywhere, a firework burst, shooting white sparks through black. Then nothing.

CHAPTER SIXTY

Someone's there.

Men with deep voices call loudly to me, asking if I can hear. Firm hands check me over, then lift me, swinging my weight.

I can't move.

Ed. His smell. His skin, the scent of his soap. My insides tighten.

I can't force my eyes open but inside, I'm smiling. I want to open my arms to him, to tell him how much I love him. I want to hold him and ask so many questions. *Why're you here? Have they let you out early? Were you coming to find me?*

His voice sounds inside my head. *I'm sorry, Louise. So sorry. But it's because of you, you know. All of this. Because of you and me.*

The skin on my arm feels a sudden chill, then, my arm tightly held, the sharpness of a needle.

I sink back and again disappear.

Something wet and cold on my lips. Parched tongue. It's a supreme effort to prise open my eyes.

The light is hard and bright and hurts. I blink.

The feathery pressure lifts from my lips. 'Lou?'

A rustle of clothes. Jo, my sister, looms and fills my vision.

'Lou? It's me. Jo. Can you hear me?'

I try to nod. My head is the weight of a cannonball. The slightest movement sends shoots of white pain through my neck and shoulders. I sink back and blink up at her. Her eyes are full of worry. 'You OK? You came off your bike.'

I'm lost, confused. I look past her at the dappled cream panels of the ceiling. A hospital.

A pink foam square appears and she runs it along my lips. Ice cold and wet, trickling water into my mouth.

I've been here before. All this, it's happened before. I manage to say: 'My leg.'

She looks puzzled. 'Your legs are fine, Lou. You're just concussed. Well, probably bruised, too.'

I try to remember. I was cycling home. I'd seen Ed. I found out the truth.

I whisper: 'It wasn't Ed. It really wasn't.'

Jo frowns. 'What wasn't who?'

'Ed didn't hit me.'

She narrows her eyes. 'No one hit you, lovely. The car behind saw everything. You just skidded. You must've hit a patch of oil or something. It's no one's fault.'

She strokes my forehead and I close my eyes and lie very still.

After a while, the mouse-squeak sounds of hurrying soft shoes on a polished floor.

A loud, clear voice. 'How are you feeling, Louise?'

I open my eyes. A nurse leans over me, her hair pinned back severely. She peers for a moment into my face and asks me a couple of questions. Finally, she says: 'The doctor's happy for you to go home now and get some rest. Your sister can take you back now, OK? Do you think you can stand for me?'

She sits me up and lifts my legs round. I sit there, swaying, taking in the tiny examination room, filled by the three of us. A large interactive screen on the wall changes picture and a photograph of a prowling cheetah melts into the emerging outlines of a swimming turtle.

'We'll get a taxi,' Jo says. 'Ready?'

She laces her arm under my shoulders and helps me stand. I'm dizzy but my legs are sound, both of them, bearing my weight with equal strength.

Jo and the nurse guide me to the door and out into the sterile corridor.

'You gave me a fright,' Jo says. 'Good job you were wearing your helmet.' She hesitates. 'Your bike looks fine, by the way. We'll have to see if we can get it in the back with us.'

She thanks the nurse and steers me along the corridor and through heavy double doors towards the entrance to Accident and Emergency and the taxi rank beyond.

'I haven't told Toby,' she says. 'Didn't want to frighten him. I thought you'd better do that.'

I shake my head. 'Toby? That's over, Jo. You know it is.'

'You've had another fight?' She pulls a face. 'I didn't know, actually. I can't keep up with you two.' She presses me forward. 'Anyway, maybe talk to him later when you've had some sleep.'

I don't answer. We make our way slowly through the reception area, past rows of hard plastic seats. About a dozen people, clustered in small family groups, are slumped here and there through the waiting area, silent and motionless, with the air of the eternally abandoned.

Outside, it's pitch dark, rain lashing the windows.

I glance across at the reception staff, screened from the public in a plastic box. Then I stop dead and stare.

Jo says: 'What?'

My eyes are fixed on the bold corporate calendar on the wall behind the receptionist. 'Why's it still on November?'

CHAPTER SIXTY-ONE

Jo takes me home.

'You should get some sleep.'

I sit heavily on the sofa while she bustles around the flat, putting the kettle on and complaining about how little I've got in the fridge. She finds some stale cheese in the back, barely enough to make me a sandwich.

'How're you feeling? Headache? Dizzy? Any sudden changes, anything at all, you call me, OK? Doesn't matter how late it is.'

I'm not really listening. My eyes are fixed on the shabby lounge walls, with their familiar stains. They're just as they were in November. Just as they were, before Ed appeared at my door and worked his magic.

'What happened?'

Jo says carefully, as if to a child. 'You came off your bike. Don't you remember?'

'Not that.' I shake my head, frustrated. 'What happened to the walls? He painted them. Ed. Remember?' I pull my eyes from the faded paintwork and look at Jo.

She's frowning, concerned.

I think about Ed. His broad back and strong arms as he worked. His smile. His shyness when he first called to see if he could come and see me, as a friend.

'You need to rest.' Jo doesn't want to argue. I know my sister. But it's clear too that she doesn't believe me. 'Let's talk about it tomorrow.'

She bustles round me, tidying, organising. I sit very still, eyes on the walls, trying to make sense of what's happening to me.

'You OK?' Jo stops rushing for a moment and looks down at me. 'You're very quiet.'

'Just a bit dizzy.' I hesitate, wondering how much more to say. I think of our snatched conversation as we left the hospital, about the calendar. 'Jo, tell me again. What's the date today?'

'November the twenty-third.' She misreads my expression. 'I know. Soon be Christmas. Where did the year go?' She bustles back to the kitchen to make me a cup of tea. I follow the familiar sounds of the kettle steaming and popping, pouring water, the clink of as teaspoon in a mug. The noises seem muffled, drifting over to me through a thick fog.

November the twenty-third? That was the date of my first accident, when Ellie hit me. When I broke my leg. I look down now at my legs now, trembling but whole. It isn't November. It's February.

So much has happened in the last three months. I think about hobbling on my crutches as my leg slowly healed. About Tanya and Ellie and Mia going missing. About Ed.

Jo carries in the cup of tea and sets it down on the coffee table. 'You need help with anything else?' Already, she's looking at her watch. 'I'd stay, Lou, but I left Mia with Mike and he's got to be somewhere. Some parents' thing at school.'

I try to get her to slow down, to look at me and listen. 'Jo. Just wait a minute. We already had Christmas.' I try to keep my voice calm and steady to show her I'm not hallucinating. 'I came to your place. Remember?'

She pauses, her forehead creased.

I struggle to remember. 'You got Mia new colouring pens and chocolate coins and a book about some puppy going missing. It was blue, with a brown and white puppy sketched on the front. Massive eyes.'

She shakes her head, at a loss.

'And you got her a nightie, remember?' I burble on. 'Sort of brushed cotton. Pink. It had a unicorn on the front. She loved it.'

She just stares.

'And you got me a new bike helmet. Dark blue with a red flash. Yes?'

'All great ideas.' She swallows. 'I guess you will need a new helmet.'

For a moment, we lock eyes. Neither of us speaks. Finally, she breaks away. 'You said you're feeling a bit dizzy. Do you think you could get to bed?'

'I'm fine,' I lie.

Jo hesitates. She needs to go, I feel the pull, but she's concerned about me. 'Take a couple of painkillers. Shall I get you some water?'

'You go.' I try to smile. 'I'm fine, really.'

Jo stoops to kiss me on the cheek. 'You will call me, won't you, if you don't feel well?' She gathers her things and heads for the door to let herself out, then pokes her head back into the lounge. 'Give Toby a call. I know you said you'd had a row, but he adores you, you know he does. He'll be over in a flash. Bet you.'

'It wasn't just a row, Jo. It's really over.'

'Oh, come on—'

I shake my head. 'Stuff happened with Toby. It's not what you think.' I hesitate. 'I think we've both finally figured out that we're not right for each other. I have, anyway.'

She gives me a questioning look but doesn't stop to argue. Her footsteps recede and the door slams shut behind her.

I sit very still, my mind in flux. Jo wouldn't lie to me. I trust her with my life. So what the hell's going on?

I take a sip of tea, then get a little shakily to my feet and go to fetch my laptop from the desk.

I switch it on and, as it powers up, I frown round at the messy, stained walls. My head aches. It's an effort to concentrate. Jo's right, I do need to sleep, but I need to figure this out first. The screen flashes as my work programme opens, bringing up an old piece of work. I check the bottom right-hand corner for the date. November the twenty-third. Just as she said. Last year.

I blink, feeling suddenly sick. None of this makes any sense. I dig my phone out of my coat pocket. It shows the same date as my laptop.

I swallow two painkillers and lie on the sofa, very still, eyes closed, trying to tamp down rising panic.

CHAPTER SIXTY-TWO

Every time I close my eyes and try to drift into sleep, I see Ed.

I see the sadness in his face when he caught sight of me as I entered that depressing visiting room; his closed, haunted look when he sat apart from me at the table, his eyes cast down, as I tried to press him, to force him to tell me the truth, to admit he made a false confession to protect Tanya.

I shake my head. Not Tanya. Ellie, after all. A reckless teenager who grew up without her father. It was all for her, then.

What was it Tanya murmured to herself the day we went to her house, as she watched Jo and Mia cross the road together, holding hands? *That's all that matters, really, isn't it? Keeping our kids safe.*

She agreed to this. She knew. She stood back and let him take the rap. No wonder she looked so stricken in court. She knew this was Ed's way of paying his debt to his friend. His way of trying to give his mate's daughter a second chance.

I remember the way Ed bowed his head as he headed slowly back to the main prison building. When I promised to keep visiting, to wait for him, he didn't look pleased, just sorrowful, weighed down by regret. As if there were something else, something so painful he couldn't bear to tell me. And as he queued at the door, waiting to be let back in, why was he the only prisoner who didn't look back?

I sit up, heart pounding. I reach for my laptop, google the prison website and then phone.

'I need to contact a prisoner, please. It's urgent.'

The woman on the other end of the line sounds bored. 'Are you on the prisoner's friends and family list?'

I hesitate. I don't know. 'Well, I just visited him. Earlier today.'

She breathes heavily. 'If you're on his approved list, if you've had security clearance, he can telephone you. If he has phone credit.'

'Can I call him?'

'I'm afraid that's not possible. Prisoners can't accept incoming calls.'

I run my hand through my hair, exasperated. 'So how can I get a message to him?'

'I'm afraid we don't offer a message service.' Her tone's clipped. 'You can write to him, if you like. Put his full name and prisoner number on the outside of the envelope. Do you have the address?'

'Please.' I grip the phone hard. 'If I give you his name, can you check his prisoner number for me? I'd be so grateful.'

She huffs for a moment. 'It might be better if you call back in the morning. In office hours.'

'It's really important.' I must sound as desperate as I feel. 'His name's Spencer. Edward Jonathan Spencer.' I spell it all out.

The silence is broken only by the clack of keyboard strokes. 'I'm sorry, madam. I'm afraid we don't have any prisoner listed with that name.'

'But you must have! I've just—'

'Perhaps you should check the spelling. Or he might be registered under a different name?'

'I'm sure he isn't.' I hesitate, thrown for a second. Is this something else I don't know about him? No, it can't be. His name was on the guards' lists when they checked me through security. 'Please could you check again? We must have made a mistake. Let me spell it out again.'

The woman sounds sniffy. 'I suggest you call back in the morning, madam, if you need further assistance. After eight thirty.'

'Can I ask you one more question? Please. I know it sounds strange, but can you tell me what the date is today?'

She's had enough. With a click, the line goes dead.

I go to bed, but I have very little sleep that night.

I toss and turn, restless, my head aching, my mind in knots. All night, I keep replaying that conversation with Ed. His misery when I interrogated him. The hopelessness in his drooping shoulders, his bowed head. And, at the end, the words he spoke as he got up to leave which seemed so desolate, so final.

You've changed me more than you will ever know. I'm sorry it has to be like this. I truly am.

He made one mistake in his life, a terrible mistake, just as I did. He's been paying for it, denying himself happiness, ever since.

I try to imagine him lying in his cell. I strain to feel him with me. But something's changed.

Before, in those painful weeks after I saw him in court, even though I was grief-stricken, struggling to make sense of what he'd done, of the way he seemed to have betrayed me, he was still there. He was still part of me. When I thought of him, I sensed, however absurd it seems, that he was thinking of me too.

I remember the times I woke in the small hours, hearing the ghostly sound of his voice, whispering my name.

But now, as hard as I try to reach out to him, all I can sense is emptiness and absence in a deeply silent room.

CHAPTER SIXTY-THREE

In the morning, my phone and laptop still tell me it's November.

November the twenty-fourth.

I've already had this day. I should be in hospital, being treated for a broken leg and concussion. Later, Toby would visit me with flowers and we'd fight while the middle-aged man sitting by the next bed pretended not to hear.

Instead, I'm here, my ribs bruised, my legs stiff and sore but whole.

My side aches. I swallow down painkillers from the bathroom cabinet and stand for a long time under a hot shower, trying to come back to life. Later, I sip a strong coffee and stand in the lounge, staring at the tired, stained walls and trying to imagine them freshly painted.

At eight thirty-one, I call the prison. Again, they claim to have no knowledge of Ed, no record of any such prisoner.

I force myself to swallow down some breakfast, then grab my jacket, keys and phone and head out. There's something I need to see for myself.

I hurry down the high street towards the river. The shop windows are gaudy with Christmas decorations and displays. Strings of coloured lights run between the lampposts. I press through a stream of commuters heading towards the station, and weave my way around groups of out-of-season tour groups: Chinese and Japanese couples, retired, by the look of it, gathering on corners to gape at the architecture as their guide addresses them through a megaphone.

I reach the river and turn left, taking the road past the docks, past the new Millennium Quay development, with its brightly lit windows, and then turn inland again towards Ed's flat.

The first, modernised building, with its sandblasted walls and metal-framed picture windows, glistens with sunlight. Steam puffs up from adjacent grills set alongside the pavement, heady with the aromas of coffee, bacon and toast. I imagine the middle-class couples inside, finishing breakfast and getting ready to leave for work.

Several balconies are hectic with Christmas displays. A plastic Santa endlessly climbs a rope ladder towards the roof. A set of glittery reindeers peers through the railings. Baubles and tinsels festoon outdoor shrubs and plants.

I'm too agitated to spend time looking. I hurry straight past, then, a moment later, stop abruptly and gape.

I can hardly believe what's in front of me.

The second building, that neglected twin, ripe for development, where Ed had his cavernous flat, now looks just the same as the first. I stare from one to the other, suddenly disorientated, doubting my memory.

This second building too has been renovated. The dark, impacted grime has been stripped off the outer stone walls. The façade is neatly divided into floors, each one with two or three neat apartments. Miniature balconies protrude along the front, adorned with trailing pot plants and window boxes, children's bicycles and wrought-iron balcony chairs, shining in the light streaming out from the glass panels of balcony doors.

I look around me, stupefied, then walk down the alley between the two blocks. I'm sure I'm in the right place. Aren't I?

I quicken my pace and rush to the spot where the old metal door stood, the door which led to the metal staircase to Ed's makeshift flat.

The outline is visible, there in the wall, neatly filled by fresh, matching bricks. The entrance itself has disappeared, absorbed into the new design.

Ed's voice sounds in my head. *'On paper, this building's ripe for development. The developer's a mate of mine, slowing things down, if you see what I mean. Keeping a roof over my head.'*

I stagger blindly, groping for the wall to stop myself from falling, suddenly very dizzy.

CHAPTER SIXTY-FOUR

Somehow, I get myself down to the waterfront and fall onto a bench overlooking the river. I hunch my shoulders, trying to steady my breathing, and huddle against the cold. The Thames, littered with floating drinks cans and scraps of plastic, runs softly past towards the sea.

I don't know what to do. What's going on? What's the matter with me? I wonder if this is what it means to go mad, how lonely it feels. I feel as if I'm at the centre of an elaborate hoax, some test of my mettle. None of this makes any sense.

My phone beeps and I rush to pull it out of my pocket, heart thumping, imagining it's Ed.

It's just Jo, texting to see if I'm OK, if I managed to sleep, asking if I need anything.

I don't answer. I don't know what to say.

There must be someone who can help me understand what's going on. There must be someone who knows where Ed is and can explain why the prison officials are suddenly denying he's there.

I force myself to get to my feet and go back to the flat to retrieve my bike and dented helmet. It'll have to do for now. There's no sign of the new one, the replacement Jo bought me, that I opened on Christmas Day.

My legs ache but I push myself into a steady rhythm, too intent on where I'm going to let memories of the accident distract me. The morning rush hour has almost played itself out but the flow of traffic, although thinning, is aggressive and I force myself to be slow and patient.

I head out of the centre of Greenwich into the network of purpose-built housing estates on its outskirts, concentrating hard on tracing the route.

It takes me a little while to find the right road. They all look much the same out here. The houses, dating back to the post-war boom, are almost identical. Finally, I see the road I want and head down it, checking out the tiny front gardens and narrow paths.

I pause as I approach number seventy-two and get down from my bike, then push it slowly to the gate. My body's hot from the exercise but my palms are cold and clammy. I stand there, waiting and watching, afraid.

It doesn't look like the same front garden. A small patch of lawn at the front is neatly maintained. It's framed by a row of low, stubby bushes and well-tended plants. The crazy-paving path, which I remember as being laced with wild grass and weeds, looks pristine. The path leading round the side of the house towards the garden has a smart, wrought-iron gate.

I frown and look again at the number. It's definitely seventy-two. I turn and look for clues. A red saloon car is parked on the pavement just outside. A family car with a luggage rack fixed to the roof. It's not one I remember seeing before.

I swallow hard and steady myself. It's nearly nine thirty. I scan the house for a sign of movement. The downstairs curtains, set round the bay window, are drawn back. A row of Christmas cards stands along the windowsill. The curtains at the upstairs window, above the lounge, are still drawn. Ellie, perhaps, her teenager hormones raging, managing a crafty lie-in before class.

I take a deep breath, then wheel my bike up the path to the front door and press the doorbell as firmly as my shaking hands allow. It chimes. Distantly, a voice calls. A woman's pitch. Then footsteps sound. They're light, feminine steps, tripping down the hall towards the door.

For a second, I consider turning and fleeing for my life. Somehow, I stay firm.

Inside, a chain rattles, a bolt slides back and the door opens.

Tanya peers out at me.

I recognise her as soon as I see her face and yet she looks very different. She's fashionably dressed in a billowing white shirt, with tight jeans and black ankle boots, all showing off her slender figure. Her hair's shorter, styled in a neat bob. Her skin, covered by only the slightest trace of make-up, glows with health. There's no hint of the tension I remember from when I last saw her. She looks like a more relaxed, happier twin sister.

'Tanya?'

I'm taut, braced for her to be hostile. This is the second time I've turned up on her doorstep without an invitation. She may suspect I know the truth.

But there's a half-smile on her face. She just says: 'That's me. I'm sorry, do I...?' She blinks at me, vague, as if she can't quite place me.

I frown. She's clearly playing a game. 'Louise,' I prompt. 'Louise Taylor. Remember?'

'Is it about tennis club?' she goes on. 'I'm so sorry but Ellie...' She hesitates and looks again, realising something isn't right. 'I'm sorry, I'm terrible with faces. Are you Sara's mum?'

I shake my head. She's doing a very good job of pretending she's never seen me before.

'Look,' I say quietly. 'I don't want trouble. I'm just trying to understand what's going on.'

She looks taken aback. 'I'm so sorry, I really don't—'

'I'm trying to find Ed. Do you know where he's gone?'

A male voice echoes down the hall. 'Who is it?'

I try to peer around her to see into the hall. It's too dark. All I can make out is the broad shape of a man approaching.

'Ed?' I strain to look. 'Is that you?'

Tanya opens the door a little wider to make room for him at her side. It's a man I've never seen before. He's thick-set, with a receding hairline. His face is tanned and weathered although, as I look more closely, I see he's probably just this side of forty. His muscular upper arms, pumped up with exercise, draw brackets on either side of his body. He's dressed in a suit, lightly creased at the elbows. The top two buttons of his shirt hang undone.

I'm sure I've never met him before but there's something in his face that I recognise. I bite my lip.

'Everything OK?' He puts a light hand on Tanya's shoulder and looks at me.

Tanya half turns to give him an uncertain look. 'She's looking for someone called Ed.'

He frowns. 'Ed? Ed who?'

Tanya turns back to me and says, as if she's trying hard to be helpful: 'There's an Eric down the road? He's quite elderly. I'm not sure which number he is, though. A-hundred-and-something, I think.'

I can't speak for a moment. I just stand there, staring, opening and closing my mouth.

The man peers more closely at me, reading my confusion. 'This is number seventy-two. Have you got the right road?'

'I'm sorry.' My knuckles blanch as I grip the bike's handlebars. I need something solid to anchor me. 'I don't understand. Who are you?'

'Me?'

He and Tanya exchange glances. His face clouds as if he's rapidly becoming suspicious of me. 'Adam Johnson. Why? Who are you? What is it you want?'

Their faces blur as I find myself, without warning, bursting into tears.

CHAPTER SIXTY-FIVE

For a moment, I just stand there, sobbing convulsively.

I feel dazed and desperately lost. None of this makes sense.

Tanya says: 'Are you all right?'

My knees buckle. Her husband grabs me, threading a meaty arm around me, holding me upright against his side. My legs are suddenly too weak to support me.

'You'd better come in a minute.' Tanya holds the door open as her husband helps me into the hall. Her face is all concern. 'Sit her down, Adam. I'll get the bike.'

He guides me into the lounge and helps me onto the sofa, then takes a seat in an armchair, across from me, and quietly watches as I struggle to get the crying under control. It's not easy.

A moment later, Tanya hurries in with a box of tissues and sets them in front of me. I pluck one out and blow my nose, wipe off my face. Tanya watches. She has the patient air of a woman who's used to crises.

'Can I get you anything? Let me get you a glass of water.' She bustles through to the kitchen at the back without waiting for me to reply.

Adam and I sit awkwardly in silence, waiting. I'm still dizzy, blinking rapidly, my thoughts jumbled. My heart thumps in my chest. Tanya reappears with a glass of water and stands over me as I sip it. Ice bobs and cracks at the brim.

The layout of the lounge is much as I remember but the furnishings have changed. The sofa I'm sitting on is plush and modern. So is the armchair. The worn carpet's been replaced by a cream one with thick pile. A bushy Christmas tree stands in the corner, glistening with multi-coloured tinsel and baubles as large as tennis balls.

Along the mantelpiece there are framed family photographs. Some are familiar: the portrait of Adam and Tanya on their wedding day, posing side by side. The school picture of Ellie at about nine or ten, all teeth. But there's a new picture too, of Adam Johnson in army fatigues, laughing, with Ellie, at the age of about four or five, perched on his shoulders.

Footsteps sound overhead as someone tramps across the upstairs bedroom. Tanya slips out and her voice sounds as she calls up the stairs to her daughter. Her tread is light as she takes the stairs. I strain to make out the hushed tones of the two of them whispering together, presumably about me: their strange, unexpected visitor.

'So, what's all this about?' His tone is civil but there's an underlying authority as if he's warning me to be careful, that if I'm part of some scam, he's not a man who's likely to fall for it.

I shudder. 'I thought you were dead.'

He frowns. 'Well, you thought wrong.'

'I thought you died years ago. In Afghanistan.'

He shakes his head. 'Someone's having you on, love.' He takes a breath. 'I did serve in Afghanistan once. Helmand. That's true enough. But I made it home safe and sound, as you can see.' He pauses. 'I was lucky.'

My eyes flick to the wedding photograph, then back to his face. He certainly looks like an older version of the same man. But I'm not sure what to believe. *He might be a cousin or a brother…*

He watches me, weighing something up. 'Who said that, anyway, that I'd died?'

'Ed.'

'Ed?' His eyes narrow. 'The one you're looking for? Ed who?'

I take a deep breath. 'Edward Jonathan Spencer. He said you were mates out there and something went terribly wrong. That you died. You were shot. And it was all his fault.'

Tanya trips back down the stairs and, a moment later, plates clatter in the kitchen.

'How did you know Ed?' Adam Johnson sits squarely in the armchair facing me, his legs apart. His thinning hair sticks up untidily. He runs his fingers through it in a nervous gesture as he speaks.

I gulp, remembering. 'Your wife gave me his number. I needed some decorating done.'

He frowns. 'Say that again?'

'Tanya.' I nod back towards the kitchen as if he might need help identifying his own wife. 'She came round to see me when I was knocked off my bike. For Victim Support. She said he was an old friend of the family.'

He narrows his eyes. 'I don't think so.'

I sigh. 'Ask her. I've been here before, with my sister when her daughter went missing.' I point. 'The carpet was different and these chairs. You've replaced them.'

He gazes at me as if I've lost my mind. 'When who went missing?'

'Mia. My niece. She tracked them down. I didn't believe her at the time, but she tried to tell us what happened, that one of you drove the car that hit me.'

'Stay there.' He gets abruptly to his feet and heads through to the kitchen. He closes the glass doors behind him and I see the two of them, Adam and Tanya, silhouetted against it, heads close together, murmuring in low tones. About me, for sure.

'Hello.'

I turn. A young woman has appeared in the doorway, grinning. It must be Ellie. It's the same teenager I saw by Tanya's side on the streets of Greenwich but with a very different look. No nose stud. No heavy make-up. She's young and sweet-faced in jeans and a baggy sweatshirt. Her hair is shoulder-length and tucked behind her ears. Her eyes are open and friendly.

I realise I must be staring because she flushes and shifts her weight from one foot to the other.

'Sorry. Did I startle you?' She sounds less certain now. 'I'm Ellie.'

I say quietly: 'You look so different.'

She blinks. 'Different?'

I give her a long, steady look. 'Do you know who I am? I'm the woman you hit that night. On the bike. I know what happened, Ellie.'

She stares at me, her eyes wide.

'I don't blame you. Don't think that. I know it was an accident.' I sigh. 'But you should have stayed. What if I'd been dying?'

She shakes her head and starts to stutter: 'I'm sorry, I don't—'

'It's all right, Ellie.' Adam's voice, stern.

I turn. He and Tanya have crept back into the room. I'm not sure how much they've heard.

Tanya lifts an arm to her daughter, inviting her to go to her side.

'Why don't you come and have some breakfast, Ellie?' She's speaking in a calm, steady voice, the kind negotiators use to soothe crazed hostage-takers. She doesn't look at me directly, but I sense her eyes flicking to me, as if she's covertly watching to see if I'll make a sudden move and is ready to spring into action if I do.

Ellie doesn't move. She looks startled.

'Come on, Ellie.' Tanya beckons her with the outstretched hand. 'You'll be late for your class. Dad's dealing with this.'

I say: 'I'm not here to make trouble. I just want to understand. To know where Ed is.'

Ellie allows herself to be persuaded away. As the two women cross the threshold into the kitchen, Tanya threads her arm around her daughter's shoulders. The glass doors close behind them, screening them off.

Adam towers over me and wags a finger. 'Look, I don't know who you are or what you're up to, but you can't come here upsetting my family.'

I shake my head. 'What did Tanya tell you? That she's never seen me before? Why would I make it up? There must be records of her visits. Call them and ask.'

He frowns. 'Call who?'

'Victim Support. Where your wife works.'

'She doesn't have a job. She hasn't worked for years, not since Ellie was born.' He pauses and his face softens slightly. 'Are you OK?'

I can't help it. My eyes brim again and I reach for a fresh tissue and dry my cheeks. What's happening to me? I shake my head and breathe hard, trying to get a grip.

'Look,' he says. 'Maybe someone thought it was funny to spin you a yarn about Ed. I don't know. But I can tell you this. If you think you've met the Edward Spencer I knew, my old army mate, you're wrong. Very wrong. OK?'

He speaks steadily and quietly. However close I feel to the end of my tether, I sense he's telling me the truth, or at least what he thinks is the truth.

'Ed was a good bloke,' he goes on, firmly. 'One of the best. If you'd really known him, you'd know what happened. Yes, we served together in Afghanistan. He was a hero. He gave his life for his country. And for us, his mates. I know he did. I was there.' He lets out a deep sigh. 'Now, I'm sorry, but I think you should leave.'

CHAPTER SIXTY-SIX

I set off slowly down the road, pushing my bike, too exhausted to start cycling.

I don't understand. I don't know what to believe. How can Ed have lost his life in Afghanistan twelve years ago? But I believe Adam Johnson. I can't help it. I think he's telling the truth.

And how can it be November?

Ellie looked so taken aback, so upset when I accused her of knocking me down that night. It wasn't the reaction of a guilty teenager who's been found out; a teenager who's broken the law and knows they might end up serving time. She seems innocent.

I stop and lean against a garden wall, run a hand over my face, close my eyes. Everything seems to be swirling around me, dizzying. I feel as if I'm falling, losing all sense of myself. I take a deep draught of cold air. *Oh, Ed. Where are you? What's happening?*

Nearby, a door opens and heels click down a path. A gate clicks. A voice is murmuring. I open my eyes. A young woman, in jeans and a short grey coat, is manoeuvring a buggy onto the pavement, two doors down. She's leaning over the child inside, smiling and chattering as she straightens up the buggy, closes the gate and heads off towards the bus stop.

'Wait!'

It takes me a moment to turn. Tanya's running after me down the road, her bob blown back, waving her arms. I hesitate. *Now what?*

'Wait.' She reaches me and stops, then bends forward, panting, as she catches her breath. 'He just told me. My husband. He said you were asking after his friend. That Ed. The one who died in Afghanistan.'

I don't know what to say. I'm too weary. How can her husband not know she has a job? She came to my flat, she helped me make a claim, she introduced me to Ed. How can it be possible that all those things never happened? I stare at her. Her face radiates kindness and concern. But this is also a woman who was prepared to stand by and let an innocent man, a friend, go to jail to protect her daughter.

She says: 'You didn't give us your name.'

'Tanya.' I sigh. 'There's no—'

'Please. Tell me.' She reaches forward and clutches my wrist. 'Please.'

'Louise.'

Her eyes brighten. 'Louise what?'

I'm about to protest. She knows exactly who I am and what happened to me. She knows everything.

I hesitate, looking at her now. Her expression is earnest. 'Taylor. Louise Taylor. Why?'

'I knew it.' She nods, slowly and thoughtfully. 'He didn't believe me.' She shifts her hand to the handlebars and lifts the bike away from me, starting to turn it around to face back towards her house. 'Come back. Please. It's important.'

As we walk back up the road, the bike between us, Ellie comes out, a messenger bag across her chest. She blushes as she sees me and dips her eyes to the pavement, scurrying past without a word.

Inside, we stow the bike once more in the hall and Tanya shows me into the lounge again, then shouts up the stairs: 'She's here.' She puts her head around the door to the lounge to tell me: 'He won't be a minute. He's in the loft. It's with his army stuff.'

I say: 'What is?'

She crosses the room without answering and disappears into the kitchen. From the kitchen, cutlery and crockery ting as she clears away the breakfast dishes and stacks the dishwasher.

After a few minutes, Adam appears at the door. He's wearing a tie now and brown lace-up shoes, further along on his interrupted journey of getting ready for work.

He looks uncomfortable. 'What did you say your name was?'

'Louise Taylor.' I'm suddenly overwhelmed with tiredness. I want to be home, to be alone, to crawl back into bed and close my eyes, to escape from all this madness.

He plonks himself down, across from me. 'Tanya reminded me.' He nods towards the kitchen. 'I told her about it at the time, you see. Years ago. But I never thought much of it. I mean, I never expected…'

I narrow my eyes. 'What?'

He hesitates. 'Can I ask you something? How old are you?'

I blow out my cheeks, weary. 'I don't how that's relevant but I'm thirty-six. Why?'

He nods, calculating. 'Thirty-six? Well, then.' He calls back to Tanya. 'She's thirty-six now. So she'd have been, what, twenty-two or twenty-three?' He turns back to me. 'When we were in Helmand, I mean. You were early twenties.'

I shrug. 'I suppose so. I hadn't really—'

He nods. 'So is that it, then? You knew him back then, when we were deployed?'

I tut with exasperation. 'Of course I didn't. I was fresh out of college then, freelancing, trying to get a job. Of course I didn't know him when he was in the army. Why would I?'

Tanya appears in the doorway, wiping her hands on a towel. 'It's what he said, though, isn't it?'

I sit forward, frustrated. 'I have no idea what you're talking about.' They're talking in riddles. I can't take much more. I just want to go home and sleep and, when I wake up, find it's early February again and this was all a bad dream.

He twists to look back at his wife.

She nods to him. 'Go on. Tell her.'

He shakes his head as if he doesn't agree but turns slowly to face me. 'Like I said, Ed and I were good mates. We served together in Helmand. That was a long time ago. Twelve years.'

I shrug. 'I know. He told me.'

He pulls a face, then takes a breath and carries on: 'He met this lad, a local lad—'

'Abdul.'

He stares at me, clearly startled. 'How d'you know that?'

I just say: 'Carry on. He met Abdul and they got a bit too friendly and it made Abdul a target. Right?'

'Right.' He nods slowly. 'Well, we went on patrol one time, in town. We were both new lieutenants, a bit wet behind the ears. Anyway, he was all hyped up that day, like he sensed something big was going to happen. God knows how. Suddenly he went haring off after some lads on a motorbike, saying they'd got Abdul. I didn't know what to do. He was breaking every rule in the book. I tried to catch up with him, but he was too fast. So, I took a few of the boys and we went after him, trying to watch his back.'

He swallows hard and hesitates a moment before he can go on. 'The Afghan lads dumped the motorbike in a side street. He seemed to know exactly where they'd gone. He jumped them in this wooden shack. By the time I got inside, he'd knocked out one lad and was trying to pin down the other one. I ran to help but the kid must've hidden a gun in there because the next thing I knew, he was twisting it free, pointing it right at me. Ed saw too. He didn't hesitate. He threw himself on that gun, just before the kid opened fire.'

He shakes, remembering. His face is anguished. 'I couldn't do a thing. Couldn't save him. I tried.'

Tanya says, firmly: 'You did everything you could.'

'He saved my life. And he saved Abdul's life. They'd taken him, see, to use as bait. He was cowering in a corner, whimpering.'

For a moment, no one speaks.

Then Tanya says: 'Tell her about the message.'

He shakes himself and looks up. 'Thing is, on our way down to town, just before it happened, he was in a strange mood. Agitated. A premonition, sort of thing. I'd been going on about Tanya, you know, and Ellie. She was just a nipper then. I missed her something chronic. I missed both of them. Then he suddenly said, out of nowhere, that he'd found someone too. The love of his life, that's what he said. Dark horse. Never said a bloody word to me about it before and we'd been together a lot. I thought I'd have known. Anyway, he said her name was Lou. Louise Taylor. He said: *If anything happens to me today, tell Lou I love her, will you? Tell her I'm sorry. I never wanted to lose her. I'm just trying to do the right thing.*'

He takes a deep breath and steadies himself. I can hardly look him in the eye.

'I tried to josh him out of it, you know. I said something like: who the hell's Lou? That's a bit sudden, isn't it? Taking the piss a bit, you know, because he'd never said a word about any girl before and now, suddenly, here he was, acting all moony, like he'd found The One. I said: how am I going to find her, anyway? If she even exists.'

He bites down on his lip. Tanya comes forward and perches on the edge of the chair. She puts her hand on his shoulders and takes up the story while he recovers himself.

She says: 'And he said: don't worry about finding her. She'll find you. But it won't be for a while. Not for years and years. Just remember, will you? Give her the message. She'll know what it means.'

Adam wipes his eyes on the heel of his hand and fishes in his pocket. 'He gave me this to give her, I mean, you. He must've just picked it up on our way out and scratched it with his knife. I know it's stupid, it's just a random rock, but I kept it with my kit all these years just, you know, just in case.'

He hands it to me. It's warm in my fingers, heated by his body. A smooth round pebble. A tiny piece of Afghanistan. I trace the scratches on the surface with my fingertips. On one side, our initials: LT and ES, with a roughly drawn heart. On the other, the neat diamond outline of a kite.

He says: 'But you said you never met him back then. So it can't have been you, can it?'

I seem to fold into myself. My mind hurts with trying to understand.

How can I explain? How can I tell them that I saw Ed yesterday? That he tried to warn me what he was going to do, that he was going back to set things right. That he was going back to sacrifice his own life so Adam could live his, here, with his wife and daughter.

I hunch forward and start again to sob. I can't stop myself.

'I guess it is you then,' Tanya says, softly. 'You poor love.'

CHAPTER SIXTY-SEVEN

I cycle home in a daze. The Afghan stone is heavy in my pocket, the only real thing I have, an anchor in all this chaos.

Inside the flat, I collapse into bed. Everything whirls and spins around me. I want to understand, I want to make sense of it. Most of all, I want Ed to be still alive.

Images drift in and out of my head as I lie there, wretched. I think about the world without him, the way things would have gone if he had died all those years ago.

No reason, then, to stall the commercial development of his building. That too would be as renovated and modern as its twin.

I think about Ellie, growing up with her father, as well as her mother. A steadier, gentler girl, no longer driving herself to take wild risks.

I think about Tanya, ageing gracefully, running a home and caring for her family. A woman who hasn't been ravaged by her past. A woman who wasn't tragically widowed but whose husband came home safely home to her from Afghanistan so they could build a life together and he could be a father to their daughter.

But what about us, Ed? Even if you could, why would you choose that? Why would you leave me? I need you too.

I sob, tearing at the sheets, at my hair. *Don't I matter? How could you choose to go back into the past and sacrifice your life if you really love me?*

I remember the message he sent through Adam Johnson: *Tell Lou I love her... tell her I'm sorry... I'm just trying to do the right thing.*

Finally, exhausted, I quieten. I sink at last into a heavy, dreadful certainty.

Of course I know the truth. I'm railing against it, I don't want to accept it, but I must. Of course this man I've come to love is decent, is selfless, will always try to do the right thing.

Even if it cost us the chance to be together. Even if it cost us our own chance at happiness.

CHAPTER SIXTY-EIGHT

Day after day, I wake and it stays November.

Each morning, I lie in bed and work out what might have happened today, if Ed had left life as it was and changed nothing.

This is the day Jo and Mia bring me home from hospital...

This is the day Tanya comes to visit, with her leaflets and false concern...

This is the day I fall and Ed picks me up, on his way to meet me for the first time...

This is the day he starts to strip back that messy wall and repaint it...

Except it isn't, not one of them, and never will be. Not any more.

I spent a lot of time walking, trying to calm myself, trying to understand.

I walk down by the docks and along the bank of the sliding river.

Some days, if the weather's dry, I walk through the park, remembering the day Ed taught Mia how to fly his battered Afghan kite. I watch the winter tourists climb the hill to General Wolfe's statue to admire the view and to straddle the meridian line and, for a fleeting moment, travel through time.

Some days, my feet take me back to Ed's building and I stand nearby for a while and consider it, looking over the lines of the new brickwork and tracing the shadow of the old, barely visible, hidden in the stone.

On one of these walks, I stay out longer than usual and by the time I head home, the darkness is already thick. The centre of Greenwich, gaudy with Christmas lights, is bustling with late-night shoppers. Music splashes out from pubs and restaurants, which heave with office parties.

I decide to avoid the crowd by carrying on along the river and only leaving the bank further down to cut through a network of quieter side streets. Most of the shops here are for tourists, selling souvenirs and postcards and they're already closed.

I'm hurrying down a narrow lane when I pass a new pizza place, one I've never noticed before.

I glance in, my eye caught by their sparkling silver decorations, and then I freeze. There, sitting alone at a corner table, close to the window, is Toby. His head is lowered as he looks over the menu, a glass of wine already at his side. There's something doleful in his expression. Something defeated in the slump of his shoulders.

I feel a pang so sharp it hurts. It's not regret but nostalgia, a sudden sadness for all the evenings we shared together, all the cosy bistros and pizza places, the long conversations over bottles of wine. I hesitate, wondering whether to go in, half wanting him to look up and see me.

Then the mood changes. A young woman, just arrived, hurries across from the entrance to join him. He looks up and smiles, a slow, wistful smile but his eyes shine nonetheless. He pushes back his chair and gets to his feet. I watch, transfixed, as they greet each other awkwardly, kissing on the cheek. He pulls out a chair for her, next to his.

She takes off her coat and scarf and folds them over a free chair, then smoothes down her dress and rakes through her frizzy, shoulder-length hair with her fingers before she sits down. She's petite, neat – I can tell, even from this distance, that she's made an effort tonight.

I'm inside and striding towards their table before I can think about it and change my mind.

She sees me first and her eyes widen. She must emit some sound because, a second later, he looks up too. 'Lou!' Toby blushes. 'What are you…?'

I manage a smile. 'Hello.' I turn to her and nod. 'Hi, Rachel.'

Toby scrambles to his feet. 'I was coming around to see you later. To talk.' He pauses, staring at me as if he still can't believe I'm there. 'Did you get my messages? I've called and called. Why won't you talk to me?'

Rachel's jaw is tight. She's turned back to her menu, scowling slightly.

I take a deep breath. 'Toby, I'm sorry. Really. But there's no point in all this. I've tried to explain. I just can't give you what you want. You have to believe me: no amount of texting or calling or turning up on the doorstep is going to make any difference. None at all. Don't do it.'

He shakes his head. 'You just—'

'I don't "just" anything. Please.' I nod down at Rachel, sitting stiffly between us, pretending she can't hear. 'She cares about you. So why not let it happen? Give it a chance? Maybe she's right for you. I don't know. But I do know I'm not. Really and truly.'

Toby takes a step towards me and lowers his voice. 'Rachel and I are just friends. Is that what this is about? Come on, Lou.'

I sigh. 'I know about August, Toby.'

He blinks rapidly, dumbstruck. 'August?'

I shrug. 'I know you two slept together.'

He's speechless for a moment, then start to splutter a denial.

I bat it away. 'You know what? It's fine. It's history. That's not why I left you, by the way. No hard feelings, Toby.' I reach over to kiss him on the cheek.

Toby gapes.

Before I turn to leave, I stoop to speak to Rachel who's still staring fixedly at the menu. 'I owe you an apology. I suspected you of something horrible, of digging up dirt on me and getting Toby to threaten me. I'm sorry. I was wrong.'

Her eyes flicker. I can tell she has no idea what I'm talking about but is determined not to say so.

I know I shouldn't, but I can't resist a final parting shot: 'But throwing yourself at someone else's boyfriend? Don't do that again, sweetheart. It's just not classy.'

CHAPTER SIXTY-NINE

I meant what I said when I apologised to Rachel.

I don't like her, but I have thought a lot about what happened. I've sat by the window at night, looking at the shifting shadows under the trees across the road, remembering how anxious I felt, trapped inside the flat, barely mobile, sensing someone hiding there, watching me.

I have a different theory now.

I think Tanya, the widowed Tanya living in that other time, dumped the cuttings at my front door that night, with their crude warning. It makes perfect sense. She must have called in a quiet favour with one of her police contacts, getting them to run a search on me, in the hope of finding something incriminating, and striking gold with the coroner's report and the press cuttings on my case. She wanted to do whatever she could to protect her daughter, to warn me off and let Ellie have the best chance she could at life.

I don't blame her, not really. Any mother would want the same, even if they weren't prepared to go to the same lengths. And Tanya nearly succeeded. If it hadn't been for Mia and her detective work, perhaps I would never have found out the truth.

And I think Tanya was the person who spied on me so often in the darkness. I wonder if she had feelings for Ed that she could never admit, if her need to monitor how much I knew about the accident, to protect her daughter, was made toxic by jealousy. I guess I'll never know, for sure.

I'm busy, packing for Chile, for that adventure of a lifetime. It seems I haven't missed out, after all, on the chance to bungee jump from a helicopter over an active volcano.

I remember how excited I was about the trip before and how desperately disappointed I felt when I was forced to pull out. I'm still excited this time but it's different now.

Everything's different.

I'm different.

All week, with each passing day, I've thought about Ed more, not less. I'm afraid of forgetting him, of losing him all over again, from memory.

I think, most of all, of the last time I saw him.

I think about his final words to me: *Go and find that woman. Mrs Collins. You must, Louise. Please.*

I don't understand why he was so insistent. But I know that, before I head to Chile, that's exactly what I need to do.

CHAPTER SEVENTY

The train out of Waterloo station is almost empty at this time in the morning.

The floor's strewn with the debris left behind by the flood of morning commuters into London: torn copies of free newspapers, empty coffee cups and discarded food wrappers. The carriage smells of stale sweat and congealed fat.

I find an empty set of seats and settle by the window as the train gathers speed. Slowly the city, with its clusters of tall buildings, its cranes, its warehouses, its balloon-letter graffiti, recedes. Gradually, here and there between the housing developments, fields emerge, dotted with horses and cows, lined with fences and hedges. It's as if we're travelling not just from city to country but back in time to a less industrial, less urban age.

As the train gathers speed and rattles along, the landscape blurs.

My phone beeps. A text from Jo:

where u now?

It's her fifth or sixth text so far today. I smile and shake my head. She's become very protective since the accident, despite the fact she's rushed off her feet, juggling work at the café with making a start on her Christmas shopping.

She's delighted with the ideas I've fed her for presents for Mia – the felt-tip pens and books and chocolate coins and the unicorn nightie and everything else I managed to recall. I'm an inspiration, apparently. I even described my new cycle helmet in detail and told her where to buy it.

As for my trip out of London today, she's surprised but supportive. She was the one who dug out the address for me. I'm grateful. Without Ed, she's the only person in my life who knows the full story.

I pull out my laptop and try to read up on Chile, but I can't concentrate. My stomach knots with tension.

The past is travelling with me, inside the railway carriage. That piercing, other-worldly scream. Mrs Collins's chalk-white face as she clutched her dead baby, her eyes, filled with hate, when she turned on me. *You killed my baby, you wicked, wicked girl.*

The railway station is a cavernous Victorian building, high-domed and echoing and ostentatiously grand for such a small town. When I climb down from the train and make my way through the ticket hall, it's almost deserted.

I select a dripping bunches of roses and lilies from the buckets outside a florist's and she makes up a bouquet. Once it's done, I pick up a taxi on the forecourt and start the short journey out to the house.

As the taxi noses its way through the traffic, my breath quickens until it becomes so shallow, it's painful. It feels as if someone's reached into my chest and tightened their fist around my lungs. I struggle to stay calm, to stop myself from telling the driver to turn back.

The driver seems utterly unaware of me. He sits low in his seat, slumped over the wheel, tapping a finger to the pop music playing on the radio.

I try to focus my thoughts on Ed to steady my resolve, and tighten my fingers around the smooth, solid Afghan stone in my pocket. I carry it with me always now and I sense I always will. I see again in my mind the compassion in his face when he came to seek me out after reading the envelope of cuttings. *It wasn't your fault.*

I force myself to take a long, deep breath. I have no idea what awaits me.

Maybe they won't even be at home and I can creep away without guilt. Maybe Mrs Collins will refuse to speak to me and slam the door in my face, once she realises who I am. Maybe she'll rail against me, give me a full, bitter account of the misery I inflicted on her, of the irreparable damage to her life. How will any of this help me? Why was Ed so determined I should come?

Mrs Collins must be nearly sixty now. I imagine her with a pinched face and greying hair. Her husband, kind, generous Mr Collins with his sweets and smiles, will be stooped and thin, prematurely aged by the tragedy I caused.

What will I say?

'Down here?' The taxi driver swings the car off the main road and takes a narrow residential street. Cars are parked in a ragged row down one side. They're medium-sized properties, semi-detached family homes, with short driveways and gaps offering glimpses of back gardens with brightly coloured plastic slides and swing sets, trampolines and tiny playhouses, grimy with mud and wet leaves.

He calls back: 'What number? Fifteen?'

I hesitate, cold with panic. 'Nineteen. But don't stop right outside, will you? Stop a little further on.'

He draws up without comment outside twenty-three.

'How long do you think you'll be?'

'Not long. Are you OK to wait?'

He shrugs and clicks the meter to waiting time, as if to say: *It's your money, suit yourself.* He plucks a newspaper from behind the sun visor and sinks even lower in his seat to read.

I sit very still, aware of the tension in my legs, the tremor in my clammy hands. I breathe deeply, reach for the door handle and scoop up the flowers from the empty seat beside me.

The house looks well-kept. A saloon car stands in the drive, parked hard against the front door. I close the door of the taxi behind me and lean back against it to steady myself. My legs don't have the strength. A fresh wave of panic rises. I can't do this.

What do I say? *I'm so sorry. I've suffered too. Please don't think I could ever forget.*

But what if she still blames me? What if she still hates me?

I stand there, unable to move.

Ed's voice comes again in my ear: *You must, Louise. Please.*

For a moment, I sense him with me. For the first time in such a long time. I close my eyes. So close, I could almost touch him. I can almost smell his skin, his hair, his leather jacket.

The straining chug of a small car engine sounds down the road. It slows as it approaches. I open my eyes to look.

It's a tiny two-door car with battered paint. It bounces lightly off the kerb as it parks, finally coming to a halt in front of number nineteen.

A young woman climbs out, swinging out long legs in heeled boots. I watch as she goes round to the passenger door and retrieves a coat and shabby leather bag, then heads up the drive to the front door. A mass of long, curly hair lifts and falls on her back as she moves. She's young – barely old enough for college – and radiant with life.

She stands for a while on the doorstep, pawing through her voluminous bag. Just as she's finally fished out a bunch of keys and is raising them to the lock, the front door has opened from inside.

A mature woman stands there, smiling.

I blink. It's Mrs Collins. I know her at once. But she's not as I feared she'd be. She's slim and elegantly dressed in slacks and a sweater, neat earrings framing her face. She's older but the love in her face, as she gazes out at the young woman, lights and transforms her features.

'Hello, beautiful!'

That voice. It brings back a rush of memory, ambushing me.

'Hi, Mum.' The young girl steps over the threshold into her arms and kisses her cheek. 'Sorry. Terrible traffic.'

Mrs Collins laughs. 'Terrible hangover, more like. Were you out partying last night?'

The young woman disappears inside and Mrs Collins turns back as she moves to shut the door and calls into the house. 'Cara's home, John. Finally!'

My knees buckle. I sink down against the side of the car until I'm in a crouch.

Cara. Twenty, now, as she should be. Healthy and well and living her life. The house blurs and shimmers as my eyes fill.

The driver opens his door an inch. 'All right there?'

I can't speak. I just nod.

That's why Ed begged me to come and find her.

I should have trusted him. I should have had faith. This is his gift to me, my second chance, his gift of love.

When I can, I haul myself back to my feet, creep past the red car and head down the drive, past the saloon car. I stand very still in front of the door, straining to make out the muffled sounds reaching for me. A man's voice, teasing, then a woman's, followed by the young woman's laughter.

I lay the bouquet of flowers gently on the step, then turn and walk back to the taxi, quickly and quietly, to start my journey home.

A LETTER FROM JILL

I want to say a huge thank you for choosing to read *I Let Him In*. If you enjoyed it and want to keep up to date with all my latest releases, just sign up at the following link. Your email address will never be shared and you can unsubscribe at any time.

www.bookouture.com/jill-childs

Have you ever wished you could go back in time and change something you did?

For most of us, it's probably something small. Tactless or mean-spirited words we've uttered in the heat of the moment, perhaps, that we'd like to take back. Or some thoughtless or embarrassing action we'd rather erase.

That's bad enough, but what if it were something more serious, an action which had unintended, life-changing consequences? Rather than living with the guilt, wouldn't you long to turn back the clock and do it differently? If only we had that power.

When I was in my twenties, I remember a close friend, who'd just fallen madly in love, saying how lucky she felt. It wasn't only miraculous, she said, that she'd found her soulmate. It was the fact that, in such a random universe, they'd happened to find each other at the right time, a time that made being together possible.

She made that remark decades ago – and yes, they've been happily married ever since – but it stayed with me. Partly because it left me wondering about someone meeting a soulmate at the wrong time, when their lives simply couldn't align. Would it be better to find that person, despite the fact you couldn't spend your lives together? Or never meet them? How might that brief encounter change you both?

It was from those thoughts about time and the mistakes of the past that *I Let Him In* was born.

I hope you loved *I Let Him In*. If you did, I would be very grateful if you could write a review. I'd love to hear what you think, and it makes such a difference in helping new readers discover my books for the first time.

I love hearing from my readers. You can get in touch on my Facebook page or on Twitter. Thank you!

All best wishes to you and yours,
Jill

 jill.childs.71
@author_jill

ACKNOWLEDGEMENTS

Thank you, as always, to my wonderful editor Kathryn Taussig and all the team at Bookouture.

Thank you to my brilliant agent, Judith Murdoch, the best in the business.

Thank you to my family for all your love and support – especially to Alice and Emily for bringing such joy. And to Nick, for everything.

Alice, this one's for you.

24795718R00173